Emmanuel Guibert   Marc Boutavant

ARIOL

A Beautiful Cow

PAPERCUT Z™

ARIOL Graphic Novels available from PAPERCUTZ™

ARIOL graphic novels are also available digitally wherever e-books are sold.

ARIOL
Just a Donkey Like You and Me
PAPERCUTZ

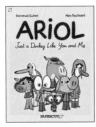

Graphic Novel #1
"Just a Donkey Like You and Me"

ARIOL
Thunder Horse
PAPERCUTZ

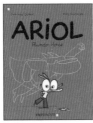

Graphic Novel #2
"Thunder Horse"

ARIOL
Happy as a Pig...
PAPERCUTZ

Graphic Novel #3
"Happy as a Pig..."

ARIOL
A Beautiful Cow
PAPERCUTZ

Graphic Novel #4
"A Beautiful Cow"

ARIOL
Bizzbilla Hits the Bullseye
PAPERCUTZ

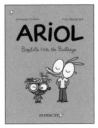

Graphic Novel #5
"Bizzbilla Hits the Bullseye"

Coming Soon

ARIOL
A Nasty Cat
PAPERCUTZ

Graphic Novel #6
"A Nasty Cat"

ARIOL
Top Dog
PAPERCUTZ

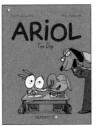

Graphic Novel #7
"Top Dog"

ARIOL
The Three Donkeys
PAPERCUTZ

Graphic Novel #8
"The Three Donkeys"

Emmanuel Guibert
Marc Boutavant
ARIOL
The Teeth of the Rabbit
PAPERCUTZ

Graphic Novel #9
"The Teeth of the Rabbit"

ARIOL
The Little Rats of the Opera
PAPERCUTZ

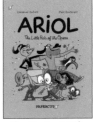

Graphic Novel #10
"The Little Rats of the Opera"

Emmanuel Guibert
Marc Boutavant
ARIOL
Boxed Set of Graphic Novels #1-3
PAPERCUTZ

Boxed Set of Graphic Novels #1-3

Emmanuel Guibert
Marc Boutavant
ARIOL
Boxed Set of Graphic Novels #4-6
PAPERCUTZ

Boxed Set of Graphic Novels #4-6

Emmanuel Guibert
Marc Boutavant
ARIOL
Where's PETULA?
PAPERCUTZ

"Where's Petula?" Graphic Novel

ARIOL graphic novels are available for $12.99 only in paperback, except for "Where's Petula?" which is $9.99. The ARIOL Boxed Sets are $38.99 each. Available from booksellers everywhere. You can also order online from papercutz.com. Or call 1-800-886-1223, Monday through Friday, 9 – 5 EST. MC, Visa, and AmEx accepted. To order by mail, please add $4.00 for postage and handling for first book ordered, $1.00 for each additional book and make check payable to NBM Publishing. Send to: Papercutz, 160 Broadway, Suite 700, East Wing, New York, NY 10038.

papercutz.com

A Beautiful Cow

To Mr. Nays,
– Emmanuel Guibert

ARIOL
#4 A Beautiful Cow

Emmanuel Guibert – Writer
Marc Boutavant – Artist
Rémi Chaurand – Colorist
Joe Johnson – Translation
Bryan Senka – Lettering
Beth Scorzato – Production Coordinator
Michael Petranek – Associate Editor
Jim Salicrup
Editor-in-Chief

Volume 4: Une jolie vache © Bayard Editions –– 2008

ISBN: 978-1-59707-513-8

Printed in China

Papercutz books may be purchased for business or promotional use. For information on bulk purchases please
contact Macmillan Corporate and Premium Sales Department at (800) 221-7945 x5442.

Distributed by Macmillan
Third Papercutz Printing

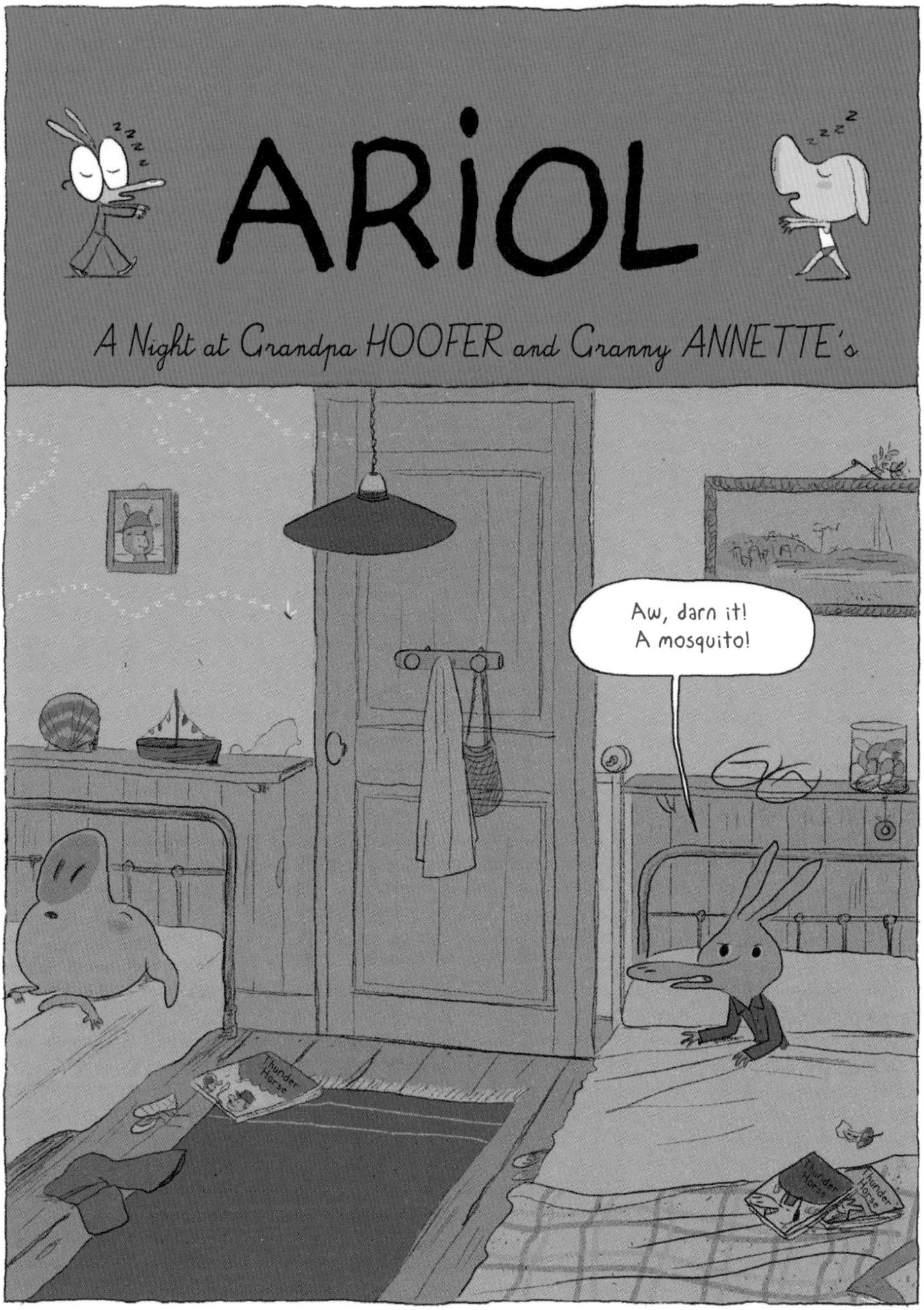
ARiOL
A Night at Grandpa HOOFER and Granny ANNETTE's
Aw, darn it! A mosquito!
Thunder Horse
Thunder Horse
Thunder Horse

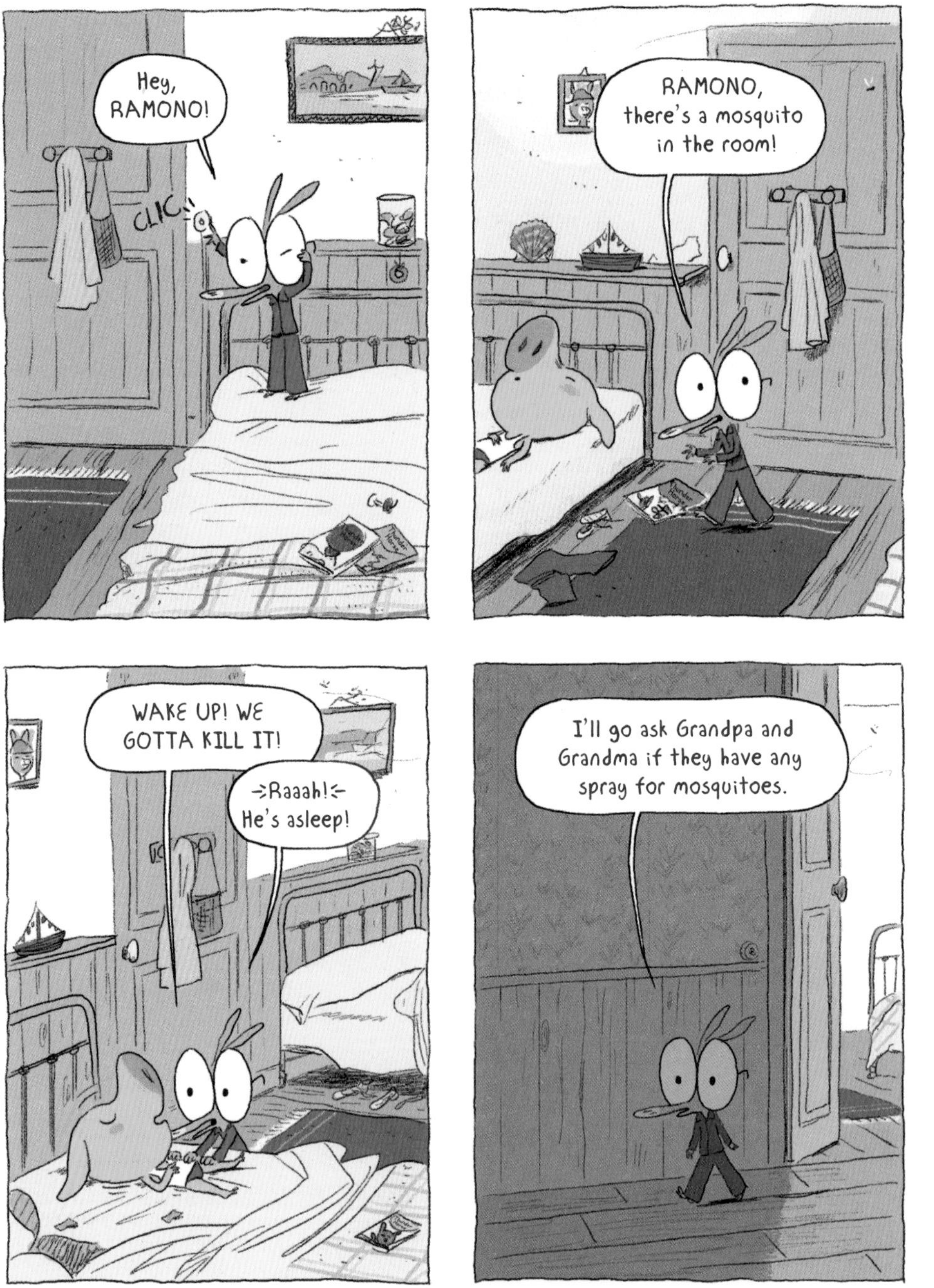
Hey, RAMONO!
CLIC
RAMONO, there's a mosquito in the room!
WAKE UP! WE GOTTA KILL IT!
Raaah! He's asleep!
I'll go ask Grandpa and Grandma if they have any spray for mosquitoes.

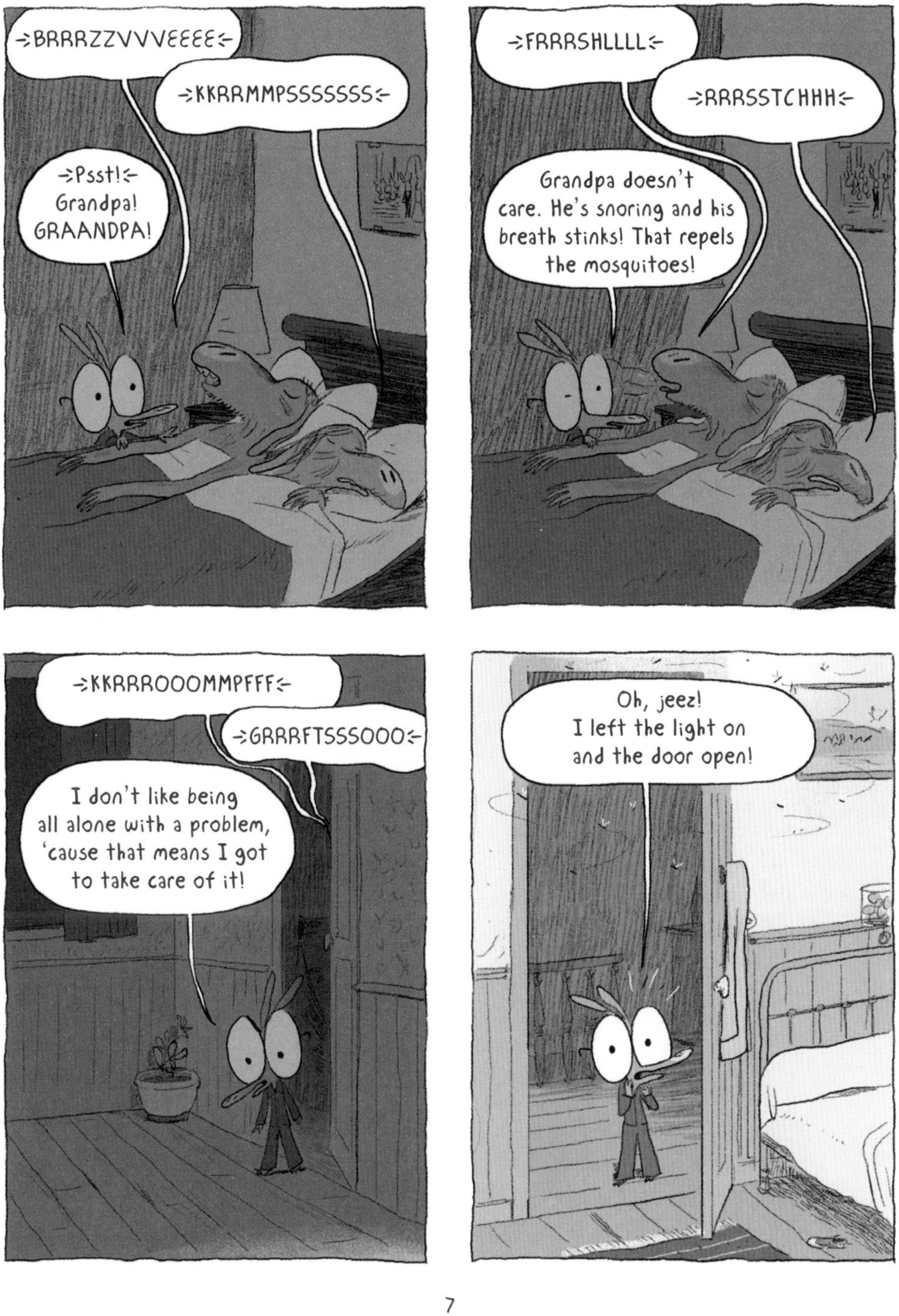
BRRRZZVVVEEEE
KKRRMMPSSSSSSS
Psst! Grandpa! GRAANDPA!
FRRRSHLLLL
RRRSSTCHHH
Grandpa doesn't care. He's snoring and his breath stinks! That repels the mosquitoes!
KKRRROOOMMPFFF
GRRRFTSSSOOO
I don't like being all alone with a problem, 'cause that means I got to take care of it!
Oh, jeez! I left the light on and the door open!

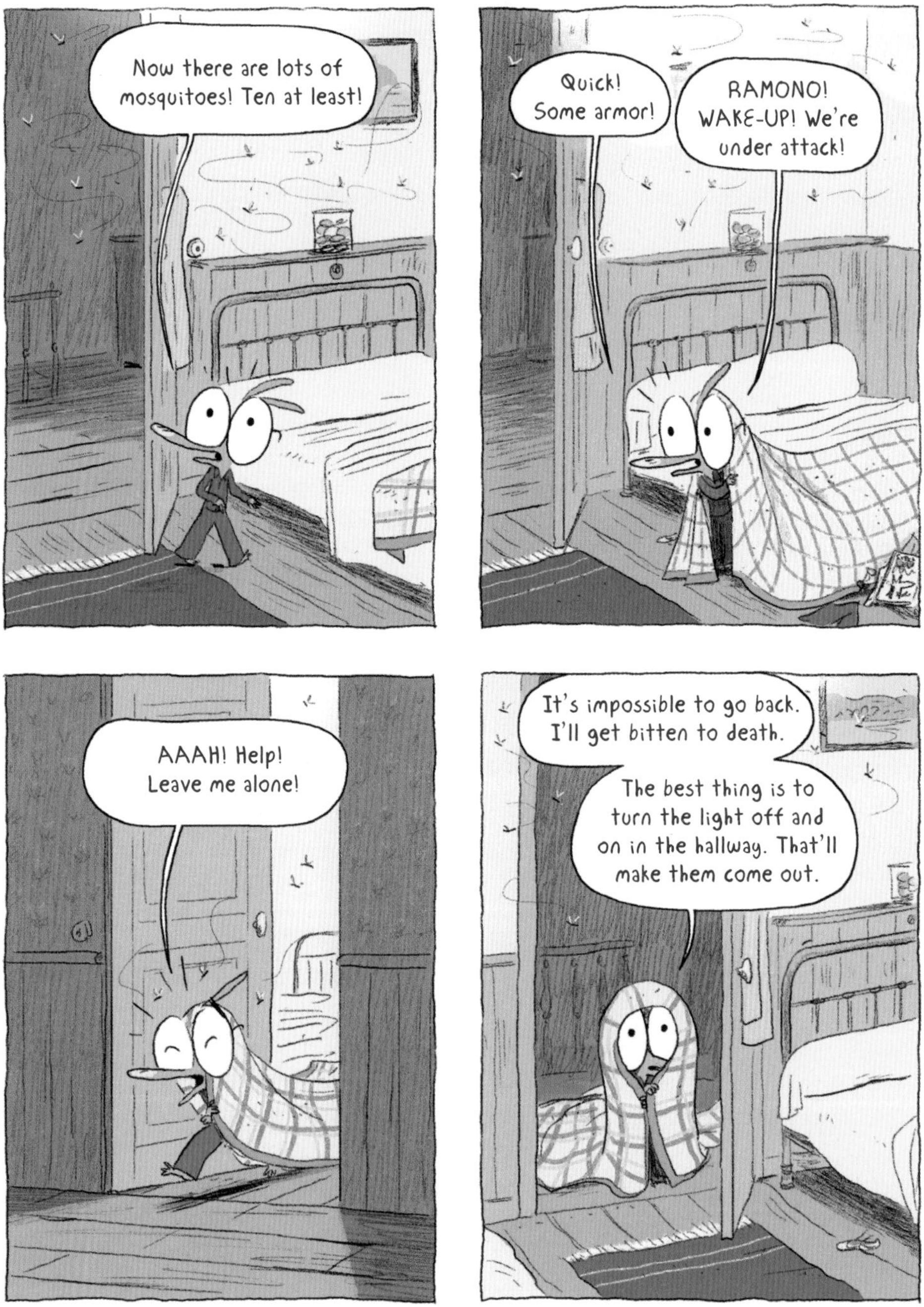
Now there are lots of mosquitoes! Ten at least!
Quick! Some armor!
RAMONO! WAKE-UP! We're under attack!
AAAH! Help! Leave me alone!
It's impossible to go back. I'll get bitten to death.
The best thing is to turn the light off and on in the hallway. That'll make them come out.

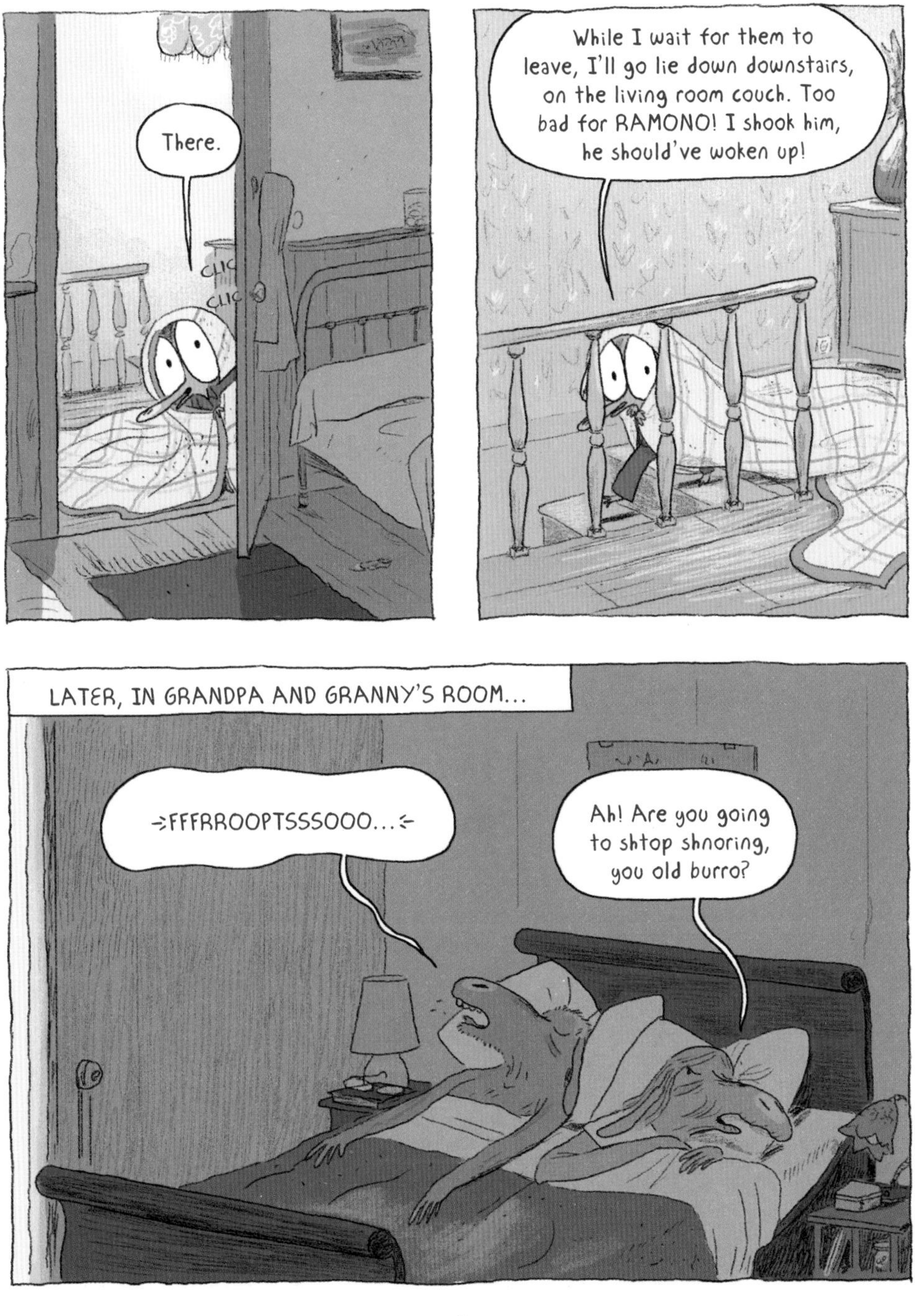
There.
CLIC
CLIC
While I wait for them to leave, I'll go lie down downstairs, on the living room couch. Too bad for RAMONO! I shook him, he should've woken up!
LATER, IN GRANDPA AND GRANNY'S ROOM...
FFFRROOPTSSSOOO...
Ah! Are you going to shtop shnoring, you old burro?

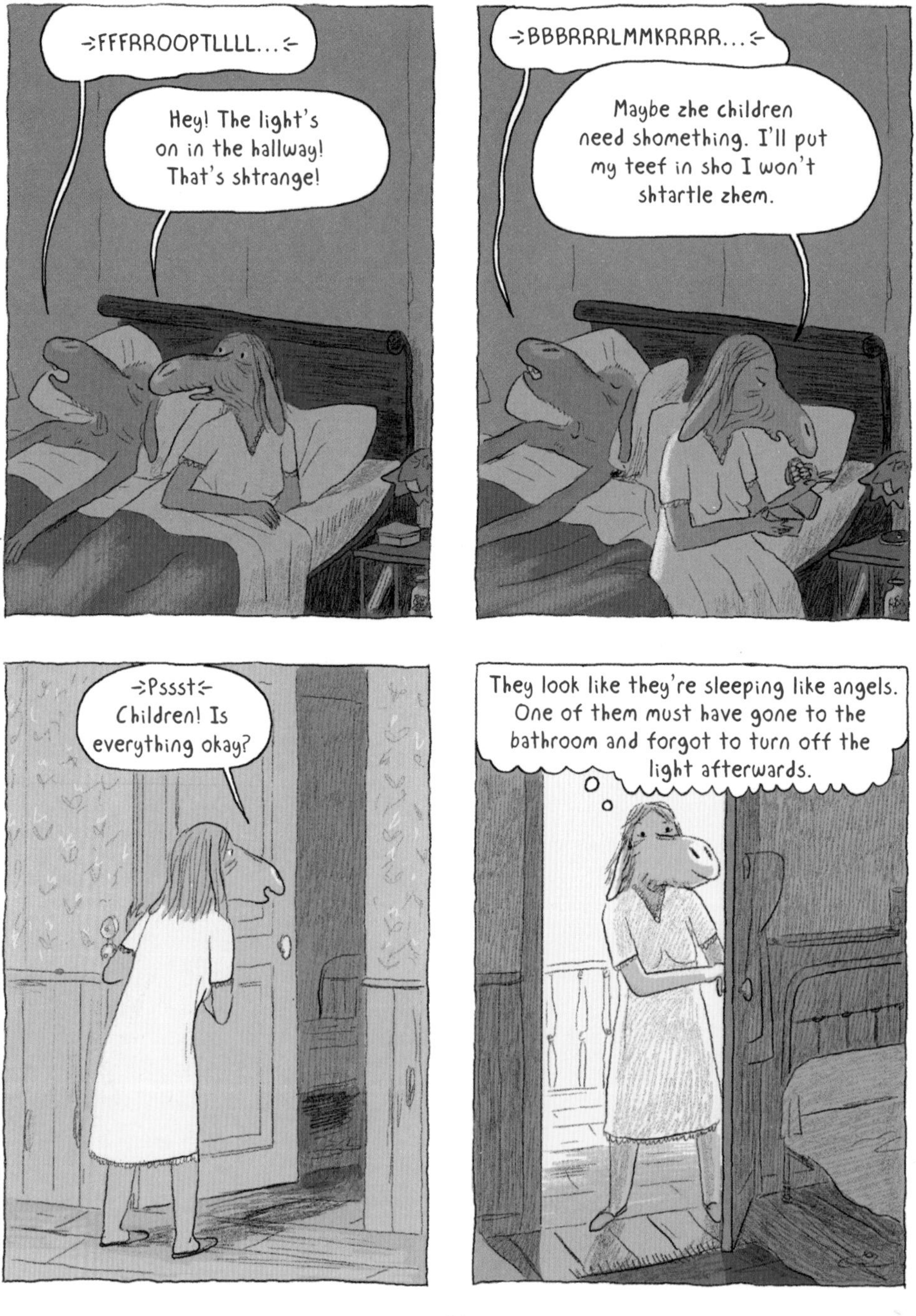

⇒FFFRROOPTLLLL...⇐
Hey! The light's on in the hallway! That's shtrange!
⇒BBBRRRLMMKRRRR...⇐
Maybe zhe children need shomething. I'll put my teef in sho I won't shtartle zhem.
⇒Pssst⇐ Children! Is everything okay?
They look like they're sleeping like angels. One of them must have gone to the bathroom and forgot to turn off the light afterwards.

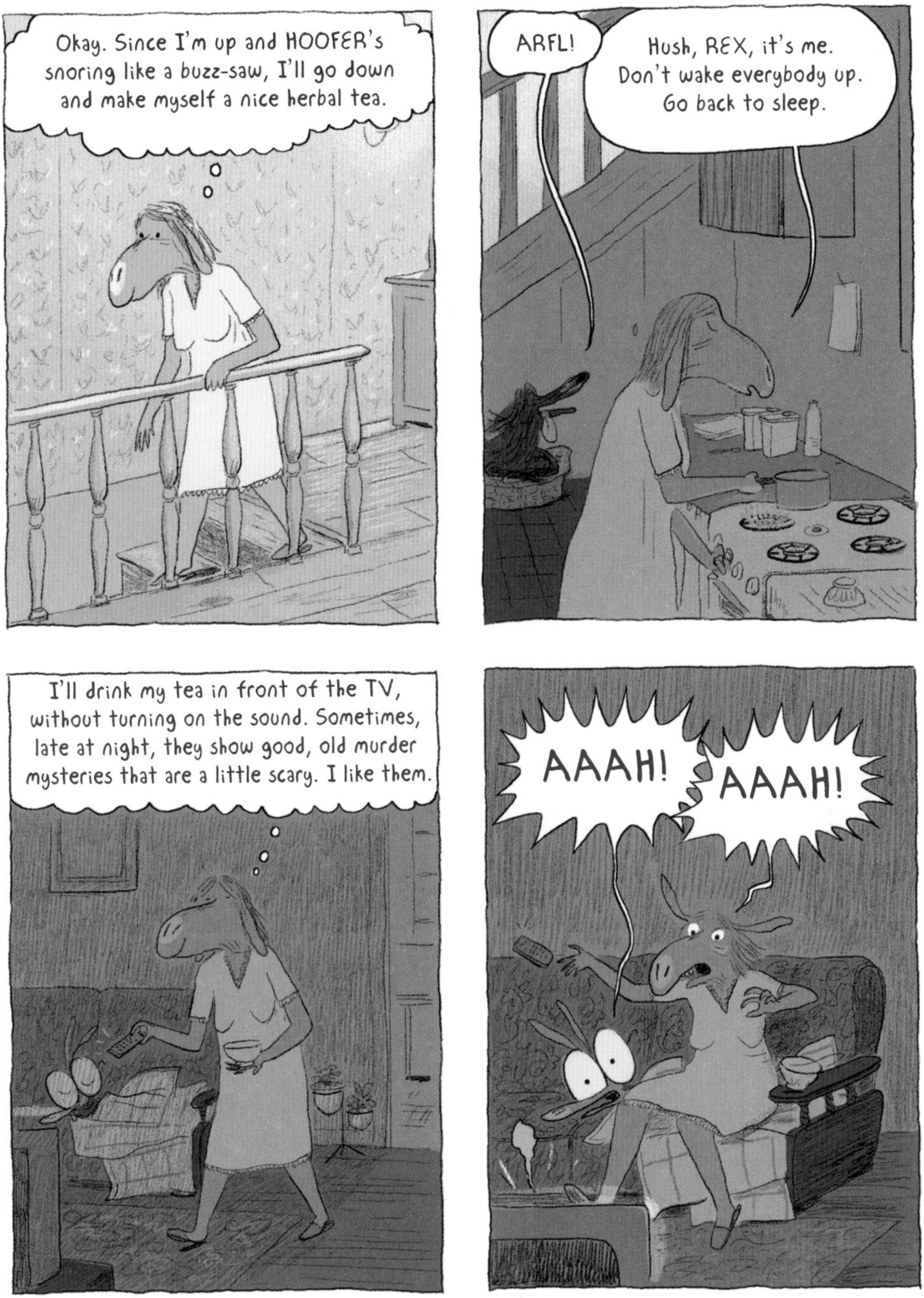
Okay. Since I'm up and HOOFER's snoring like a buzz-saw, I'll go down and make myself a nice herbal tea.
ARFL!
Hush, REX, it's me. Don't wake everybody up. Go back to sleep.
I'll drink my tea in front of the TV, without turning on the sound. Sometimes, late at night, they show good, old murder mysteries that are a little scary. I like them.
AAAH!
AAAH!

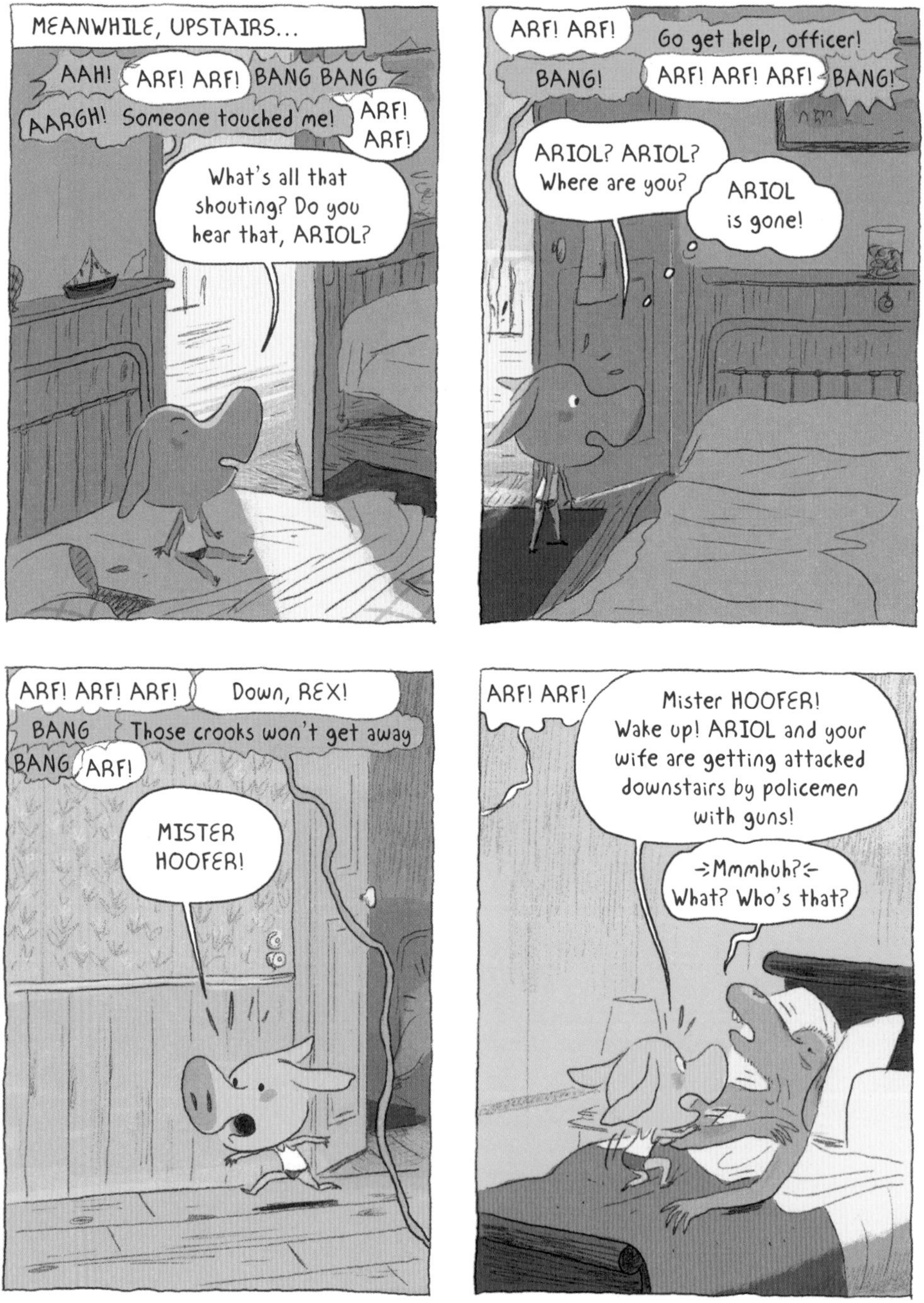
MEANWHILE, UPSTAIRS...
AAH!
ARF! ARF!
BANG BANG
AARGH! Someone touched me!
ARF! ARF!
What's all that shouting? Do you hear that, ARIOL?
ARF! ARF!
Go get help, officer!
BANG!
ARF! ARF! ARF!
BANG!
ARIOL? ARIOL? Where are you?
ARIOL is gone!
ARF! ARF! ARF!
Down, REX!
BANG
Those crooks won't get away
BANG
ARF!
MISTER HOOFER!
ARF! ARF!
Mister HOOFER! Wake up! ARIOL and your wife are getting attacked downstairs by policemen with guns!
Mmmhuh? What? Who's that?

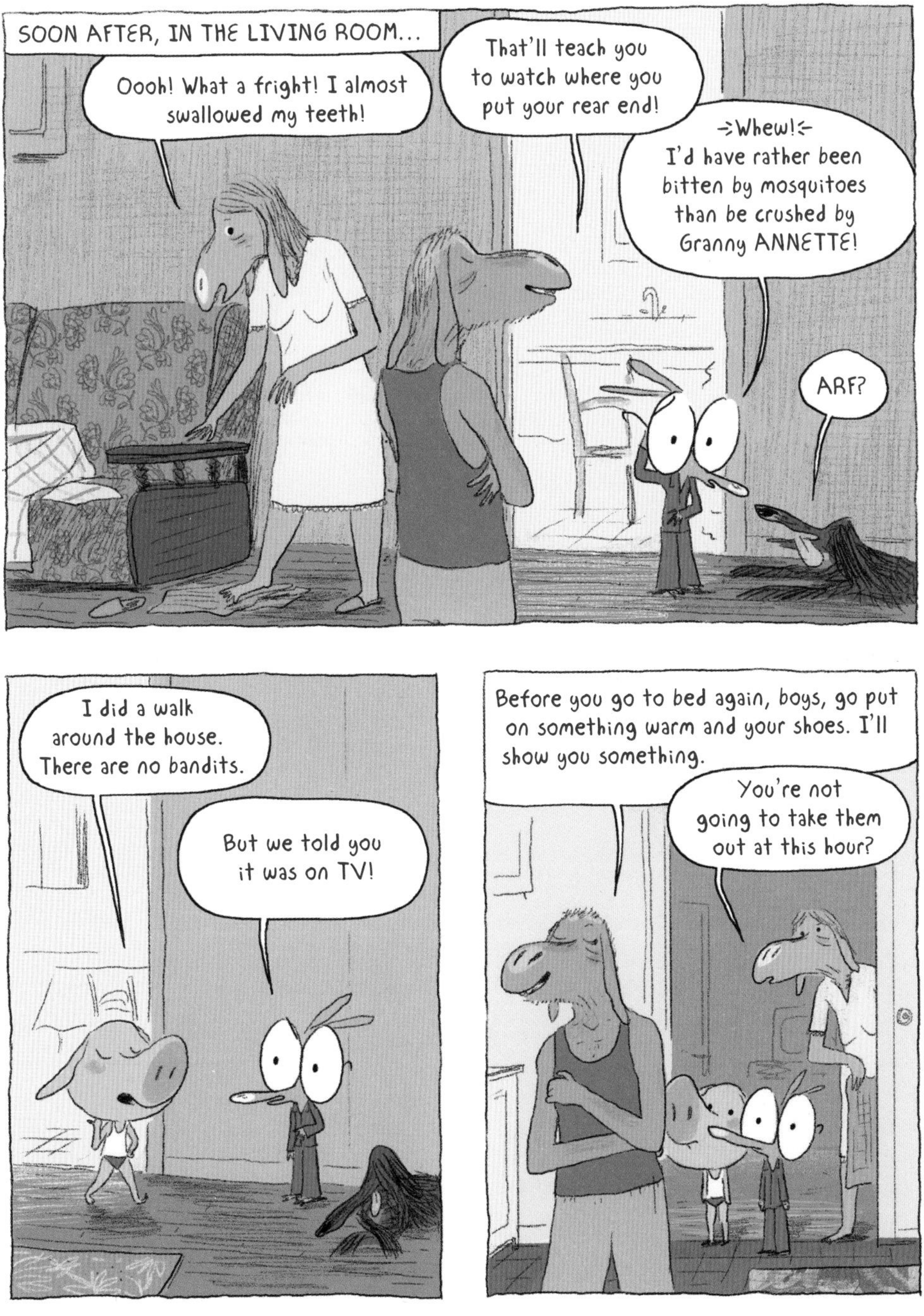
SOON AFTER, IN THE LIVING ROOM...
Oooh! What a fright! I almost swallowed my teeth!
That'll teach you to watch where you put your rear end!
Whew! I'd have rather been bitten by mosquitoes than be crushed by Granny ANNETTE!
ARF?
I did a walk around the house. There are no bandits.
But we told you it was on TV!
Before you go to bed again, boys, go put on something warm and your shoes. I'll show you something.
You're not going to take them out at this hour?

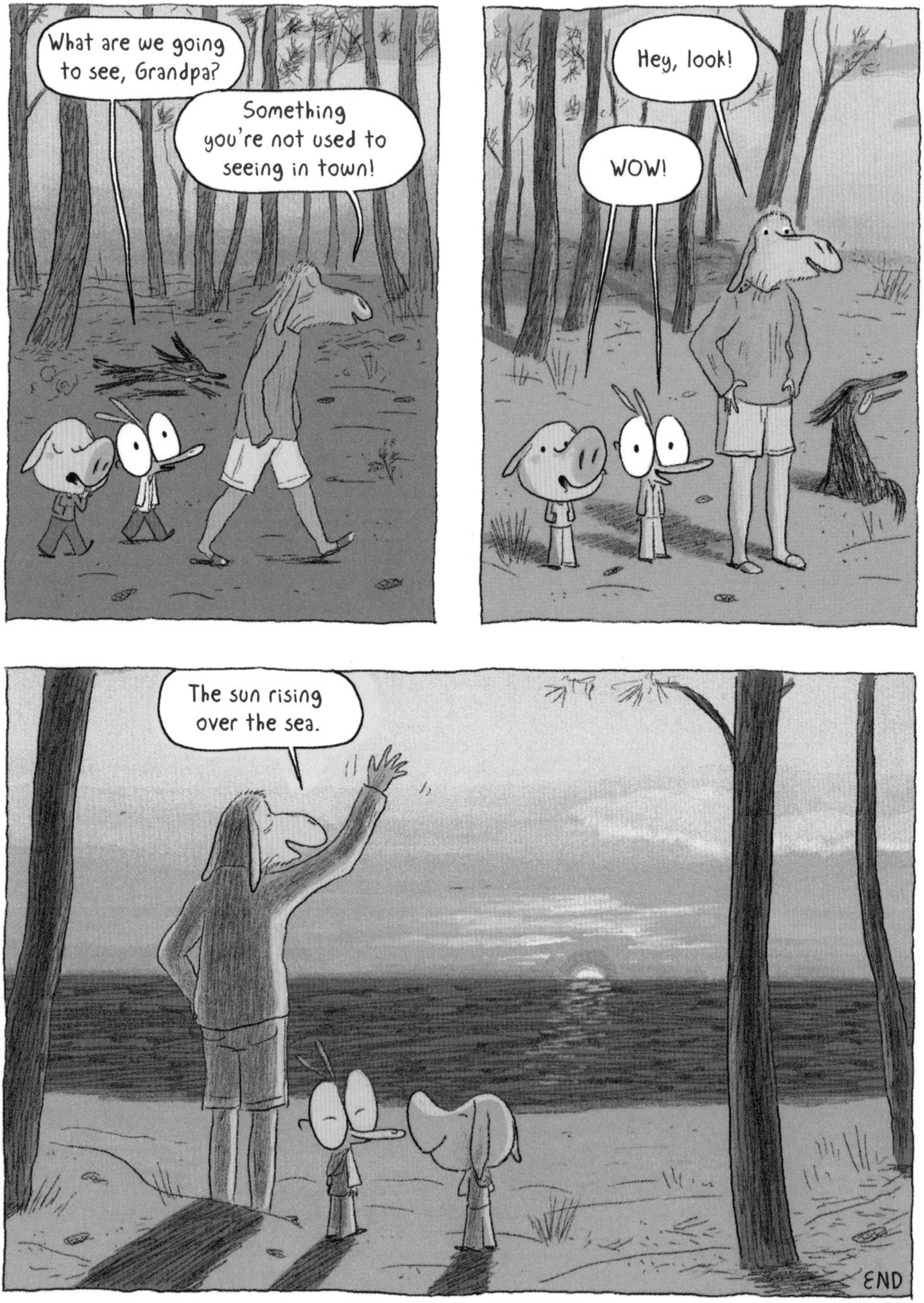
What are we going to see, Grandpa?
Something you're not used to seeing in town!
Hey, look!
WOW!
The sun rising over the sea.
END

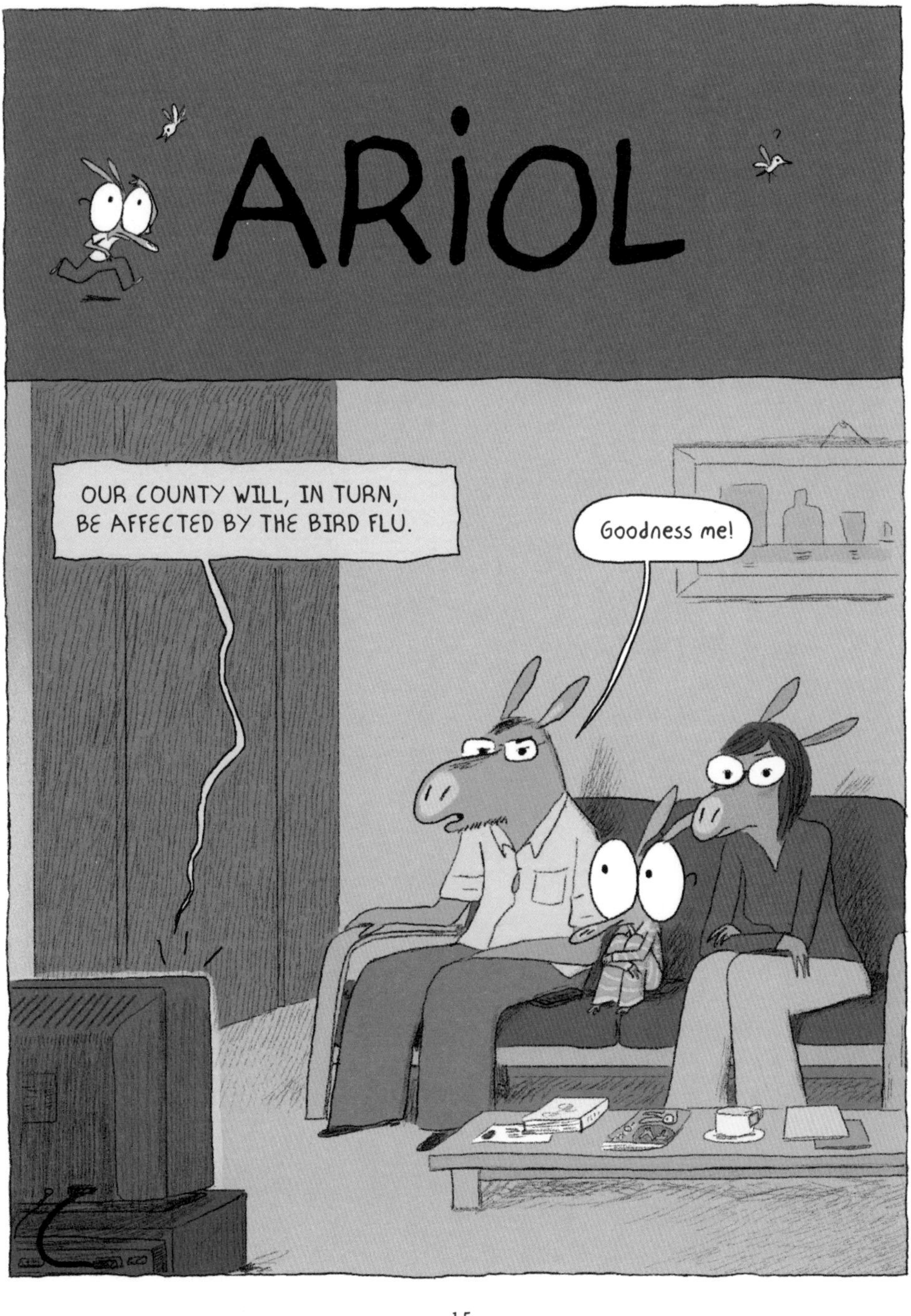
ARiOL
OUR COUNTY WILL, IN TURN, BE AFFECTED BY THE BIRD FLU.
Goodness me!

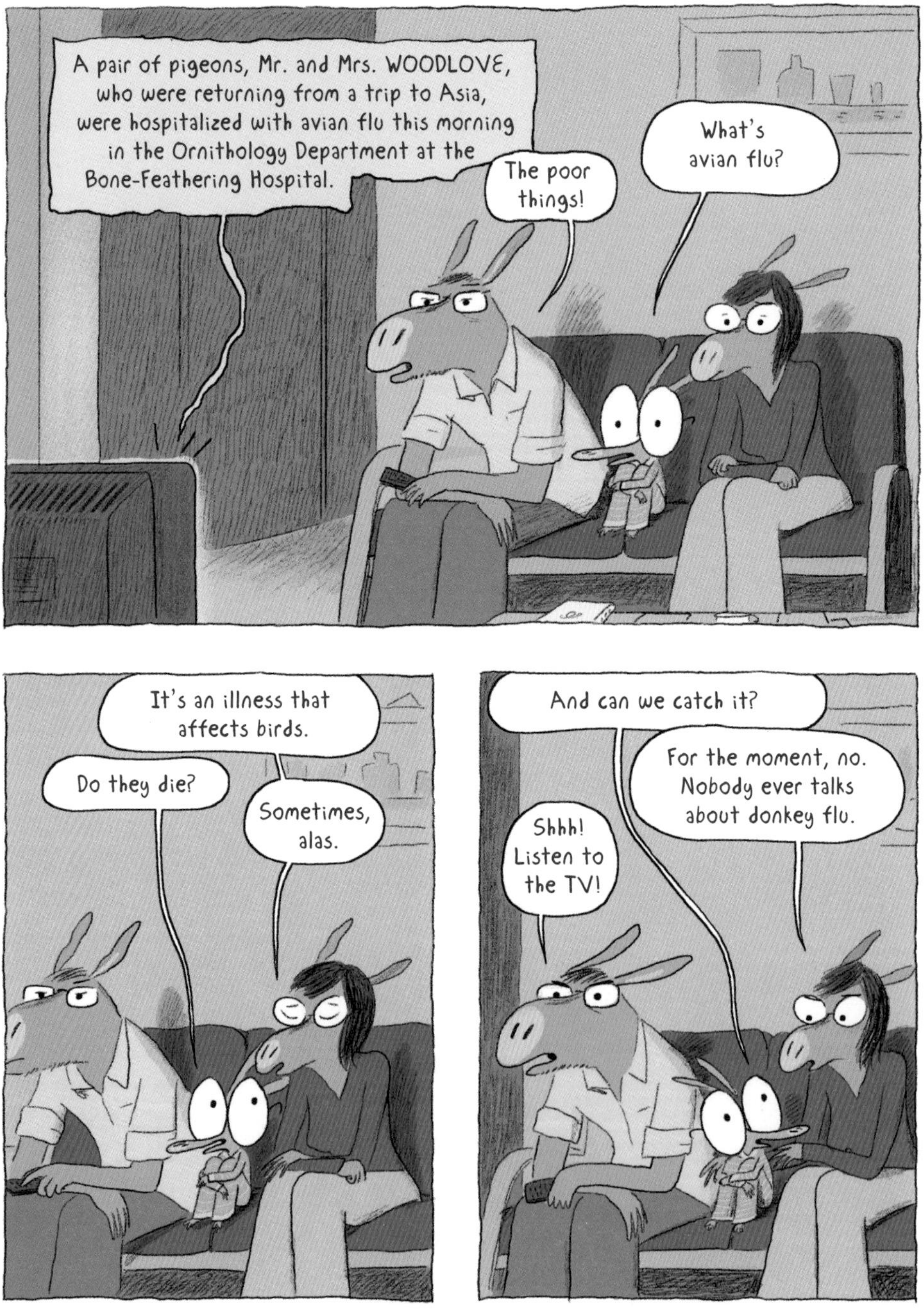
A pair of pigeons, Mr. and Mrs. WOODLOVE, who were returning from a trip to Asia, were hospitalized with avian flu this morning in the Ornithology Department at the Bone-Feathering Hospital.
The poor things!
What's avian flu?
It's an illness that affects birds.
Do they die?
Sometimes, alas.
And can we catch it?
For the moment, no. Nobody ever talks about donkey flu.
Shhh! Listen to the TV!

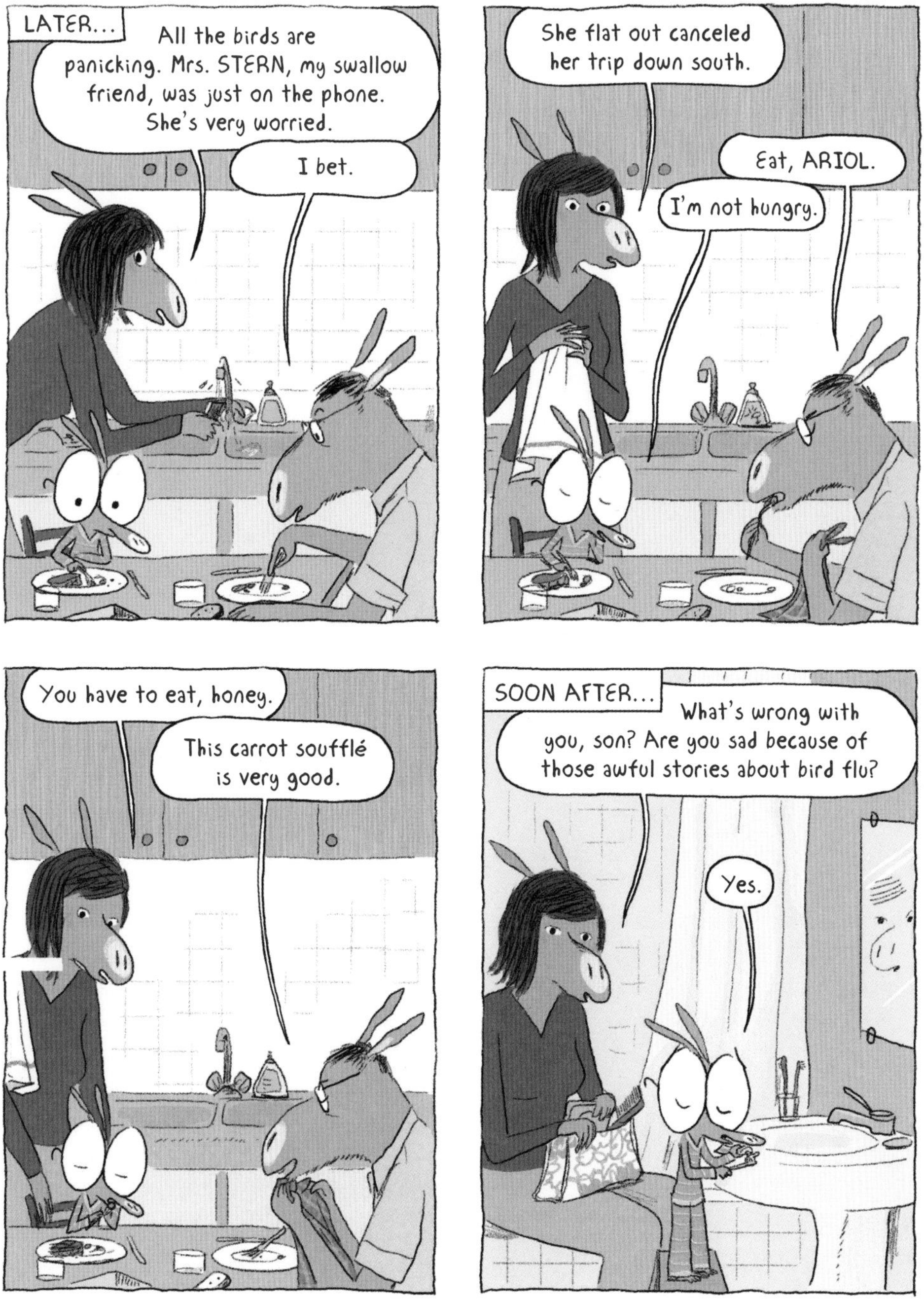
LATER...
All the birds are panicking. Mrs. STERN, my swallow friend, was just on the phone. She's very worried.
I bet.
She flat out canceled her trip down south.
Eat, ARIOL.
I'm not hungry.
You have to eat, honey.
This carrot soufflé is very good.
SOON AFTER...
What's wrong with you, son? Are you sad because of those awful stories about bird flu?
Yes.

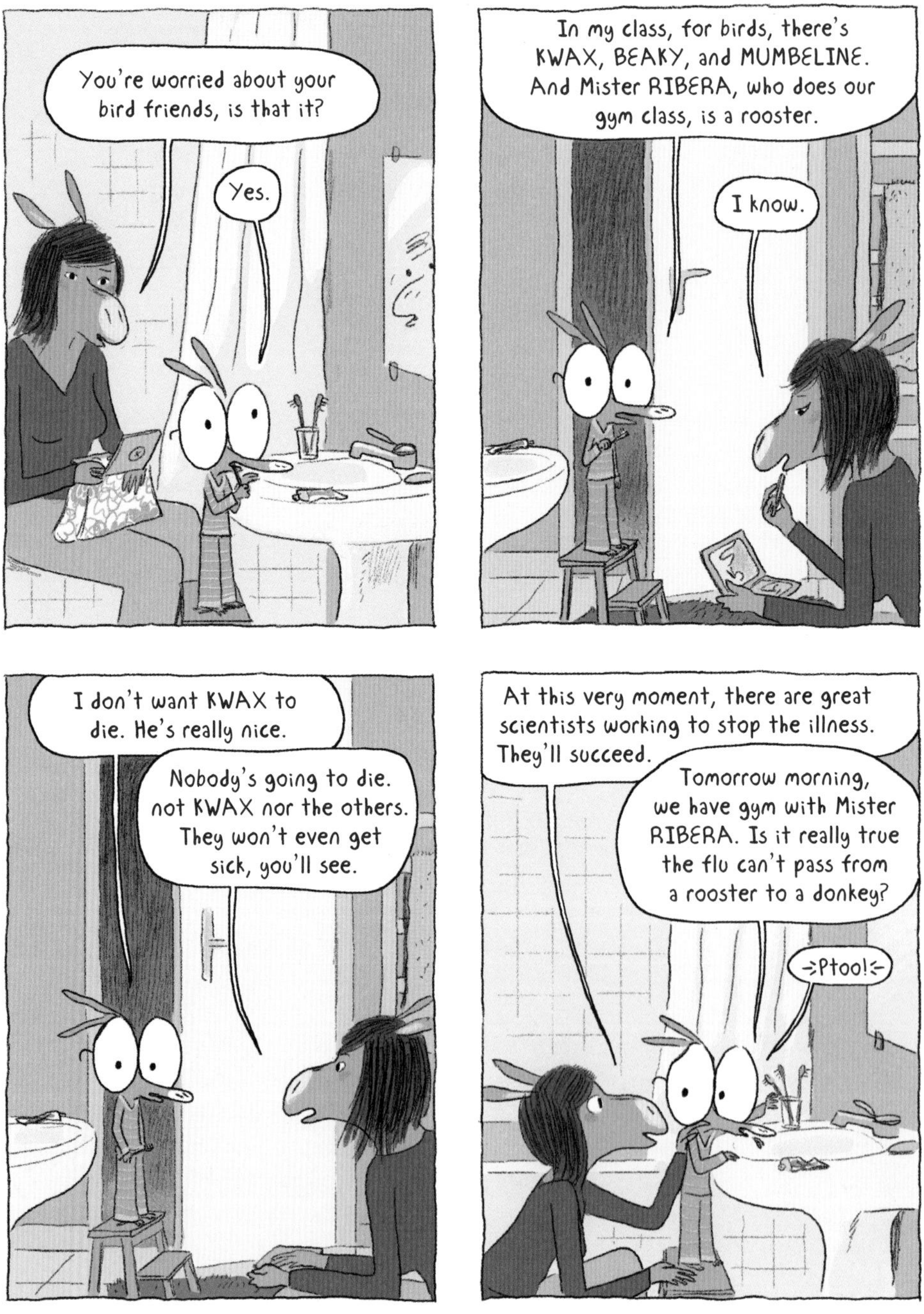
You're worried about your bird friends, is that it?
Yes.
In my class, for birds, there's KWAX, BEAKY, and MUMBELINE. And Mister RIBERA, who does our gym class, is a rooster.
I know.
I don't want KWAX to die. He's really nice.
Nobody's going to die. not KWAX nor the others. They won't even get sick, you'll see.
At this very moment, there are great scientists working to stop the illness. They'll succeed.
Tomorrow morning, we have gym with Mister RIBERA. Is it really true the flu can't pass from a rooster to a donkey?
Ptoo!

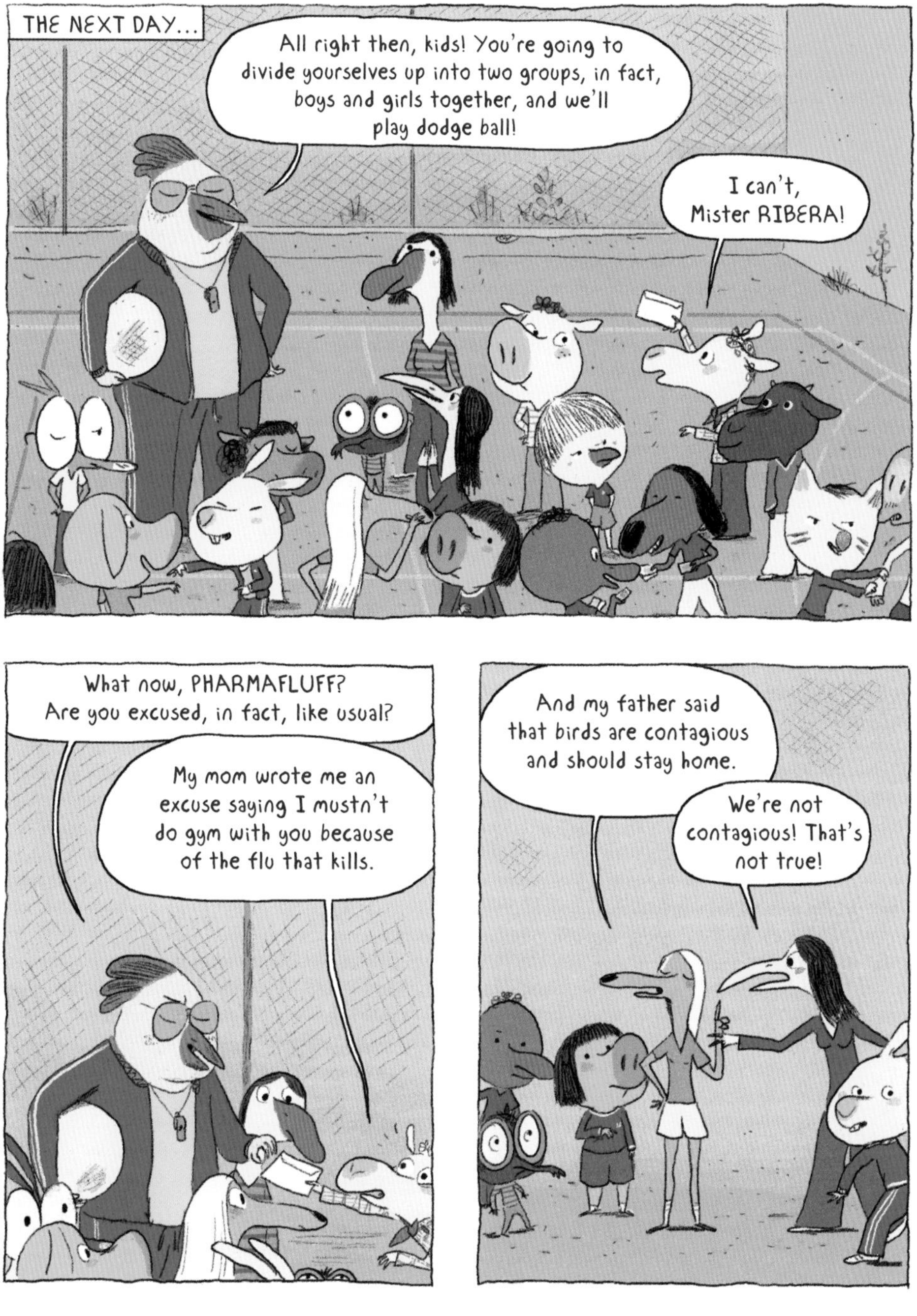
THE NEXT DAY...
All right then, kids! You're going to divide yourselves up into two groups, in fact, boys and girls together, and we'll play dodge ball!
I can't, Mister RIBERA!
What now, PHARMAFLUFF? Are you excused, in fact, like usual?
My mom wrote me an excuse saying I mustn't do gym with you because of the flu that kills.
And my father said that birds are contagious and should stay home.
We're not contagious! That's not true!

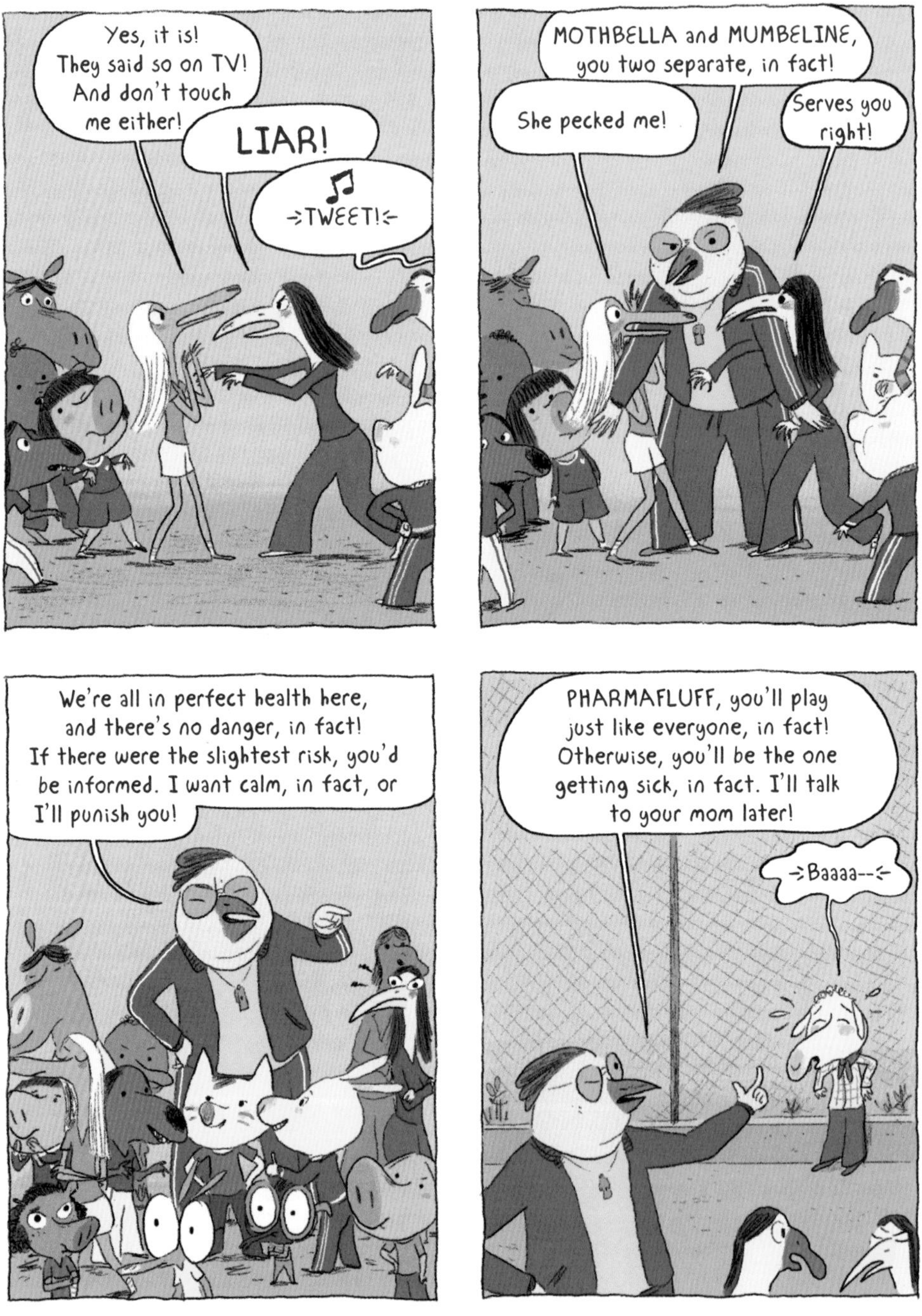
Yes, it is! They said so on TV! And don't touch me either!
LIAR!
♫ TWEET!
MOTHBELLA and MUMBELINE, you two separate, in fact!
She pecked me!
Serves you right!
We're all in perfect health here, and there's no danger, in fact! If there were the slightest risk, you'd be informed. I want calm, in fact, or I'll punish you!
PHARMAFLUFF, you'll play just like everyone, in fact! Otherwise, you'll be the one getting sick, in fact. I'll talk to your mom later!
Baaaa--

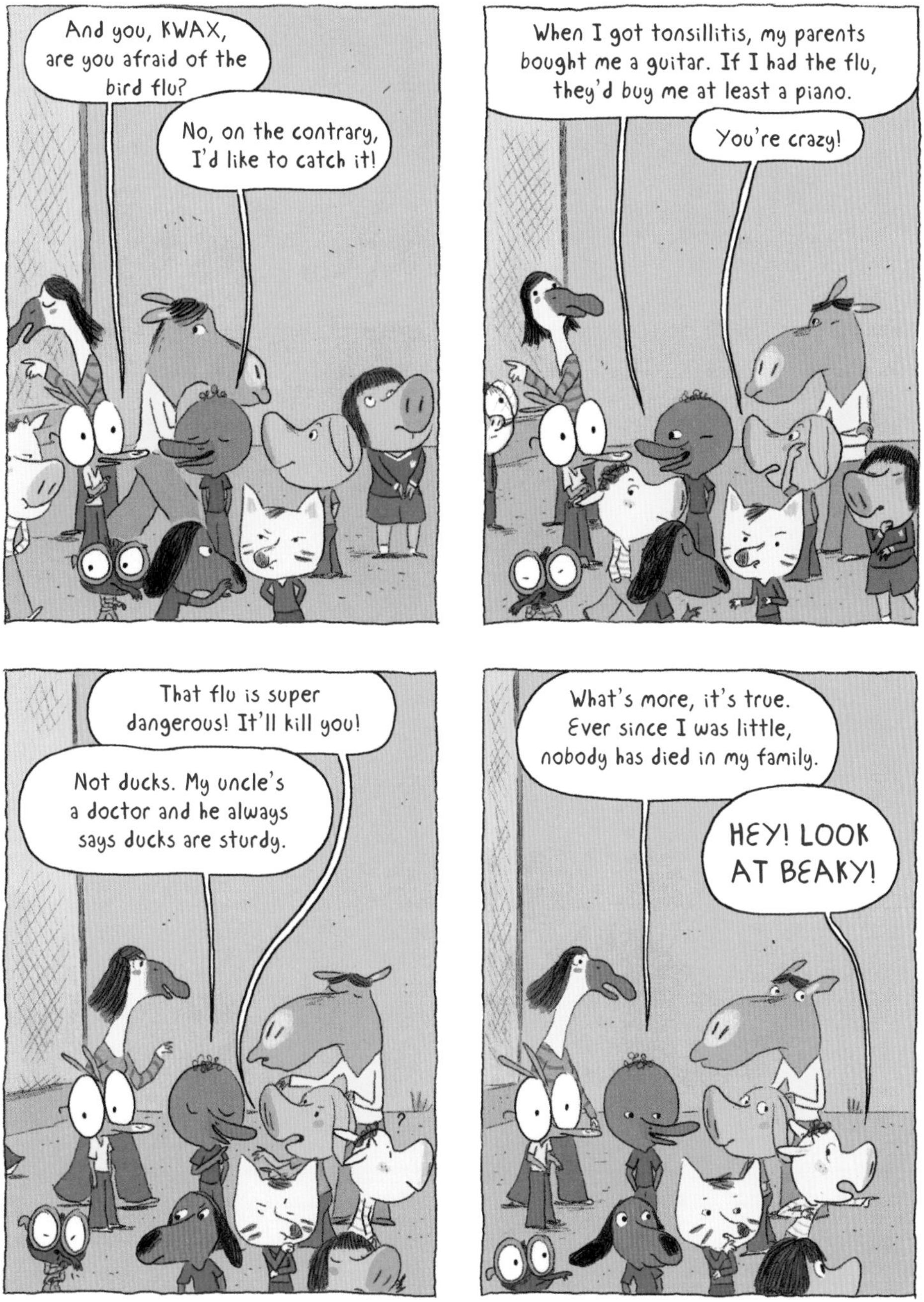
And you, KWAX, are you afraid of the bird flu?
No, on the contrary, I'd like to catch it!
When I got tonsillitis, my parents bought me a guitar. If I had the flu, they'd buy me at least a piano.
You're crazy!
That flu is super dangerous! It'll kill you!
Not ducks. My uncle's a doctor and he always says ducks are sturdy.
What's more, it's true. Ever since I was little, nobody has died in my family.
HEY! LOOK AT BEAKY!

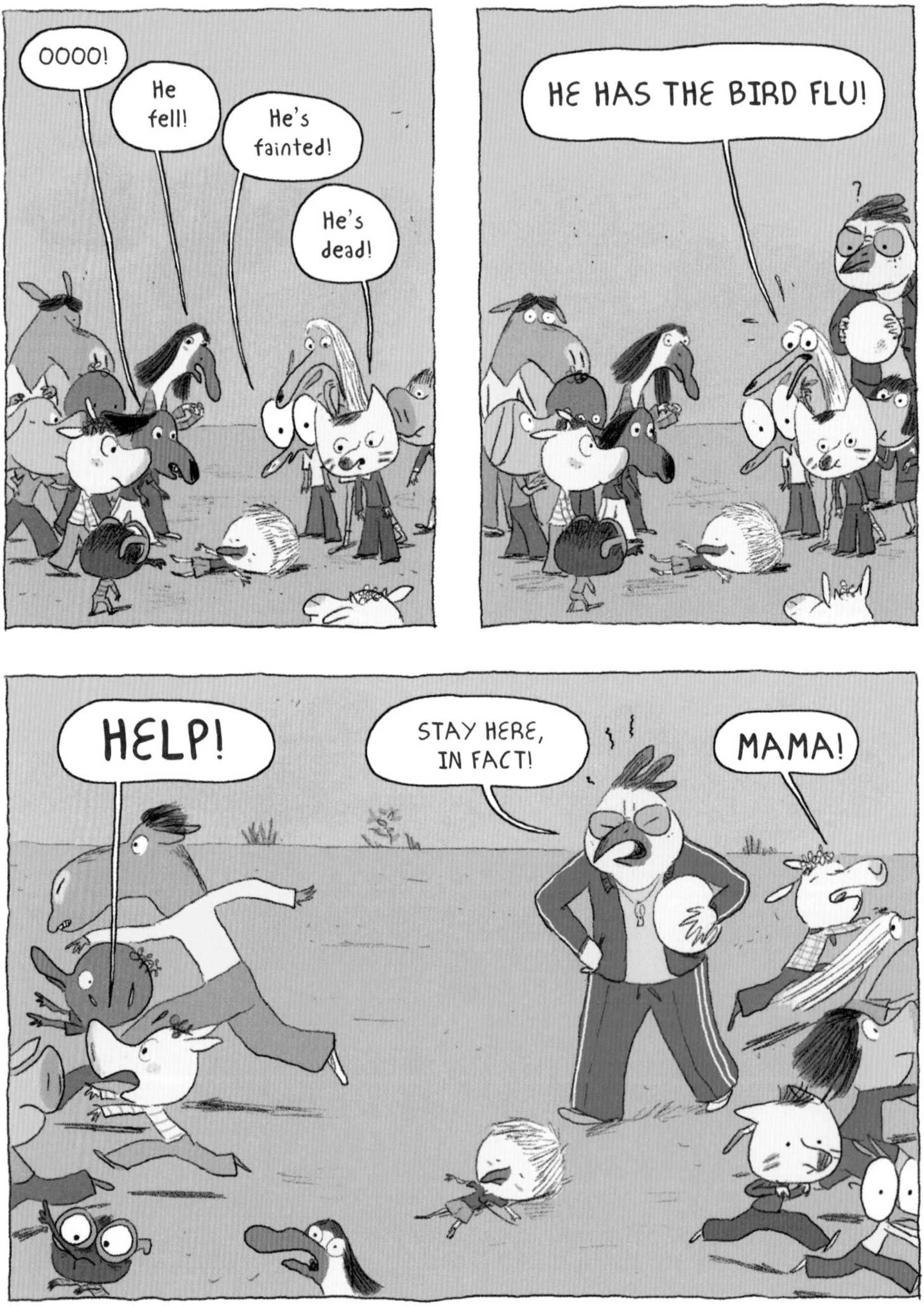
OOOO!
He fell!
He's fainted!
He's dead!
HE HAS THE BIRD FLU!
HELP!
STAY HERE, IN FACT!
MAMA!

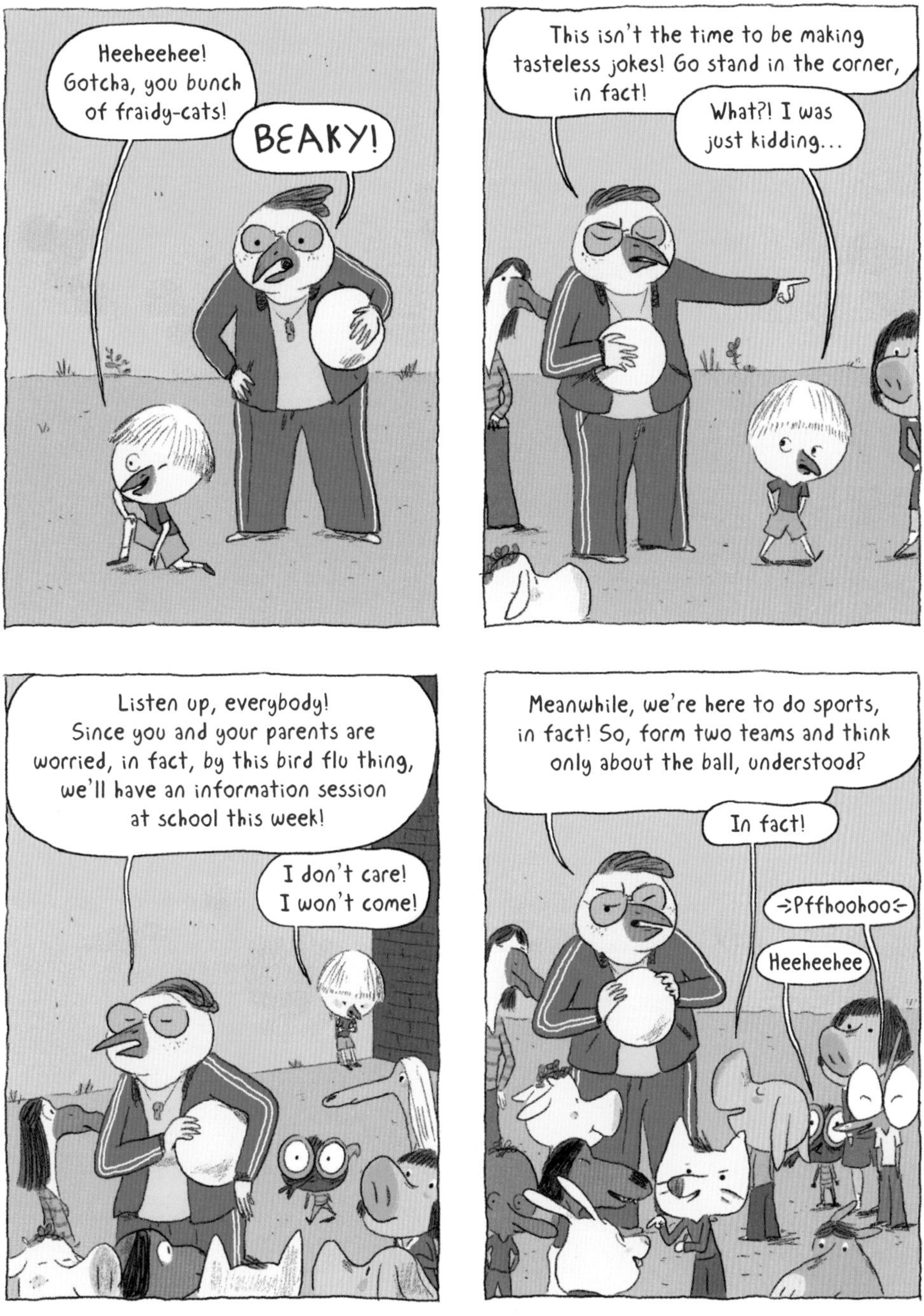
Heeheehee! Gotcha, you bunch of fraidy-cats!
BEAKY!
This isn't the time to be making tasteless jokes! Go stand in the corner, in fact!
What?! I was just kidding...
Listen up, everybody! Since you and your parents are worried, in fact, by this bird flu thing, we'll have an information session at school this week!
I don't care! I won't come!
Meanwhile, we're here to do sports, in fact! So, form two teams and think only about the ball, understood?
In fact!
Pffhoohoo
Heeheehee

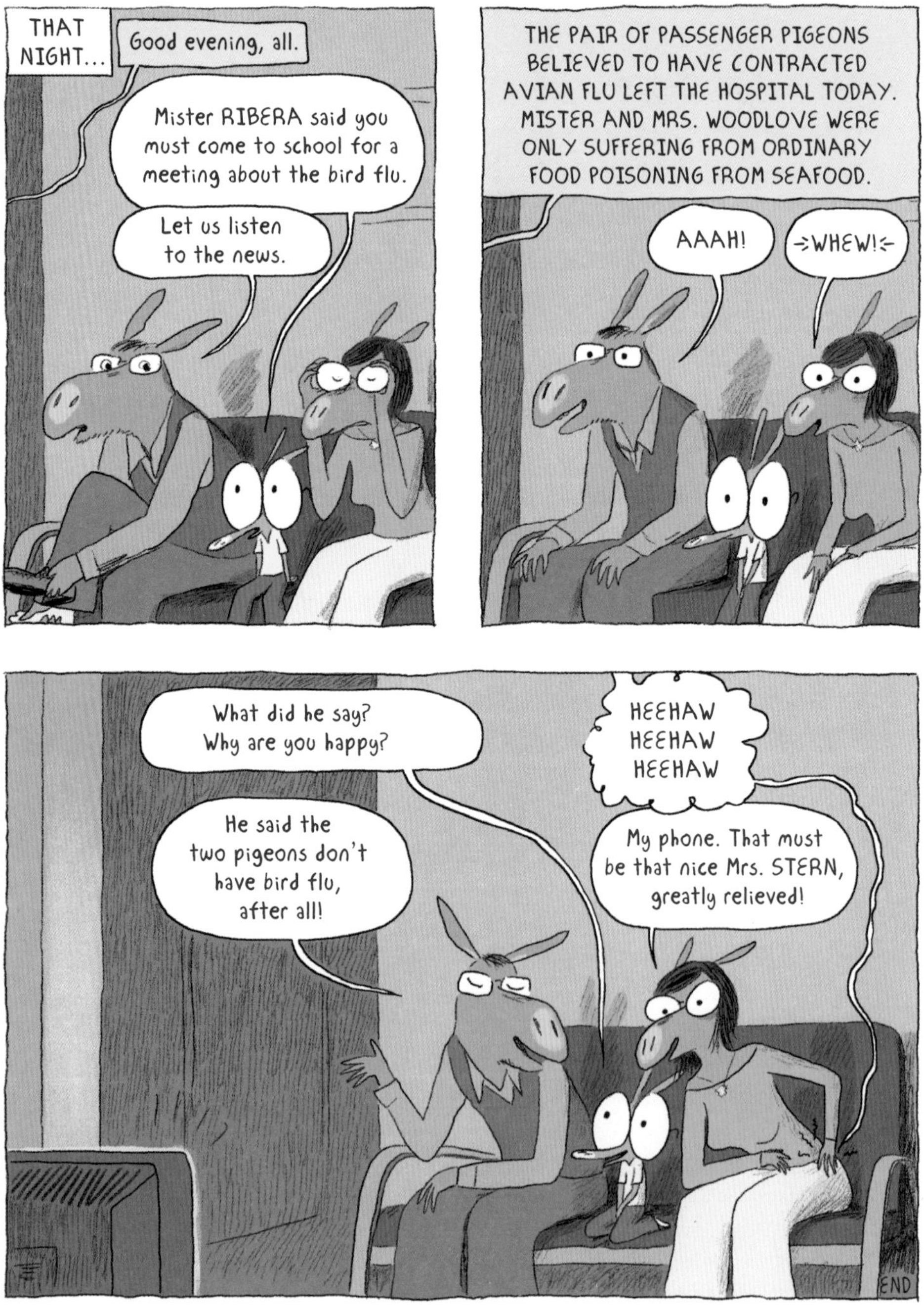
THAT NIGHT...
Good evening, all.
Mister RIBERA said you must come to school for a meeting about the bird flu.
Let us listen to the news.
THE PAIR OF PASSENGER PIGEONS BELIEVED TO HAVE CONTRACTED AVIAN FLU LEFT THE HOSPITAL TODAY. MISTER AND MRS. WOODLOVE WERE ONLY SUFFERING FROM ORDINARY FOOD POISONING FROM SEAFOOD.
AAAH!
WHEW!
What did he say? Why are you happy?
He said the two pigeons don't have bird flu, after all!
HEEHAW HEEHAW HEEHAW
My phone. That must be that nice Mrs. STERN, greatly relieved!
END

ARiOL

At the TOTO Station

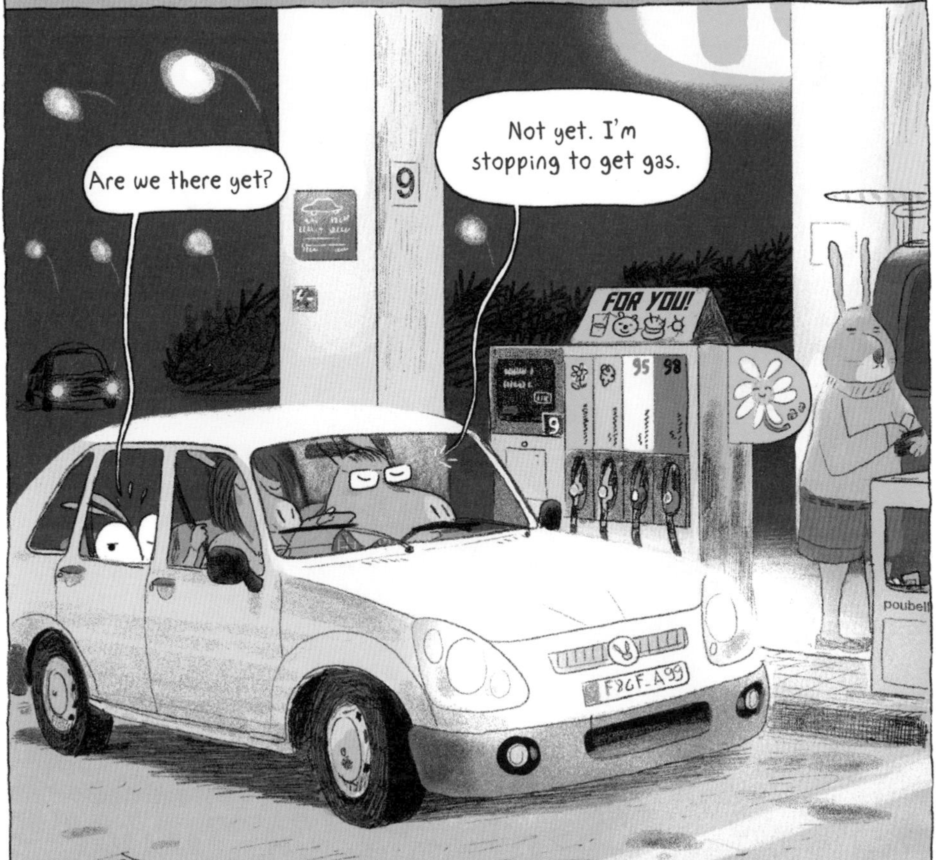

Are we there yet?
Not yet. I'm stopping to get gas.
9
FOR YOU!
95
98
F86F_A99
poubell

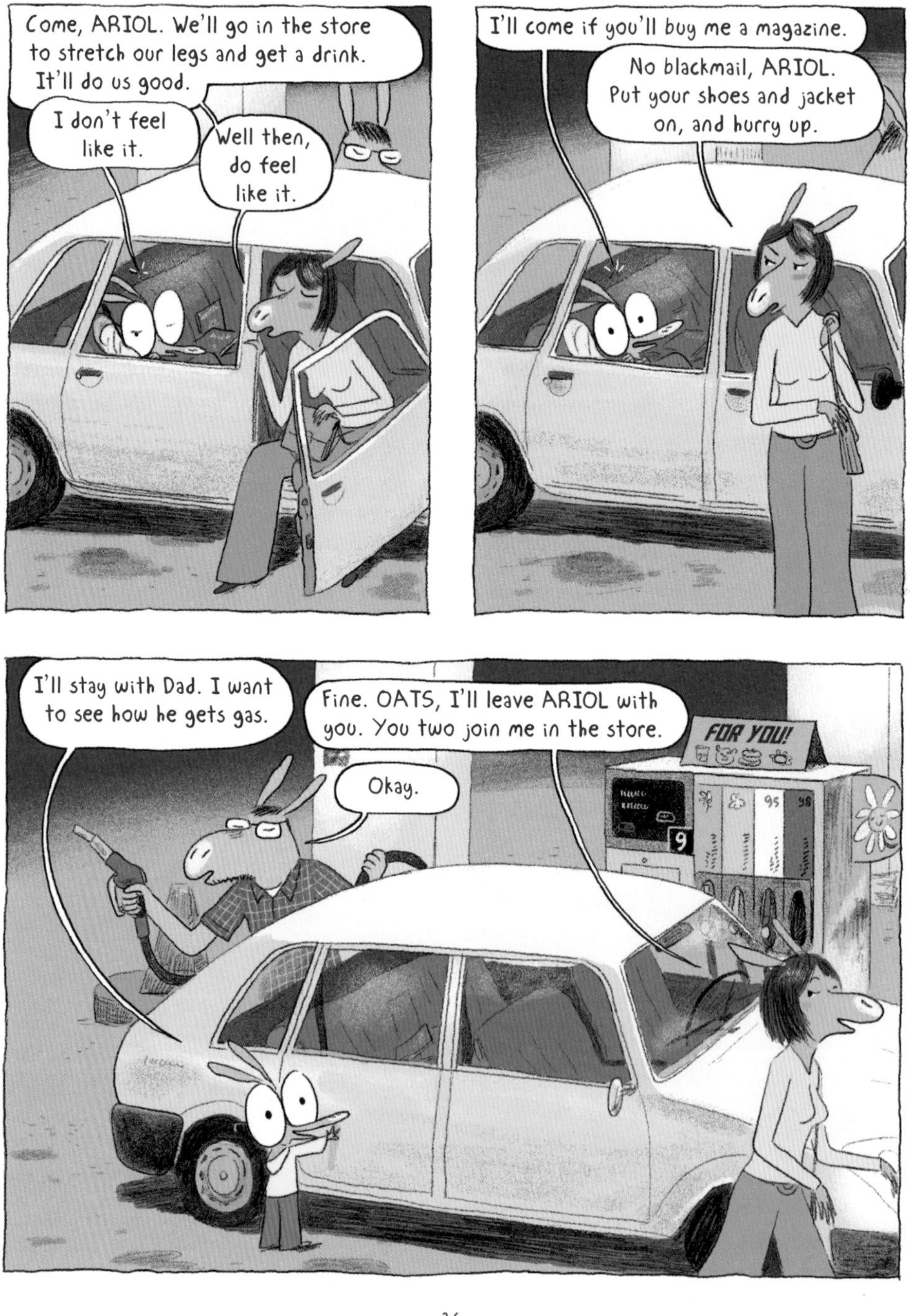
Come, ARIOL. We'll go in the store to stretch our legs and get a drink. It'll do us good.
I don't feel like it.
Well then, do feel like it.
I'll come if you'll buy me a magazine.
No blackmail, ARIOL. Put your shoes and jacket on, and hurry up.
I'll stay with Dad. I want to see how he gets gas.
Fine. OATS, I'll leave ARIOL with you. You two join me in the store.
Okay.
FOR YOU!
95
98
9

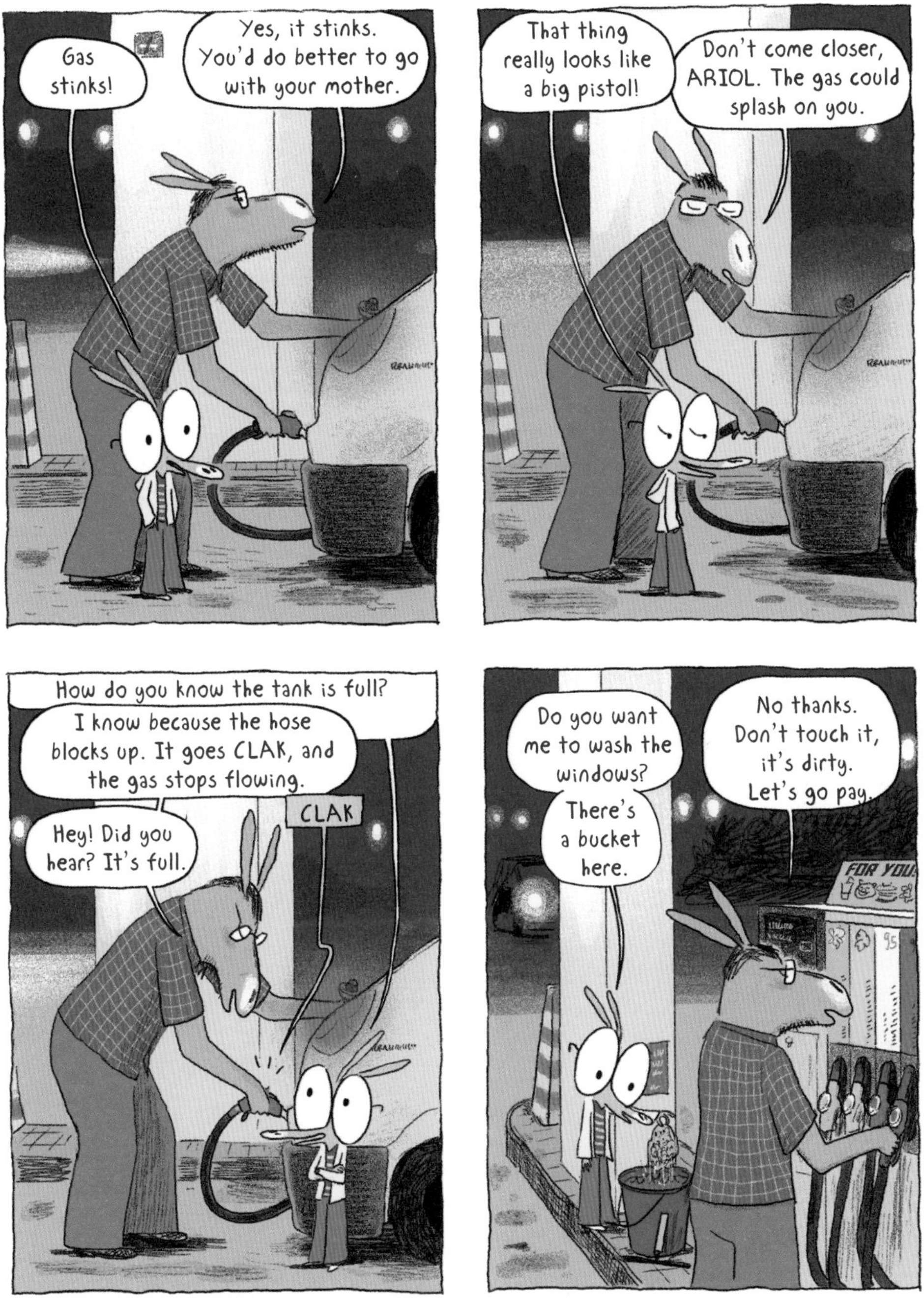

Gas stinks!
Yes, it stinks. You'd do better to go with your mother.
That thing really looks like a big pistol!
Don't come closer, ARIOL. The gas could splash on you.
How do you know the tank is full?
I know because the hose blocks up. It goes CLAK, and the gas stops flowing.
Hey! Did you hear? It's full.
CLAK
Do you want me to wash the windows?
There's a bucket here.
No thanks. Don't touch it, it's dirty. Let's go pay.
FOR YOU

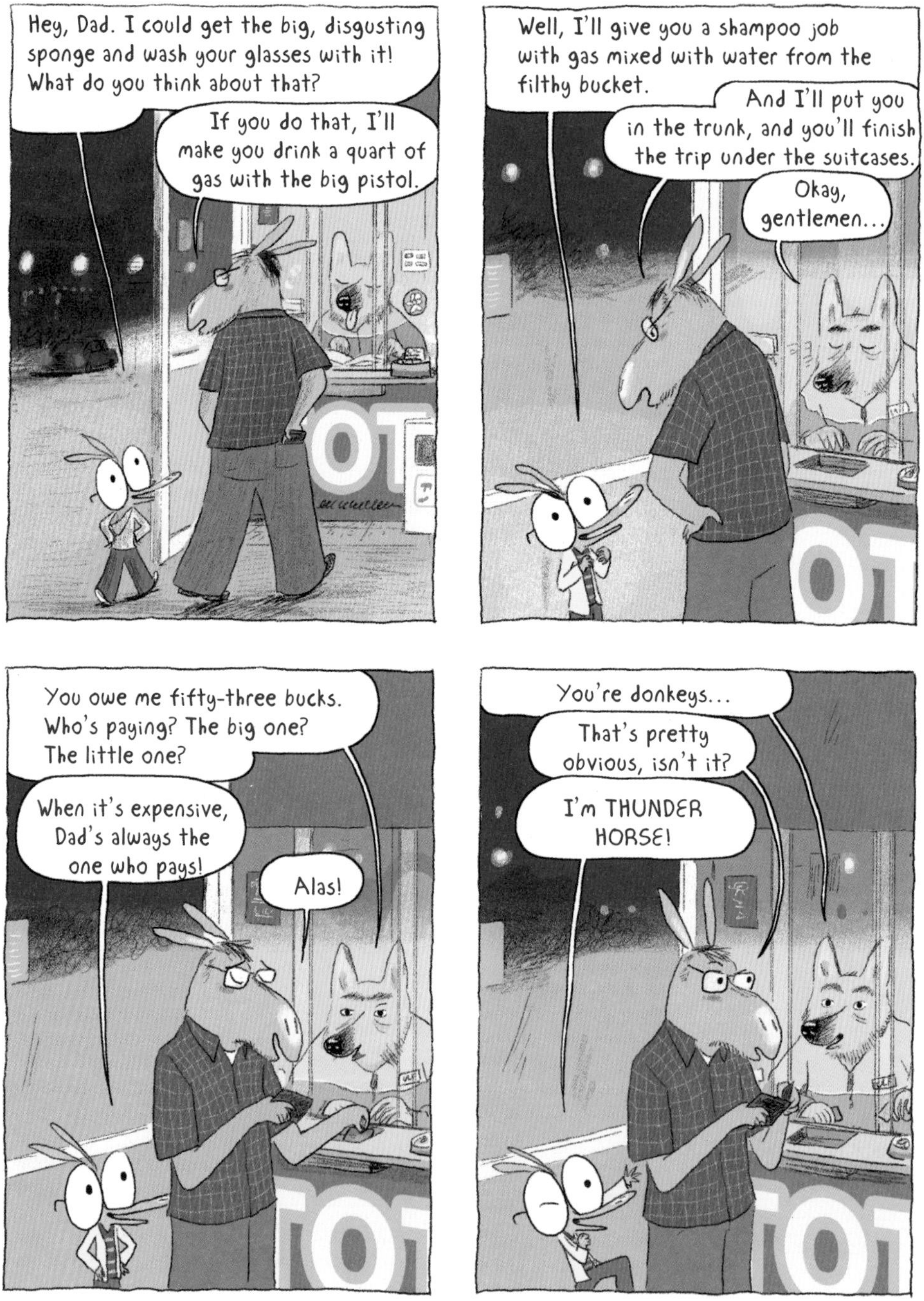
Hey, Dad. I could get the big, disgusting sponge and wash your glasses with it! What do you think about that?
If you do that, I'll make you drink a quart of gas with the big pistol.
Well, I'll give you a shampoo job with gas mixed with water from the filthy bucket.
And I'll put you in the trunk, and you'll finish the trip under the suitcases.
Okay, gentlemen...
You owe me fifty-three bucks. Who's paying? The big one? The little one?
When it's expensive, Dad's always the one who pays!
Alas!
You're donkeys...
That's pretty obvious, isn't it?
I'm THUNDER HORSE!

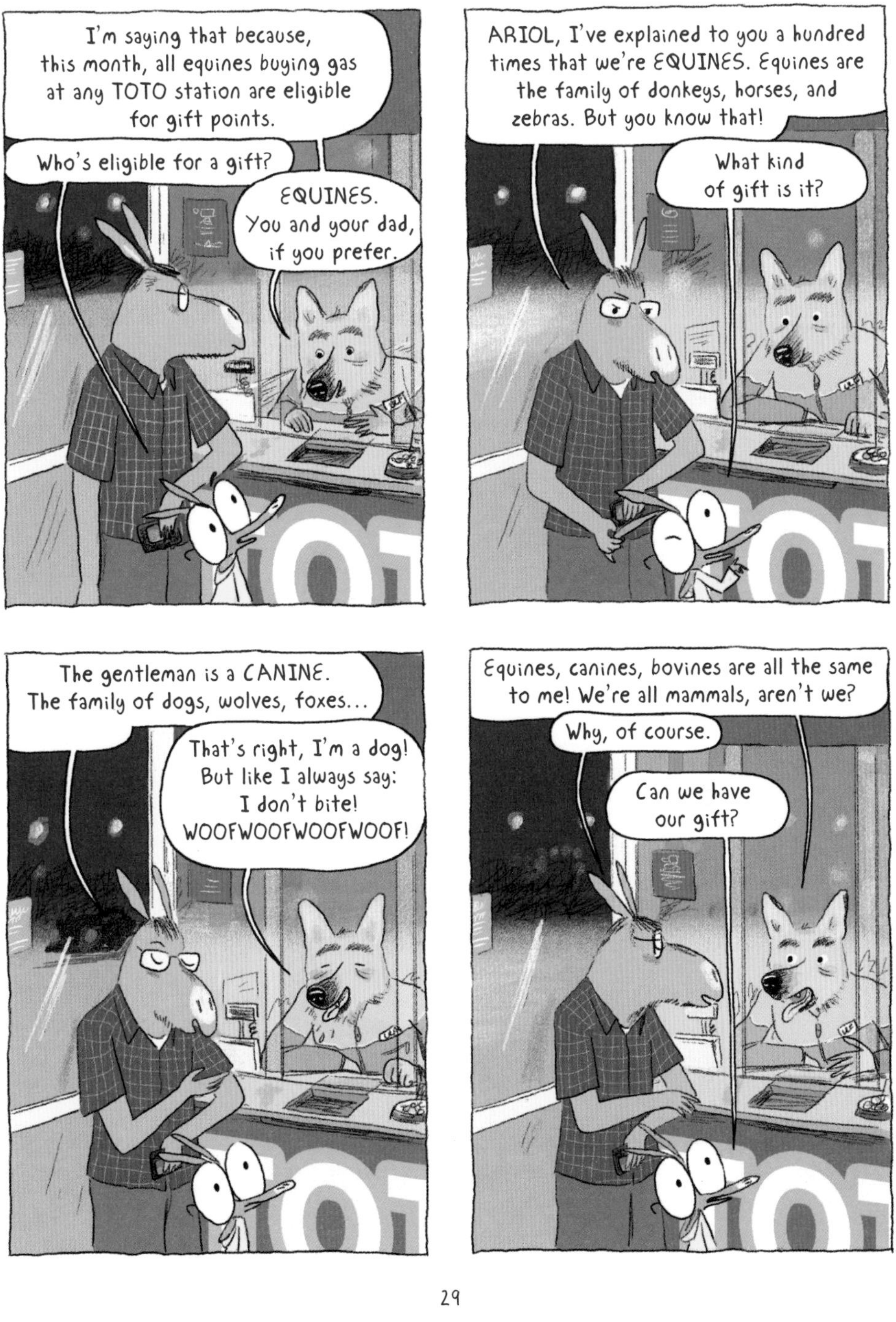
I'm saying that because, this month, all equines buying gas at any TOTO station are eligible for gift points.
Who's eligible for a gift?
EQUINES. You and your dad, if you prefer.
ARIOL, I've explained to you a hundred times that we're EQUINES. Equines are the family of donkeys, horses, and zebras. But you know that!
What kind of gift is it?
The gentleman is a CANINE. The family of dogs, wolves, foxes...
That's right, I'm a dog! But like I always say: I don't bite! WOOFWOOFWOOFWOOF!
Equines, canines, bovines are all the same to me! We're all mammals, aren't we?
Why, of course.
Can we have our gift?

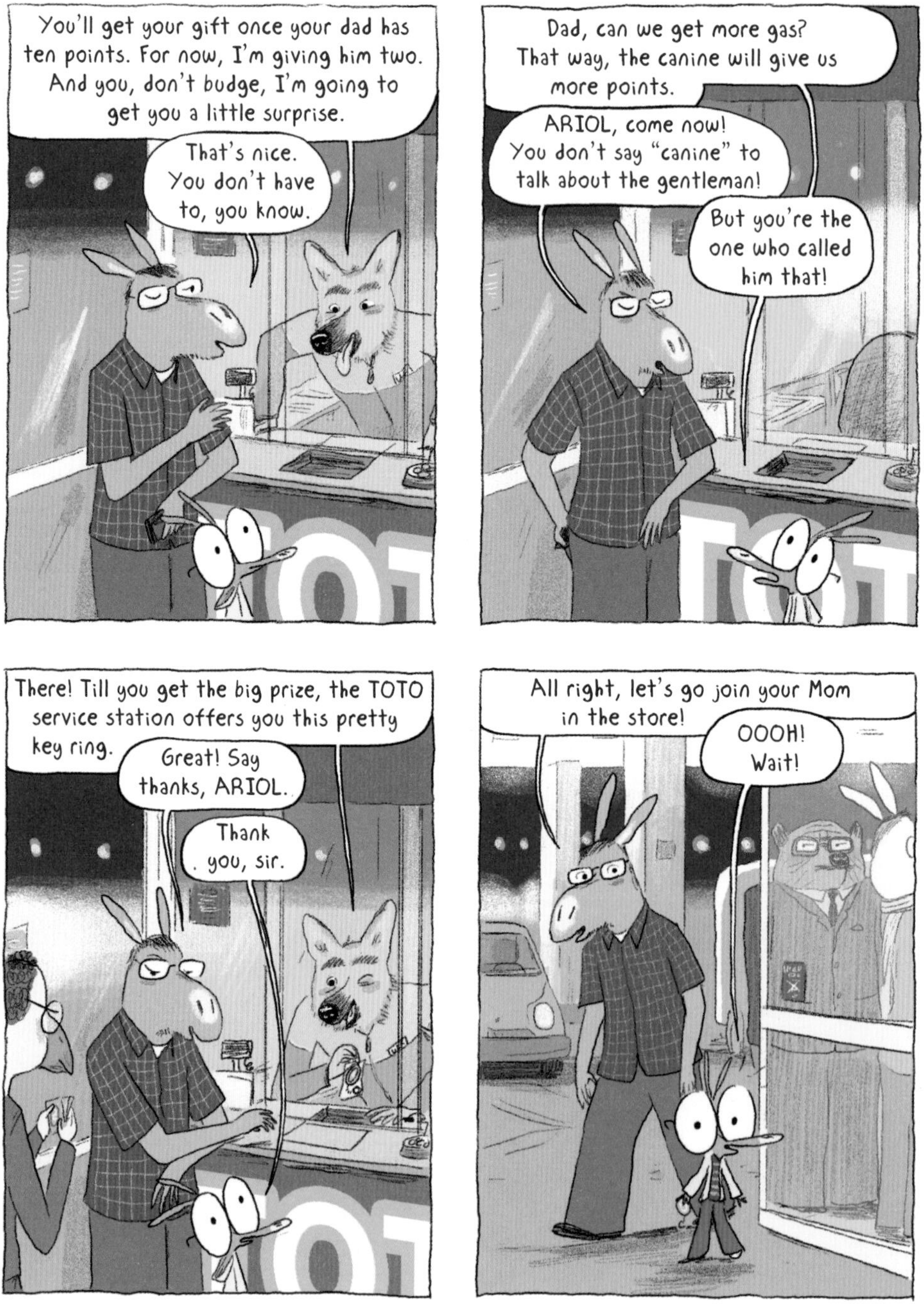
You'll get your gift once your dad has ten points. For now, I'm giving him two. And you, don't budge, I'm going to get you a little surprise.
That's nice. You don't have to, you know.
Dad, can we get more gas? That way, the canine will give us more points.
ARIOL, come now! You don't say "canine" to talk about the gentleman!
But you're the one who called him that!
There! Till you get the big prize, the TOTO service station offers you this pretty key ring.
Great! Say thanks, ARIOL.
Thank you, sir.
All right, let's go join your Mom in the store!
OOOH! Wait!

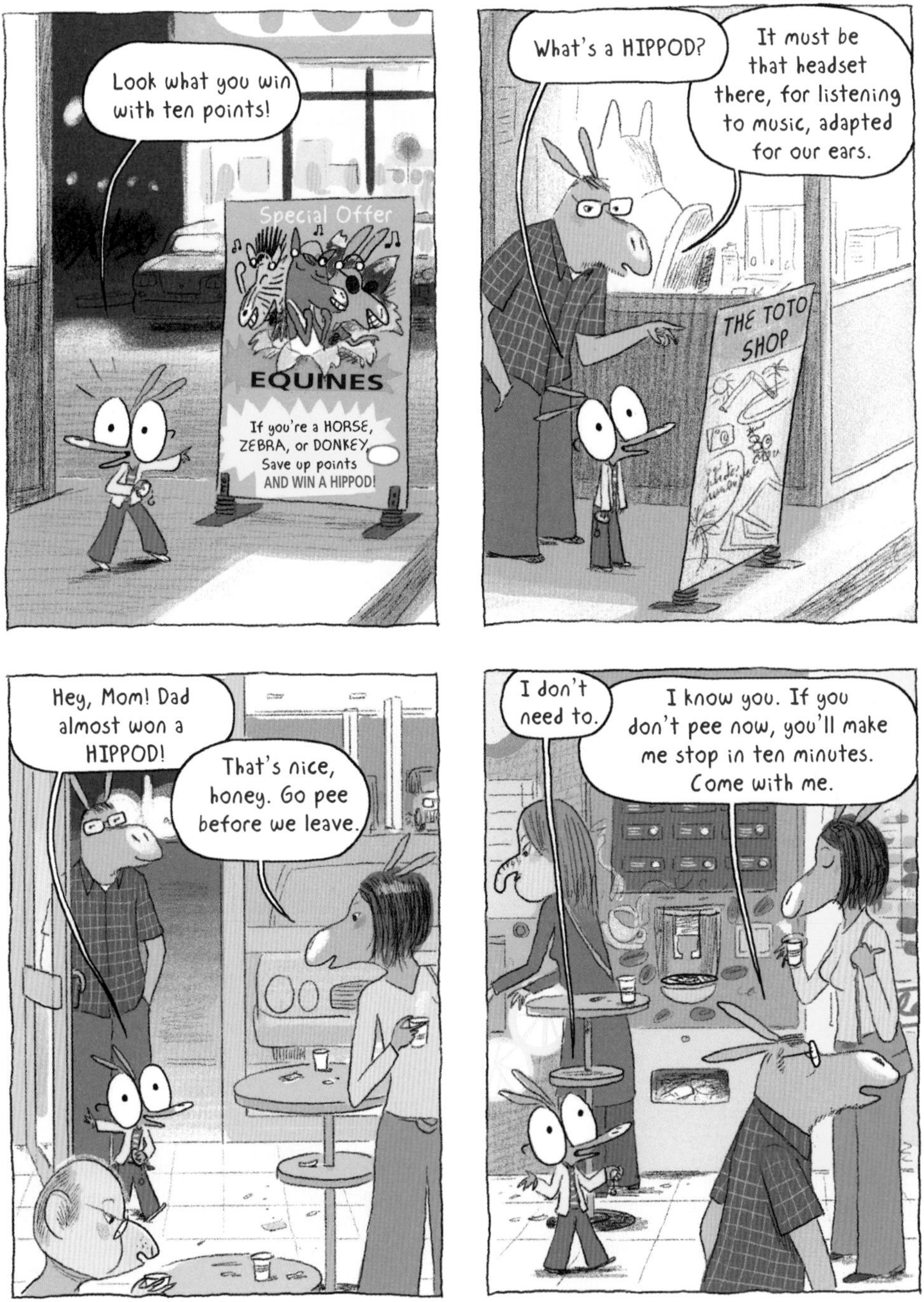
Look what you win with ten points!
Special Offer
EQUINES
If you're a HORSE, ZEBRA, or DONKEY, Save up points AND WIN A HIPPOD!
What's a HIPPOD?
It must be that headset there, for listening to music, adapted for our ears.
THE TOTO SHOP
Hey, Mom! Dad almost won a HIPPOD!
That's nice, honey. Go pee before we leave.
I don't need to.
I know you. If you don't pee now, you'll make me stop in ten minutes. Come with me.

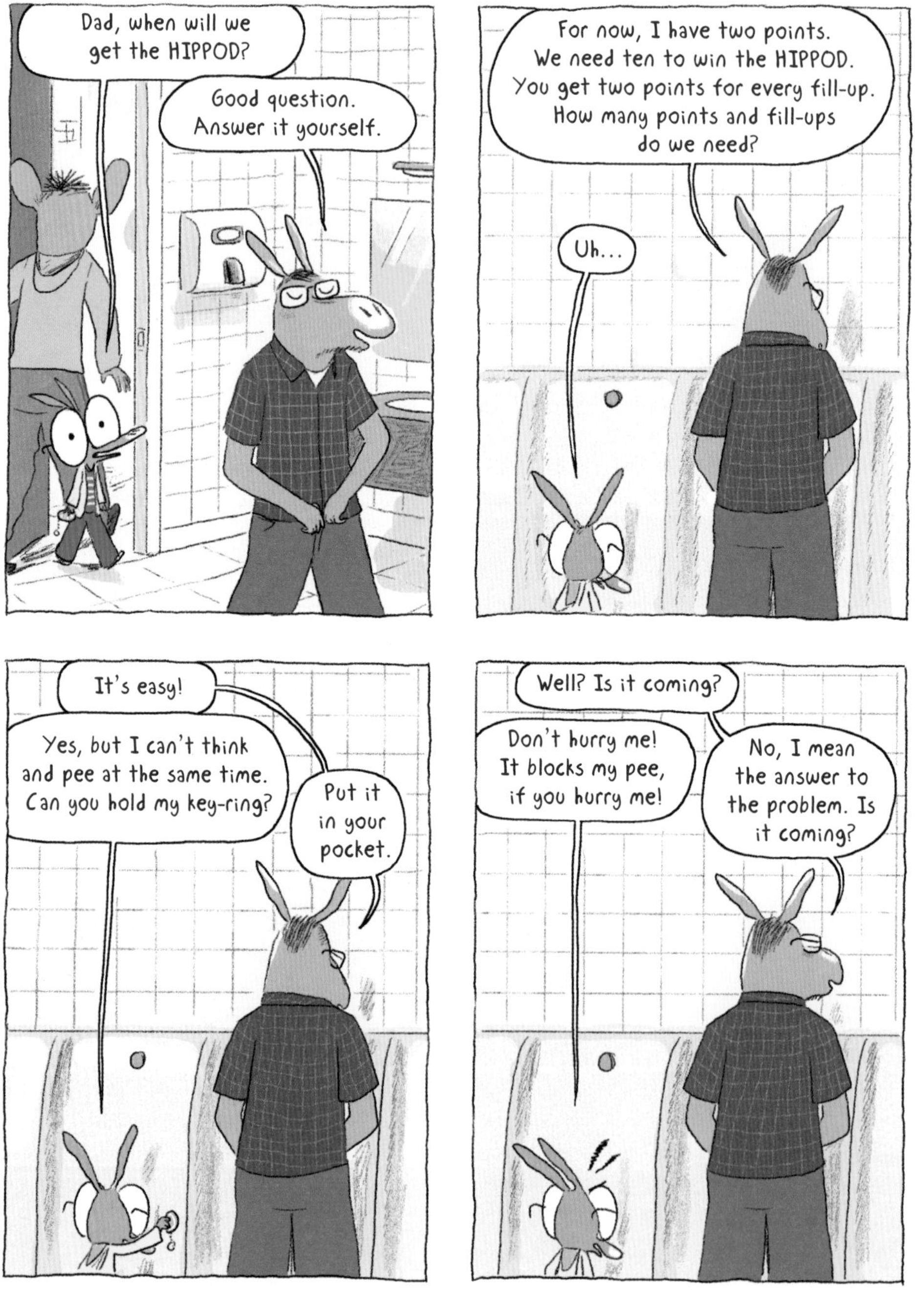
Dad, when will we get the HIPPOD?
Good question. Answer it yourself.
For now, I have two points. We need ten to win the HIPPOD. You get two points for every fill-up. How many points and fill-ups do we need?
Uh...
It's easy!
Yes, but I can't think and pee at the same time. Can you hold my key-ring?
Put it in your pocket.
Well? Is it coming?
Don't hurry me! It blocks my pee, if you hurry me!
No, I mean the answer to the problem. Is it coming?

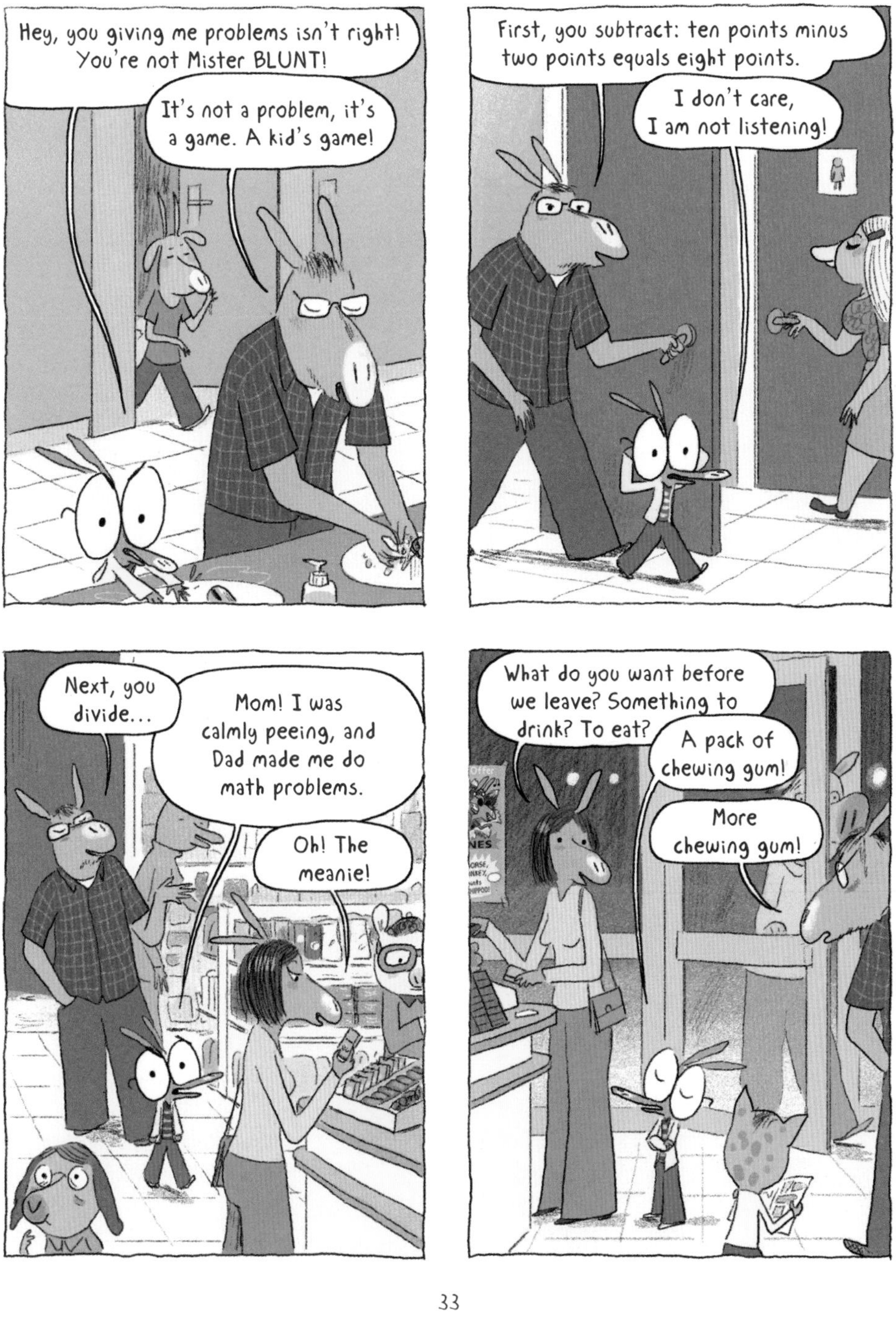
Hey, you giving me problems isn't right! You're not Mister BLUNT!
It's not a problem, it's a game. A kid's game!
First, you subtract: ten points minus two points equals eight points.
I don't care, I am not listening!
Next, you divide...
Mom! I was calmly peeing, and Dad made me do math problems.
Oh! The meanie!
What do you want before we leave? Something to drink? To eat?
A pack of chewing gum!
More chewing gum!

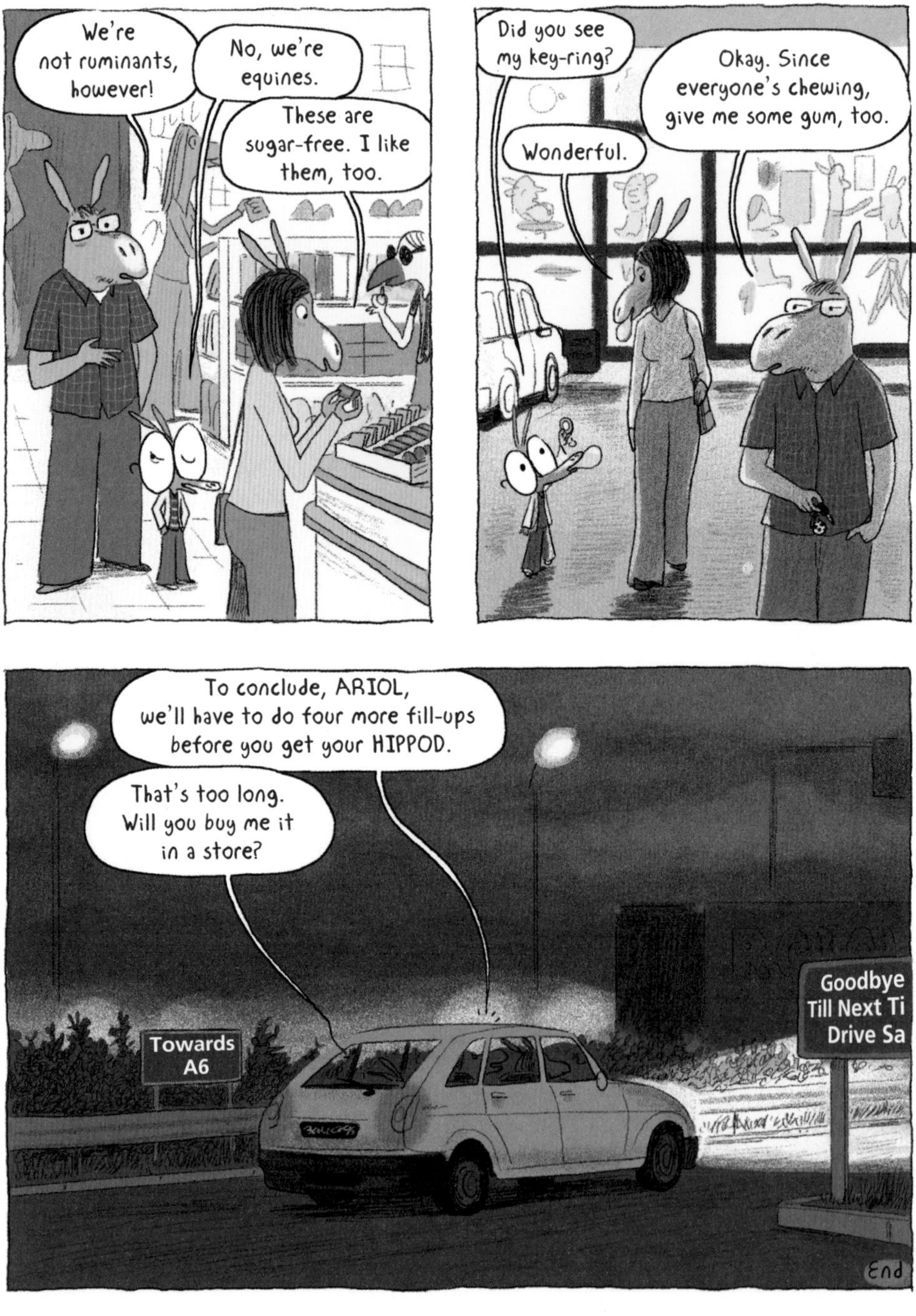
We're not ruminants, however!
No, we're equines.
These are sugar-free. I like them, too.
Did you see my key-ring?
Wonderful.
Okay. Since everyone's chewing, give me some gum, too.
To conclude, ARIOL, we'll have to do four more fill-ups before you get your HIPPOD.
That's too long. Will you buy me it in a store?
Towards A6
Goodbye
Till Next Ti
Drive Sa
End

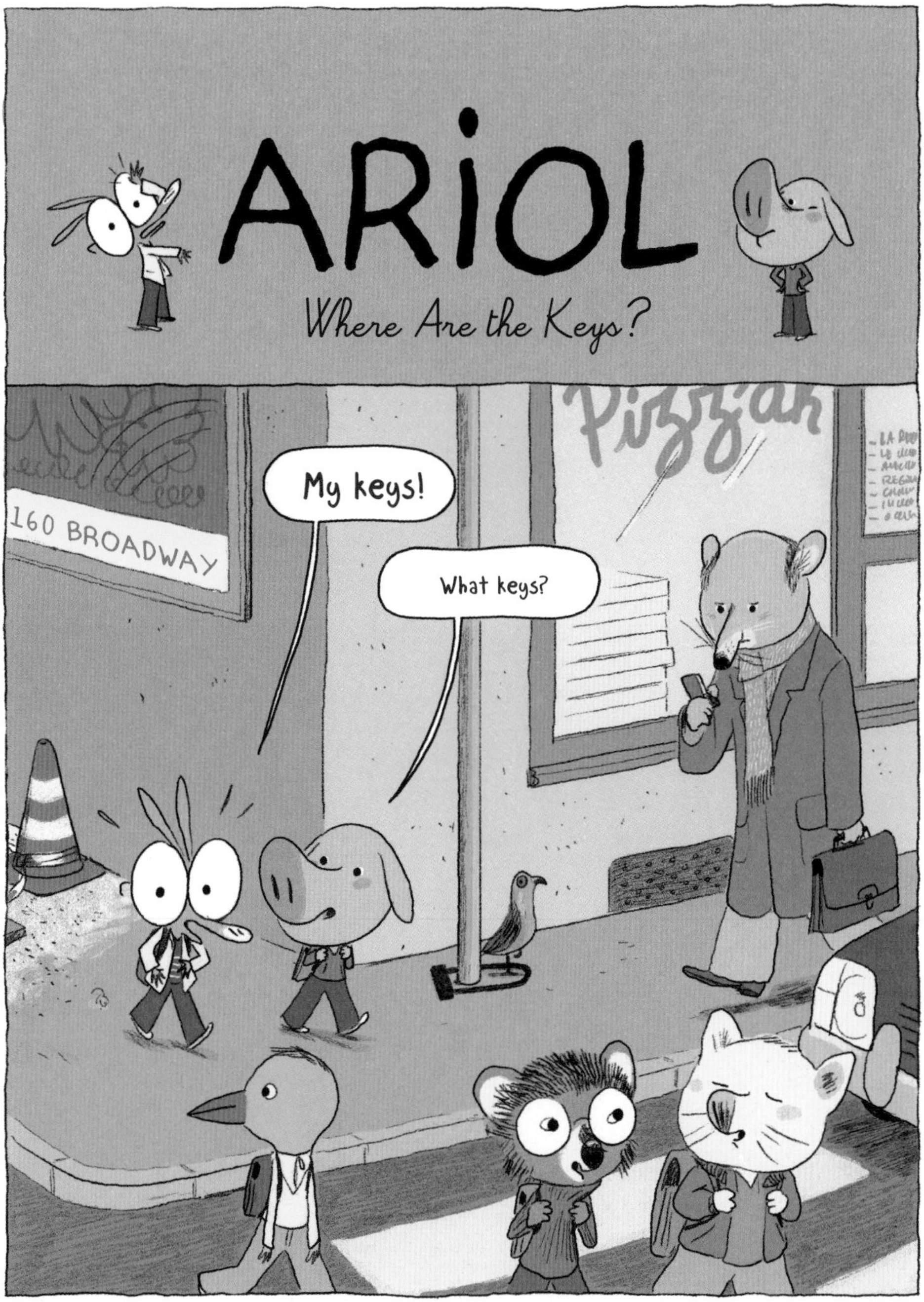
ARIOL
Where Are the Keys?
160 BROADWAY
Pizz'ah
My keys!
What keys?

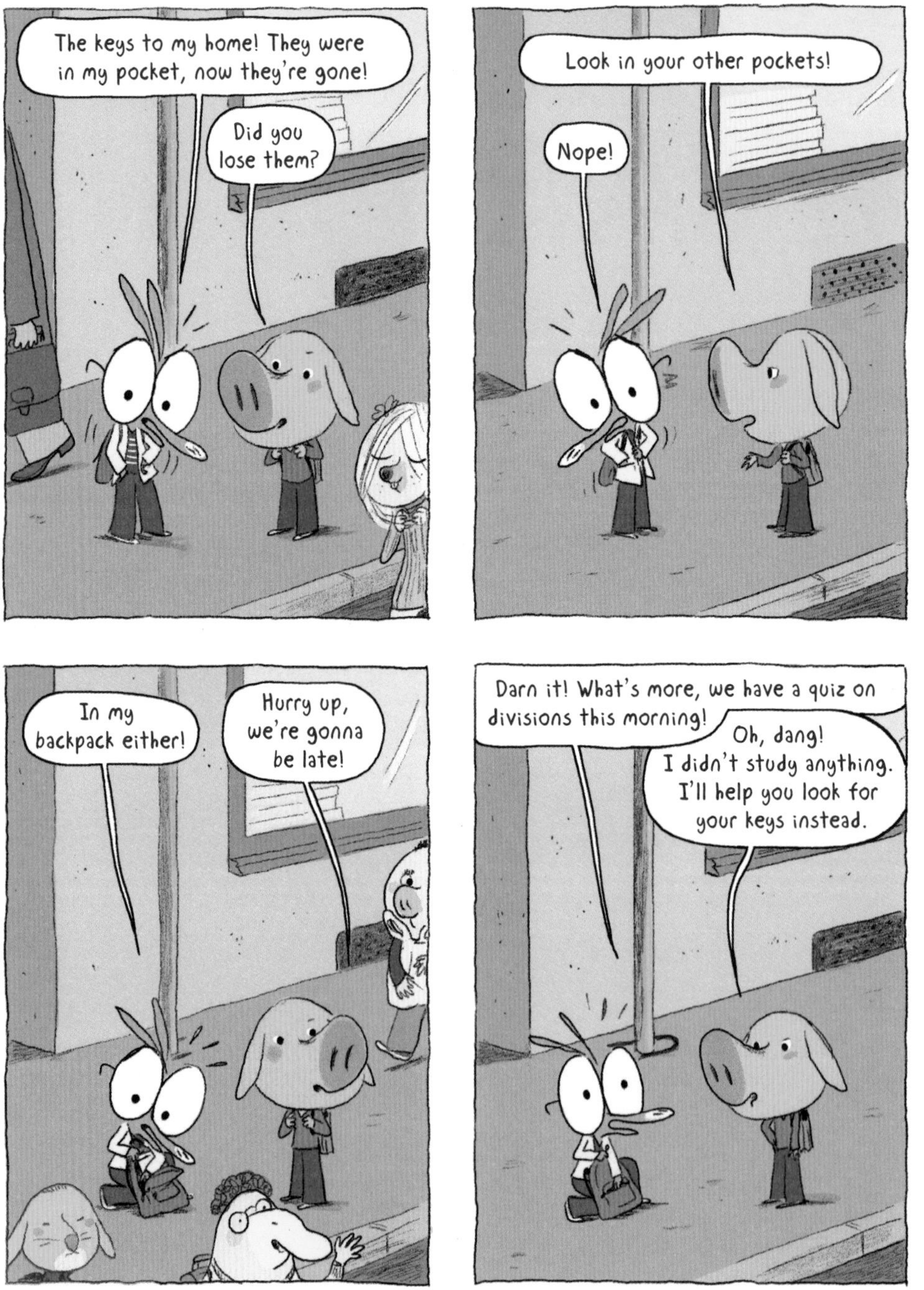
The keys to my home! They were in my pocket, now they're gone!
Did you lose them?
Look in your other pockets!
Nope!
In my backpack either!
Hurry up, we're gonna be late!
Darn it! What's more, we have a quiz on divisions this morning!
Oh, dang! I didn't study anything. I'll help you look for your keys instead.

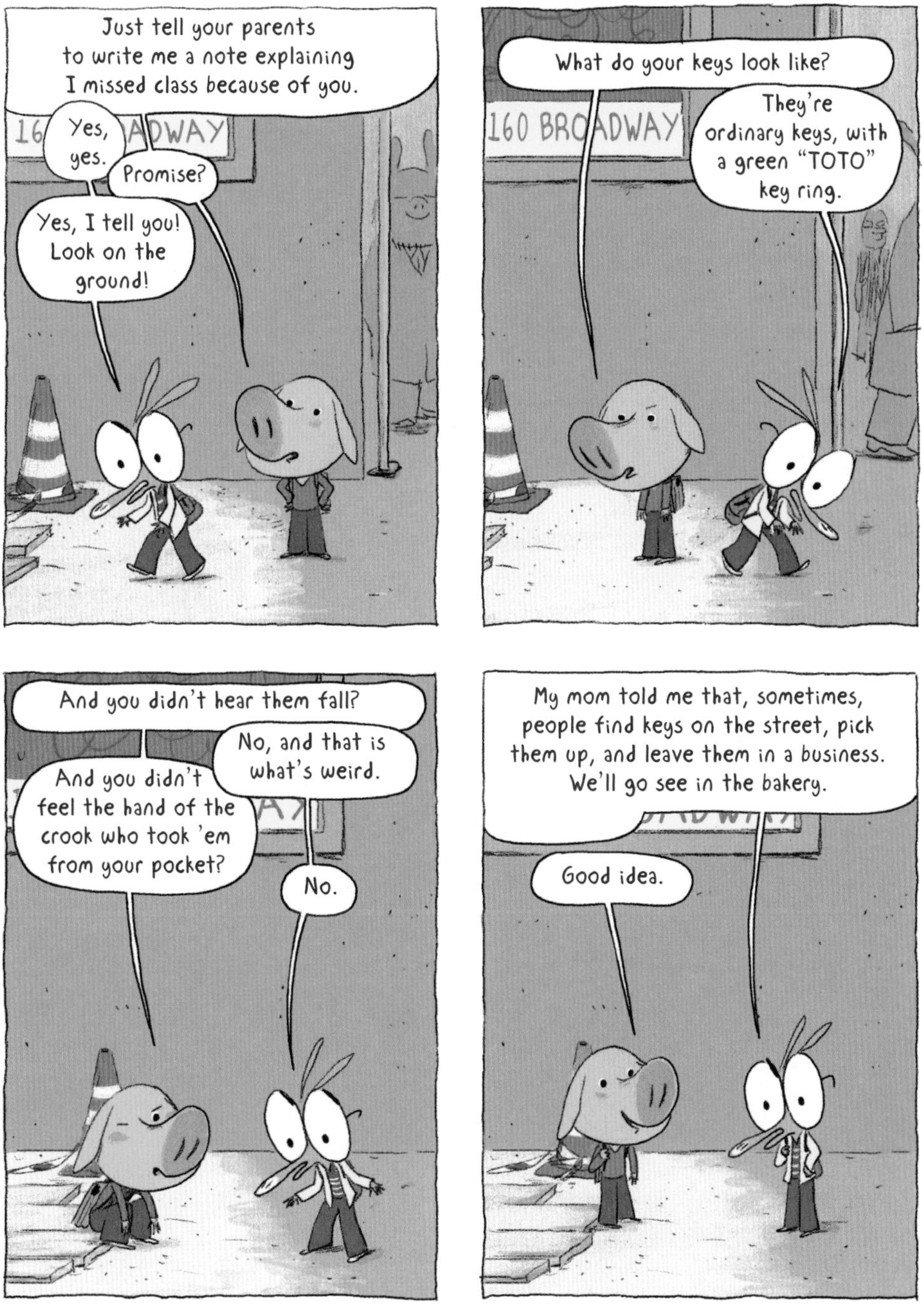
Just tell your parents to write me a note explaining I missed class because of you.
160 BROADWAY
Yes, yes.
Promise?
Yes, I tell you! Look on the ground!
What do your keys look like?
160 BROADWAY
They're ordinary keys, with a green "TOTO" key ring.
And you didn't hear them fall?
And you didn't feel the hand of the crook who took 'em from your pocket?
No, and that is what's weird.
No.
My mom told me that, sometimes, people find keys on the street, pick them up, and leave them in a business. We'll go see in the bakery.
Good idea.

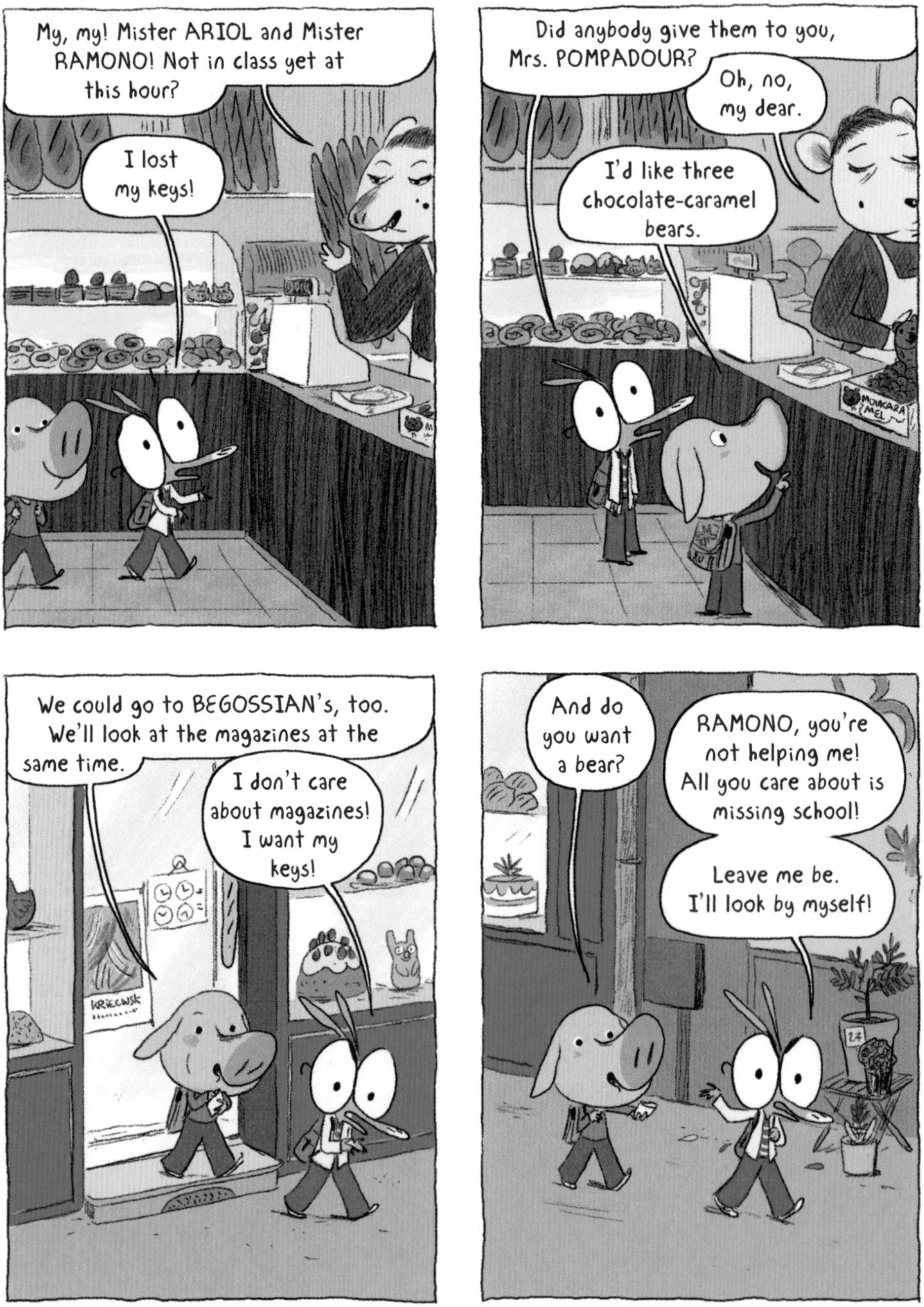
My, my! Mister ARIOL and Mister RAMONO! Not in class yet at this hour?
I lost my keys!
Did anybody give them to you, Mrs. POMPADOUR?
Oh, no, my dear.
I'd like three chocolate-caramel bears.
We could go to BEGOSSIAN's, too. We'll look at the magazines at the same time.
I don't care about magazines! I want my keys!
And do you want a bear?
RAMONO, you're not helping me! All you care about is missing school!
Leave me be. I'll look by myself!

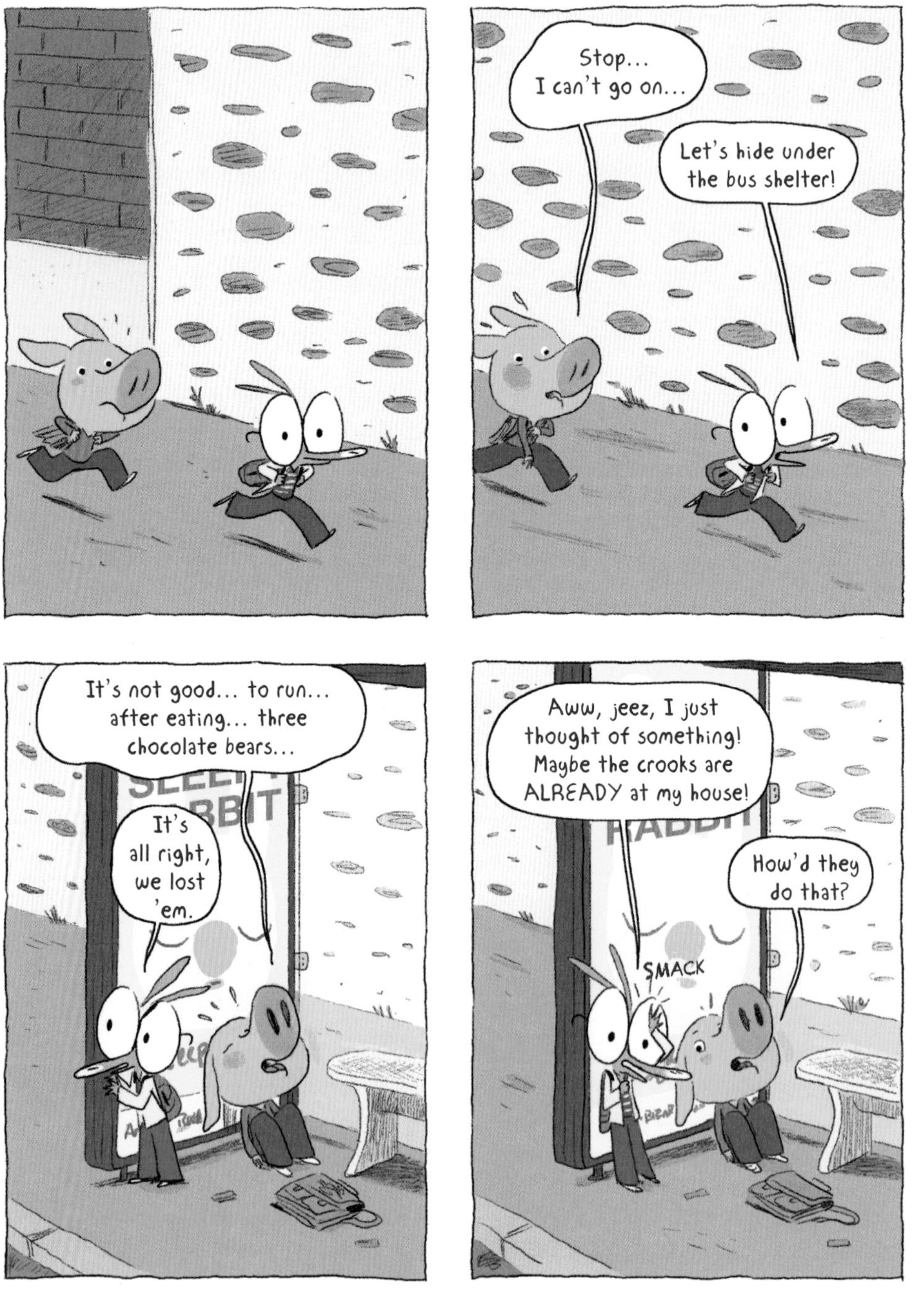
Stop...
I can't go on...
Let's hide under the bus shelter!
It's not good... to run... after eating... three chocolate bears...
It's all right, we lost 'em.
Aww, jeez, I just thought of something! Maybe the crooks are ALREADY at my house!
SMACK
How'd they do that?

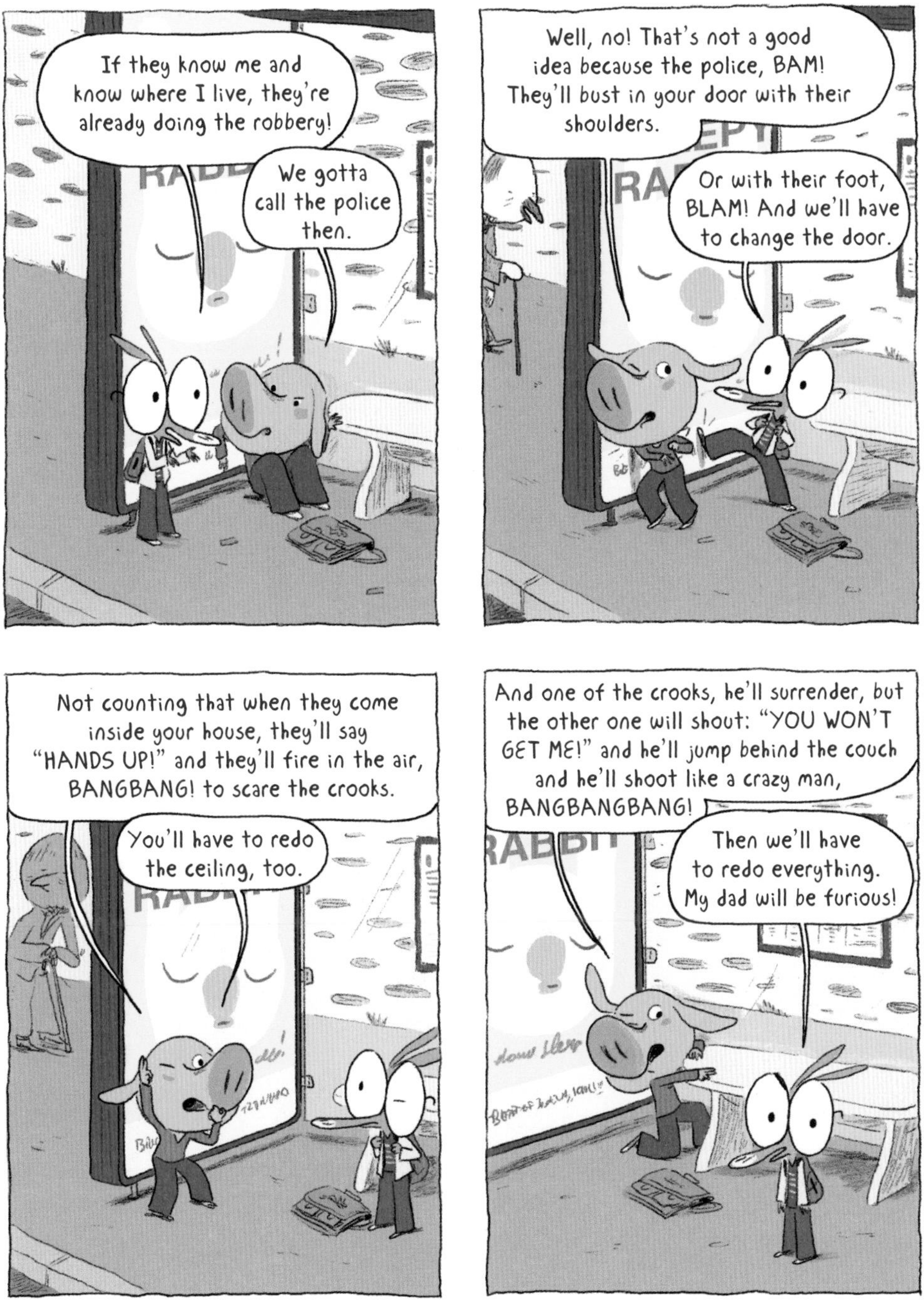

If they know me and know where I live, they're already doing the robbery!
We gotta call the police then.
Well, no! That's not a good idea because the police, BAM! They'll bust in your door with their shoulders.
Or with their foot, BLAM! And we'll have to change the door.
Not counting that when they come inside your house, they'll say "HANDS UP!" and they'll fire in the air, BANGBANG! to scare the crooks.
You'll have to redo the ceiling, too.
And one of the crooks, he'll surrender, but the other one will shout: "YOU WON'T GET ME!" and he'll jump behind the couch and he'll shoot like a crazy man, BANGBANGBANG!
Then we'll have to redo everything. My dad will be furious!

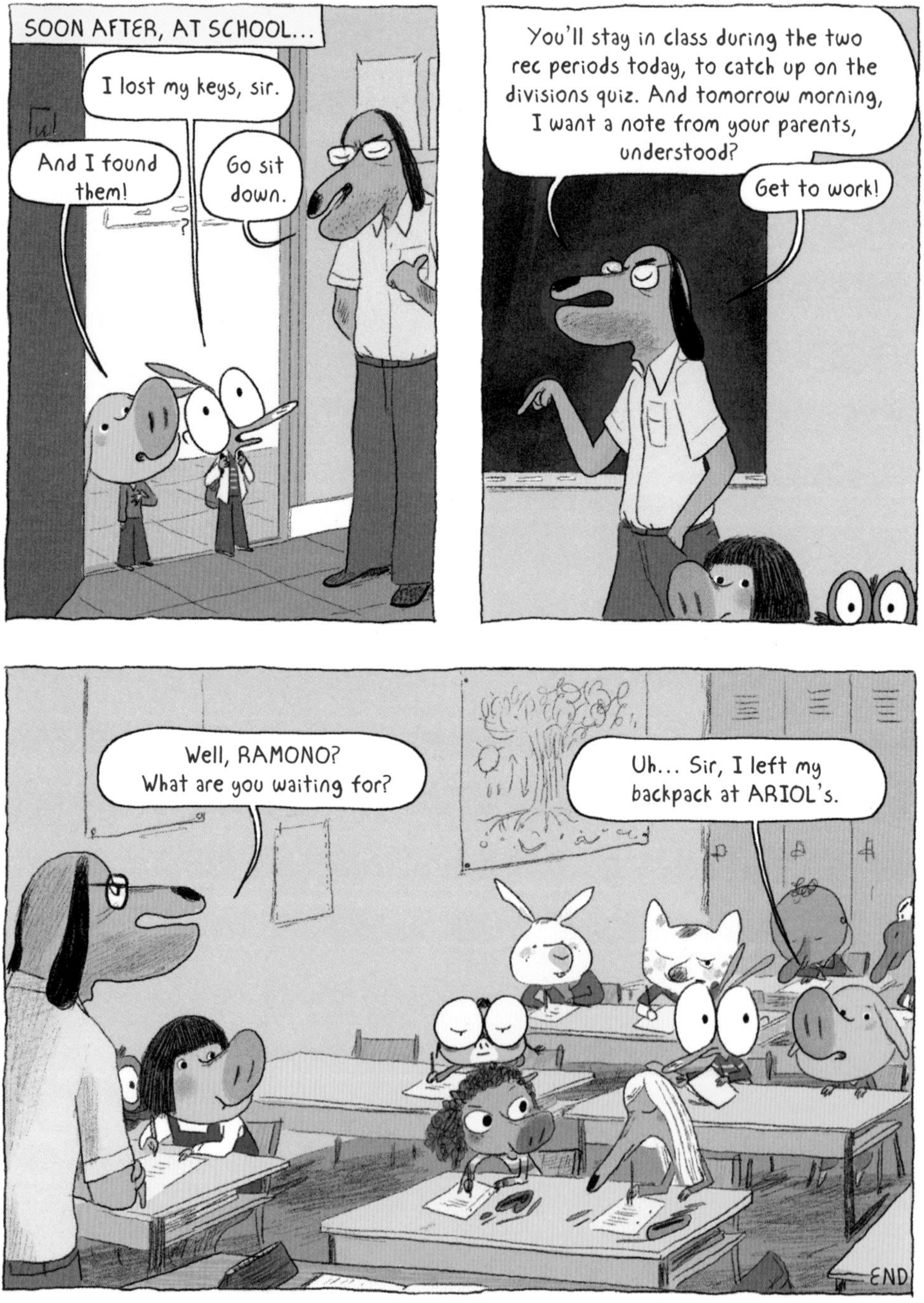
SOON AFTER, AT SCHOOL...
I lost my keys, sir.
And I found them!
Go sit down.
You'll stay in class during the two rec periods today, to catch up on the divisions quiz. And tomorrow morning, I want a note from your parents, understood?
Get to work!
Well, RAMONO? What are you waiting for?
Uh... Sir, I left my backpack at ARIOL's.
END

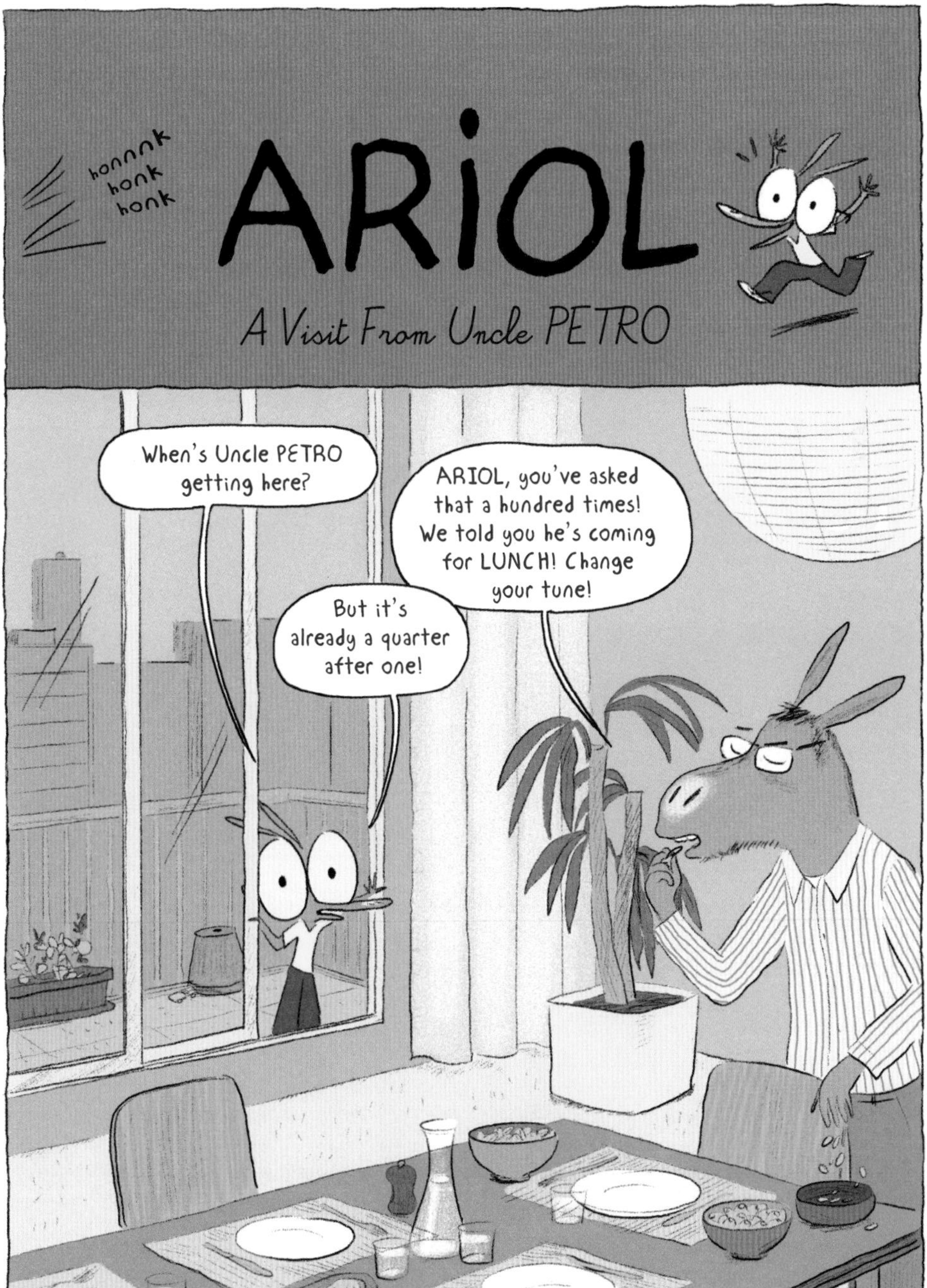
honnnk honk honk
ARIOL
A Visit From Uncle PETRO
When's Uncle PETRO getting here?
ARIOL, you've asked that a hundred times! We told you he's coming for LUNCH! Change your tune!
But it's already a quarter after one!

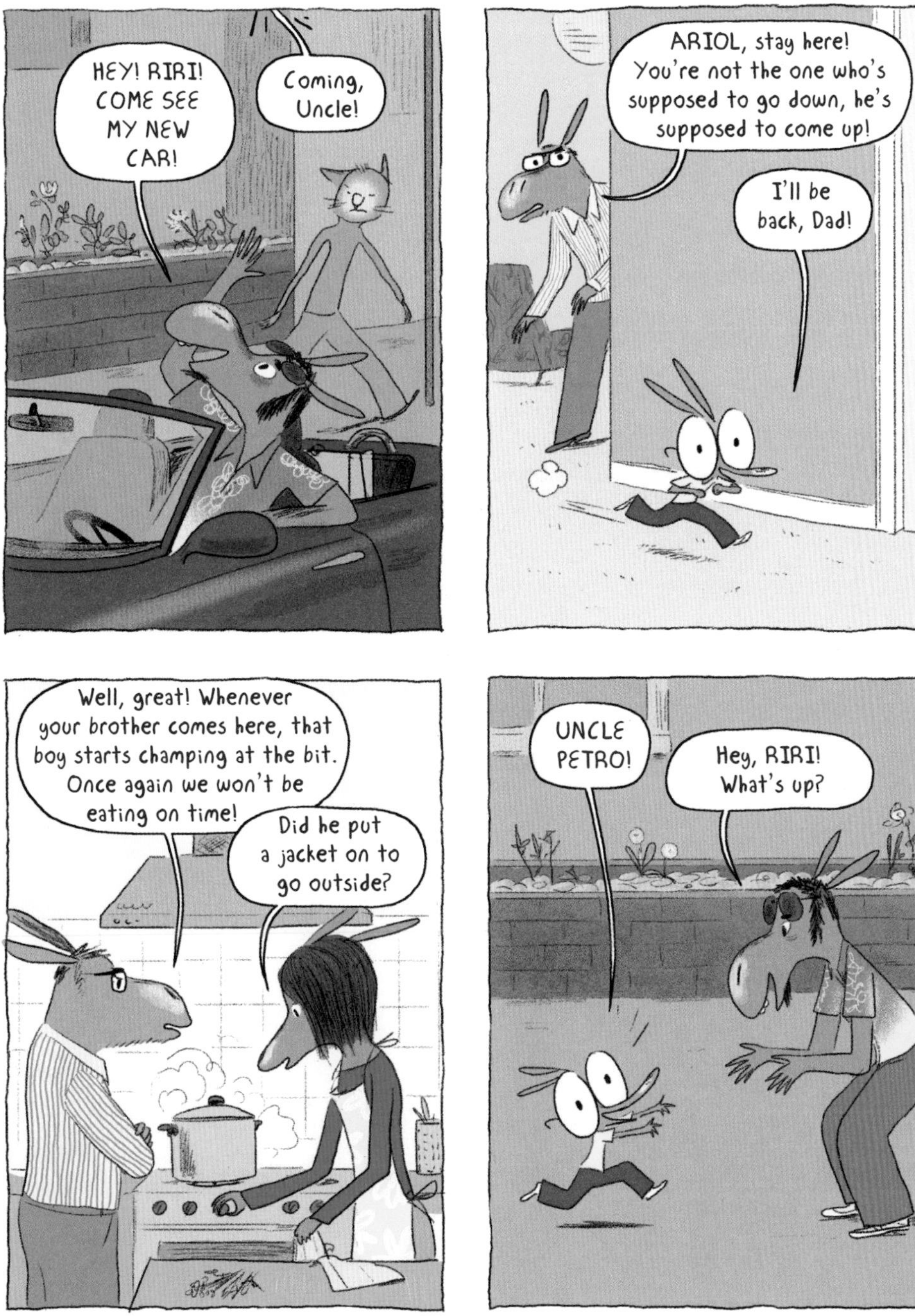
HEY! RIRI! COME SEE MY NEW CAR!
Coming, Uncle!
ARIOL, stay here! You're not the one who's supposed to go down, he's supposed to come up!
I'll be back, Dad!
Well, great! Whenever your brother comes here, that boy starts champing at the bit. Once again we won't be eating on time!
Did he put a jacket on to go outside?
UNCLE PETRO!
Hey, RIRI! What's up?

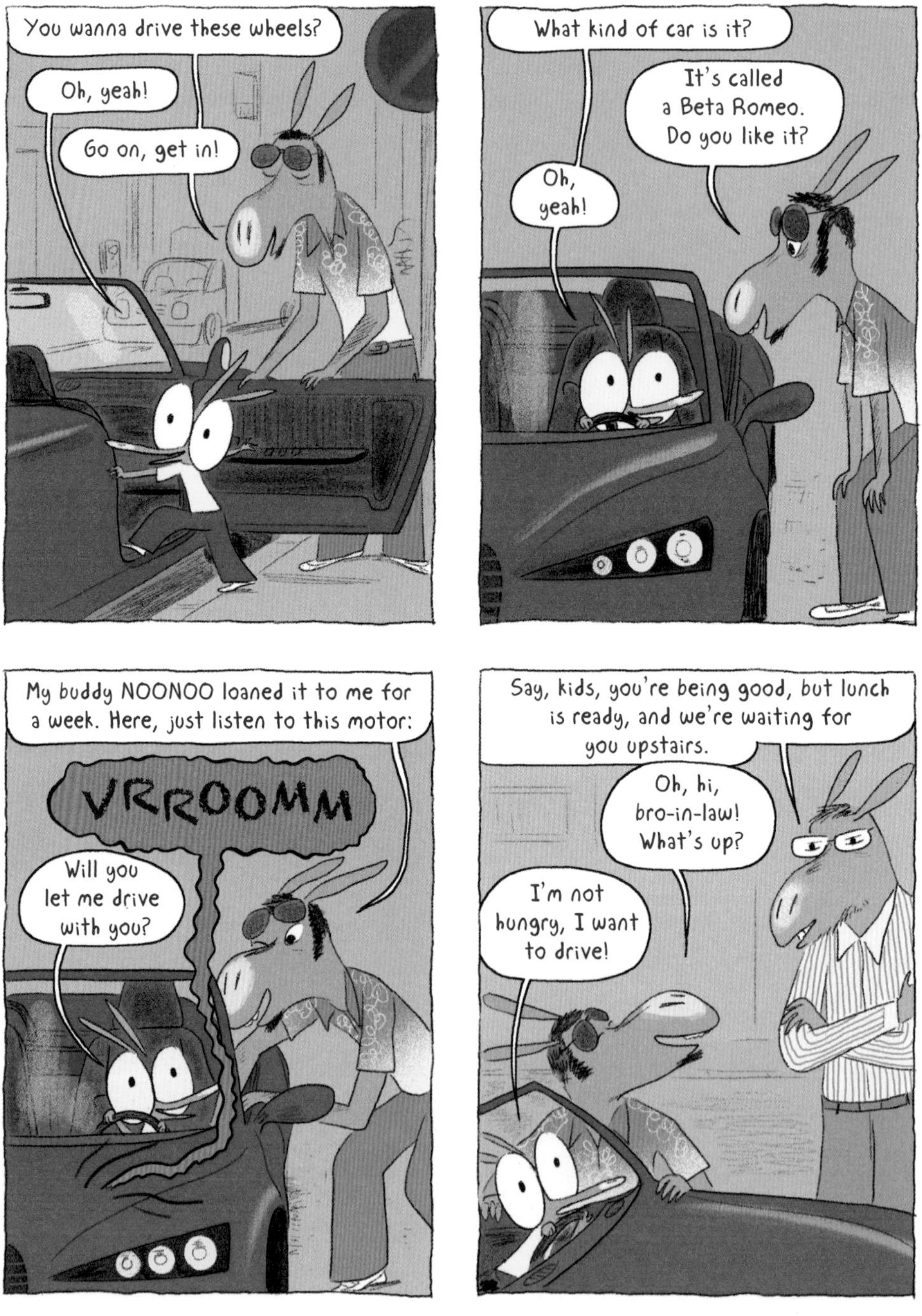

You wanna drive these wheels?
Oh, yeah!
Go on, get in!
What kind of car is it?
It's called a Beta Romeo. Do you like it?
Oh, yeah!
My buddy NOONOO loaned it to me for a week. Here, just listen to this motor:
VRROOMM
Will you let me drive with you?
Say, kids, you're being good, but lunch is ready, and we're waiting for you upstairs.
Oh, hi, bro-in-law! What's up?
I'm not hungry, I want to drive!

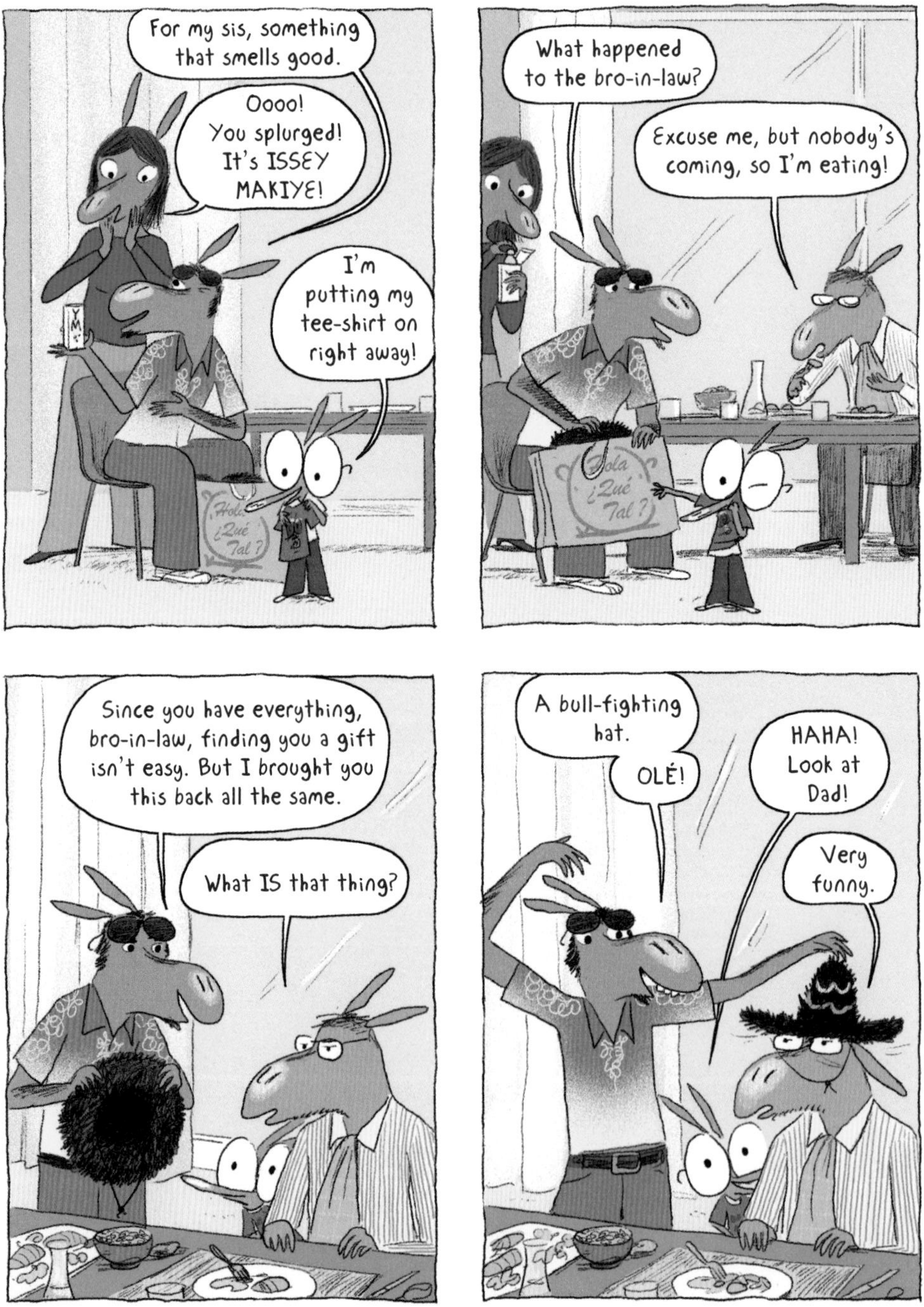
For my sis, something that smells good.
Oooo! You splurged! It's ISSEY MAKIYE!
I'm putting my tee-shirt on right away!
Hola ¿Qué Tal?
What happened to the bro-in-law?
Excuse me, but nobody's coming, so I'm eating!
Hola ¿Qué Tal?
Since you have everything, bro-in-law, finding you a gift isn't easy. But I brought you this back all the same.
What IS that thing?
A bull-fighting hat.
OLÉ!
HAHA! Look at Dad!
Very funny.

51

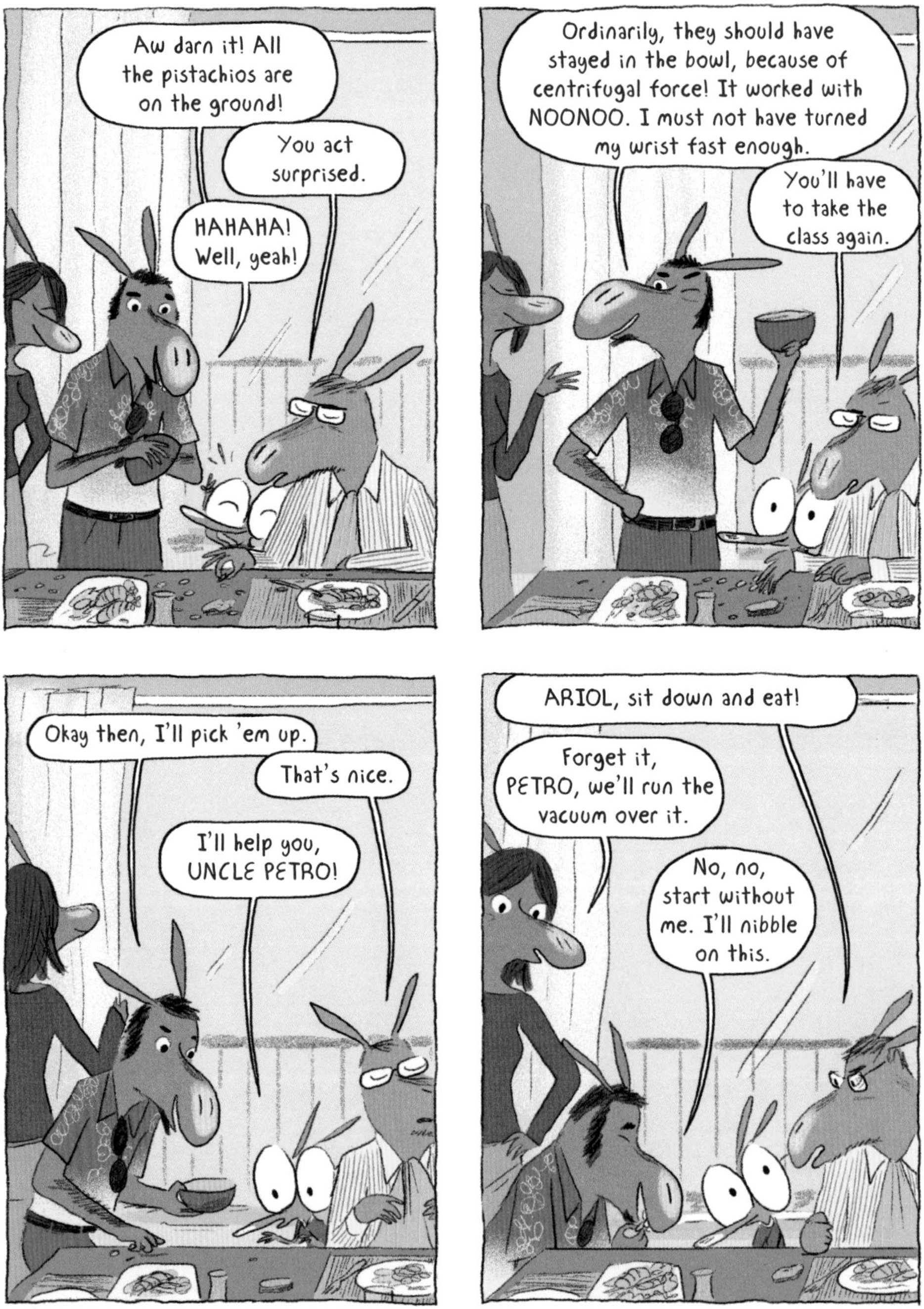
Aw darn it! All the pistachios are on the ground!
You act surprised.
HAHAHA! Well, yeah!
Ordinarily, they should have stayed in the bowl, because of centrifugal force! It worked with NOONOO. I must not have turned my wrist fast enough.
You'll have to take the class again.
Okay then, I'll pick 'em up.
That's nice.
I'll help you, UNCLE PETRO!
ARIOL, sit down and eat!
Forget it, PETRO, we'll run the vacuum over it.
No, no, start without me. I'll nibble on this.

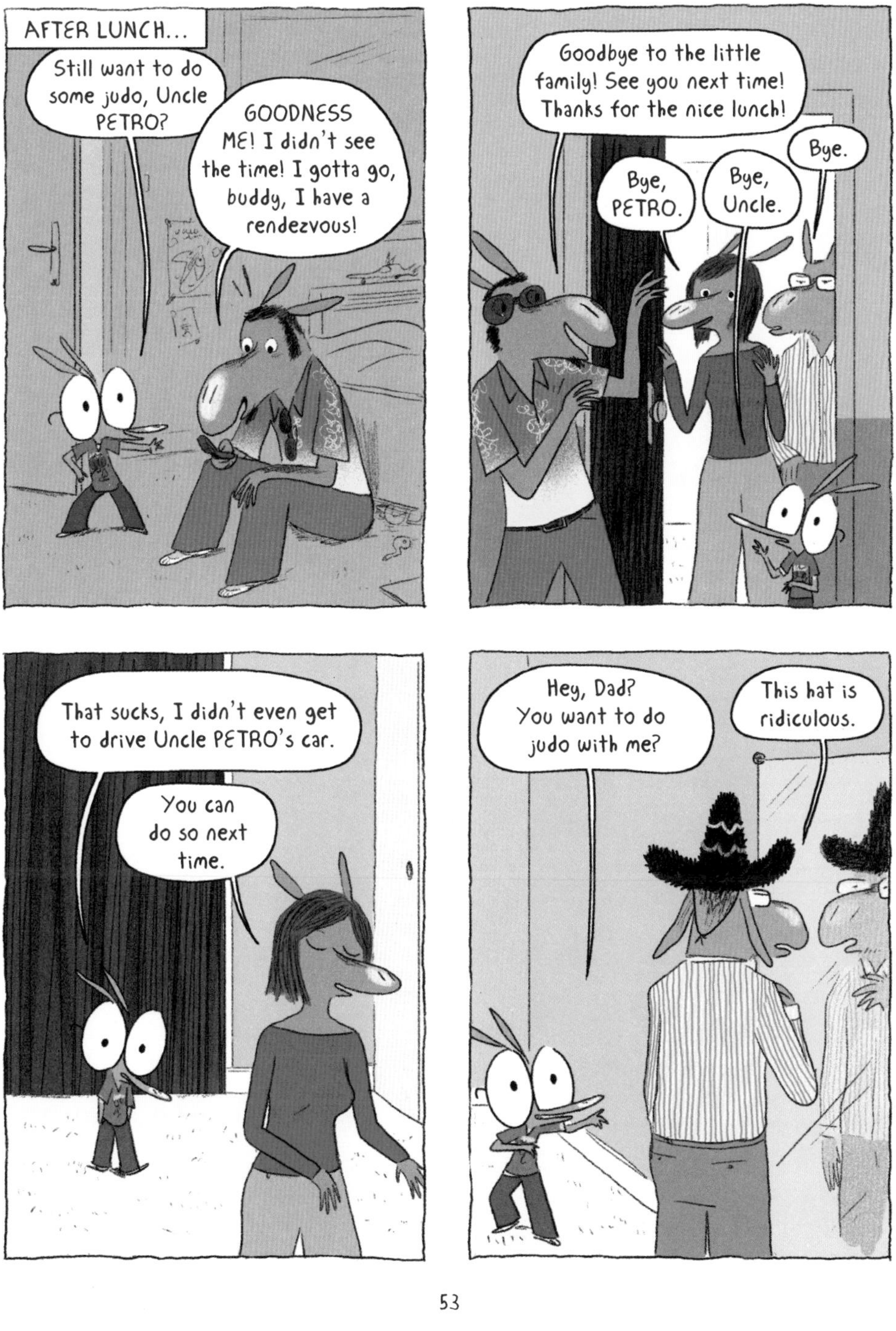
AFTER LUNCH...
Still want to do some judo, Uncle PETRO?
GOODNESS ME! I didn't see the time! I gotta go, buddy, I have a rendezvous!
Goodbye to the little family! See you next time! Thanks for the nice lunch!
Bye, PETRO.
Bye, Uncle.
Bye.
That sucks, I didn't even get to drive Uncle PETRO's car.
You can do so next time.
Hey, Dad? You want to do judo with me?
This hat is ridiculous.

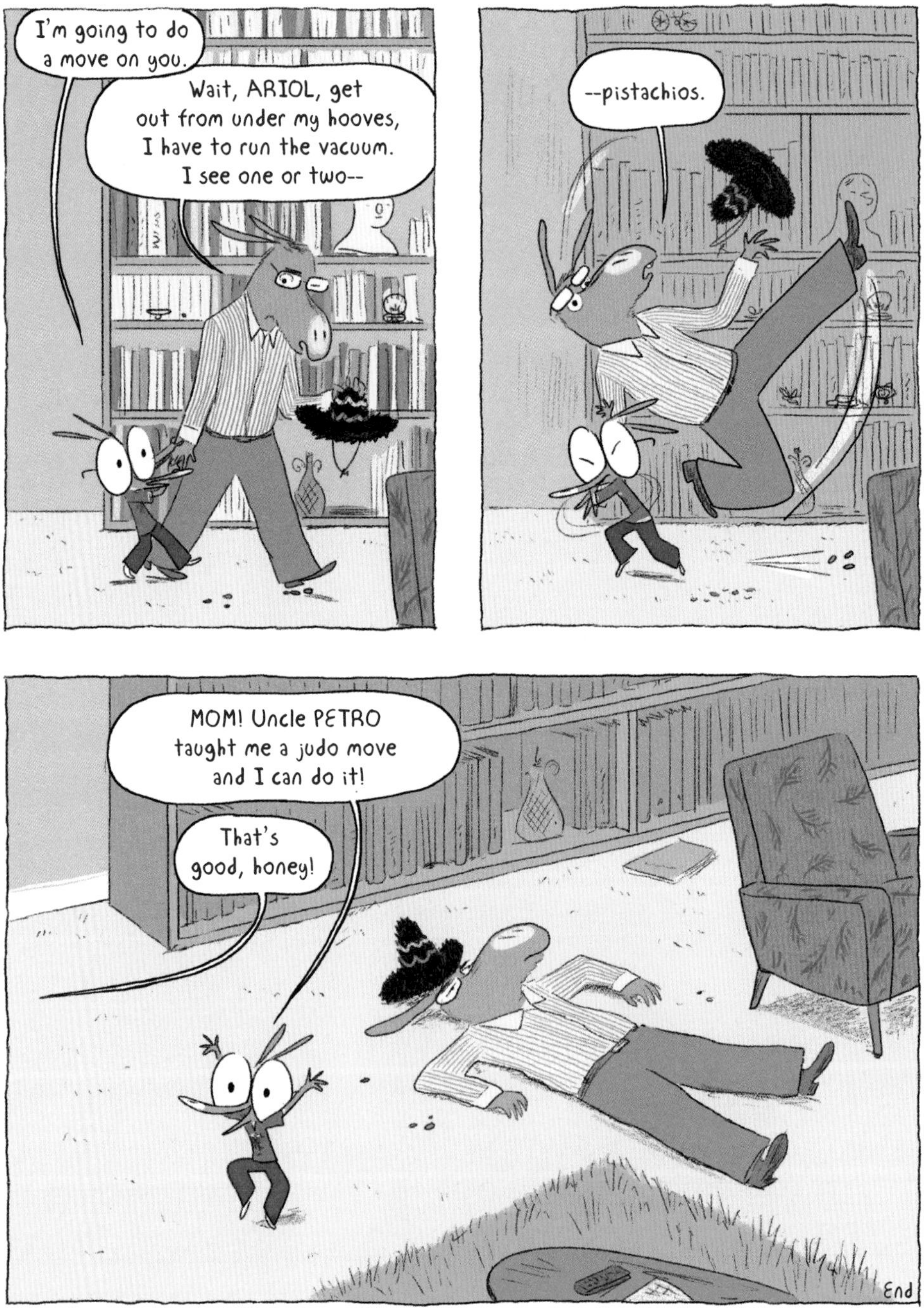
I'm going to do a move on you.
Wait, ARIOL, get out from under my hooves, I have to run the vacuum. I see one or two--
--pistachios.
MOM! Uncle PETRO taught me a judo move and I can do it!
That's good, honey!
End

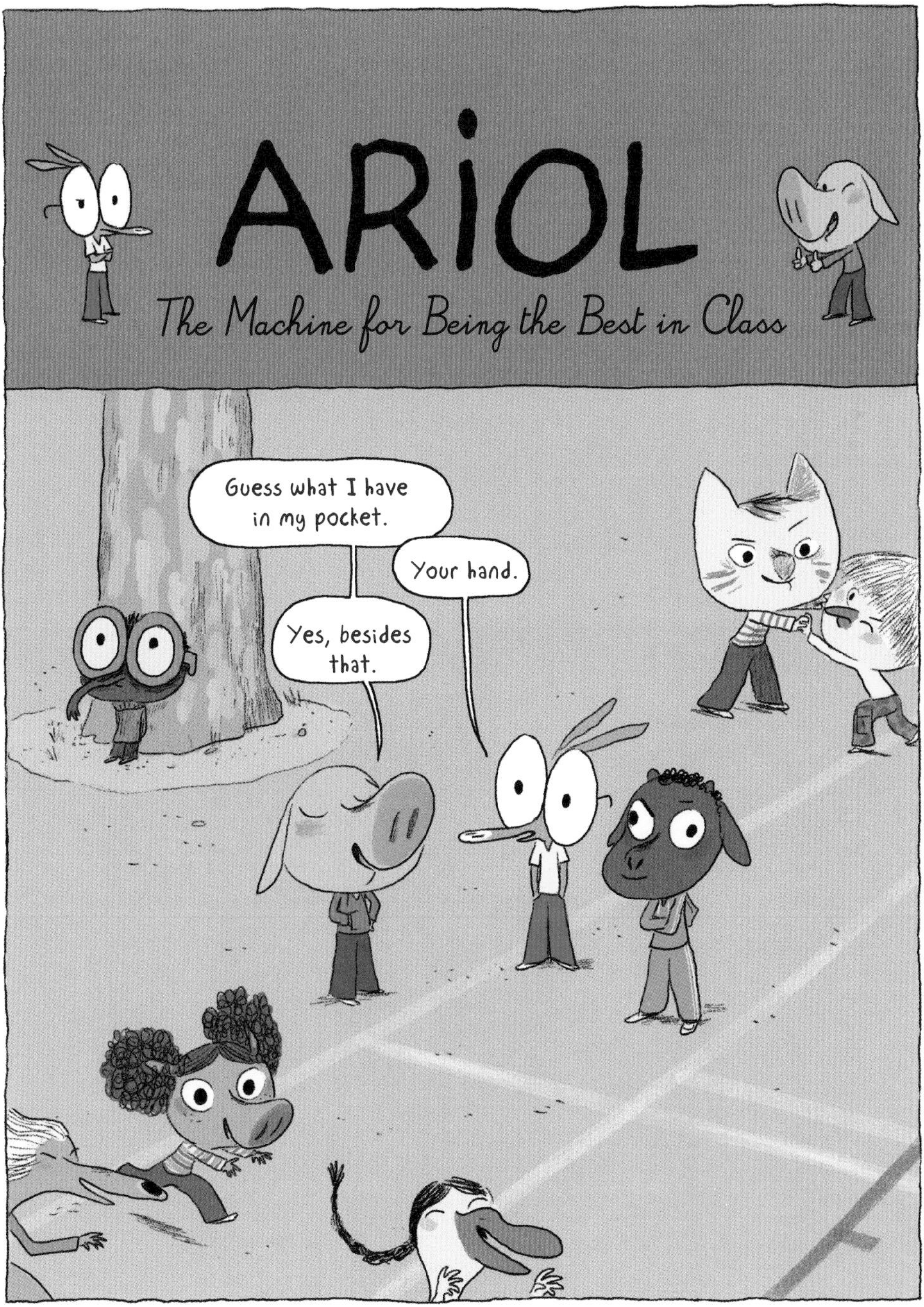

ARiOL
The Machine for Being the Best in Class
Guess what I have in my pocket.
Your hand.
Yes, besides that.

56

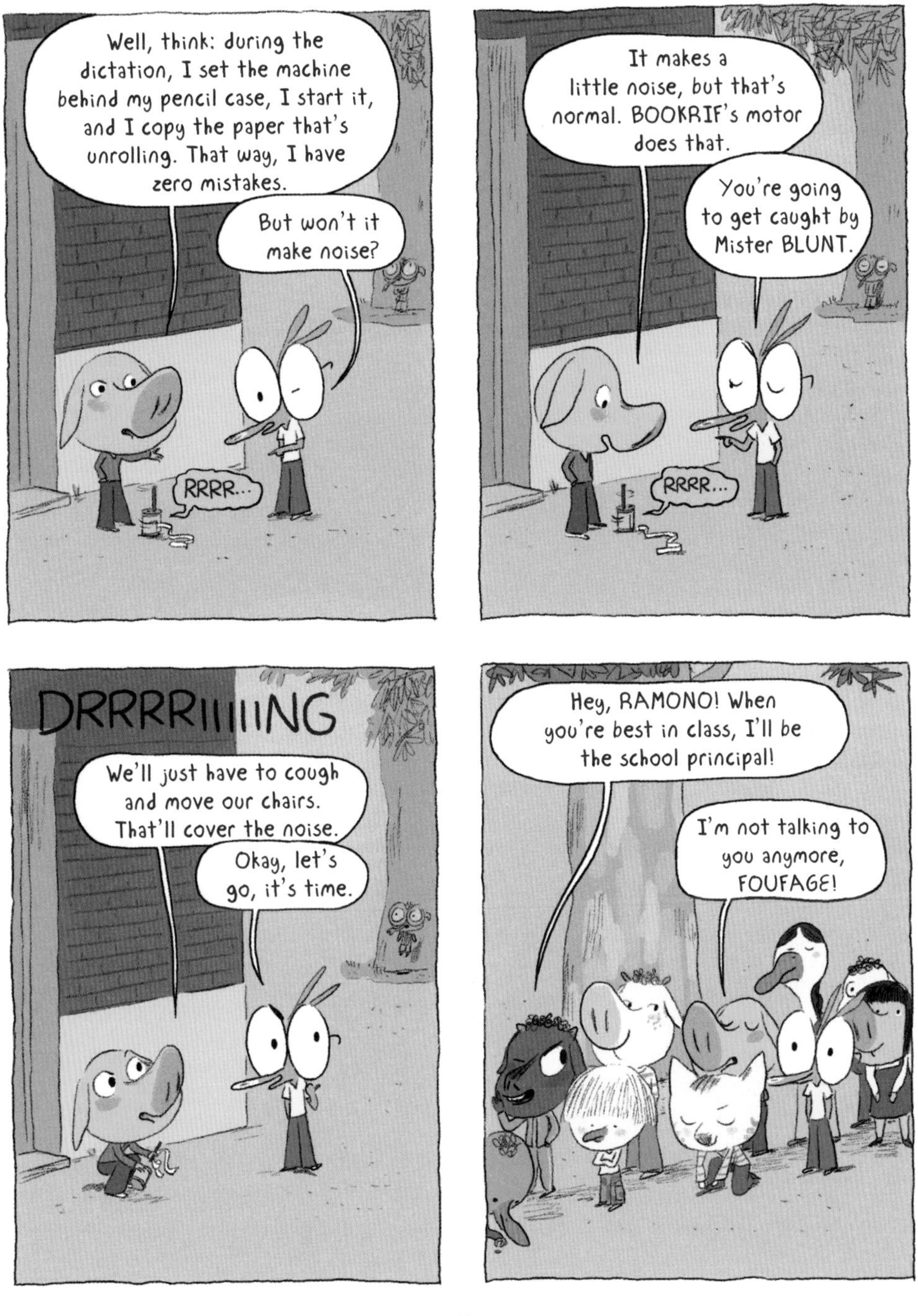
Well, think: during the dictation, I set the machine behind my pencil case, I start it, and I copy the paper that's unrolling. That way, I have zero mistakes.
But won't it make noise?
RRRR...
It makes a little noise, but that's normal. BOOKRIF's motor does that.
You're going to get caught by Mister BLUNT.
RRRR...
DRRRRIIIIING
We'll just have to cough and move our chairs. That'll cover the noise.
Okay, let's go, it's time.
Hey, RAMONO! When you're best in class, I'll be the school principal!
I'm not talking to you anymore, FOUFAGE!

62

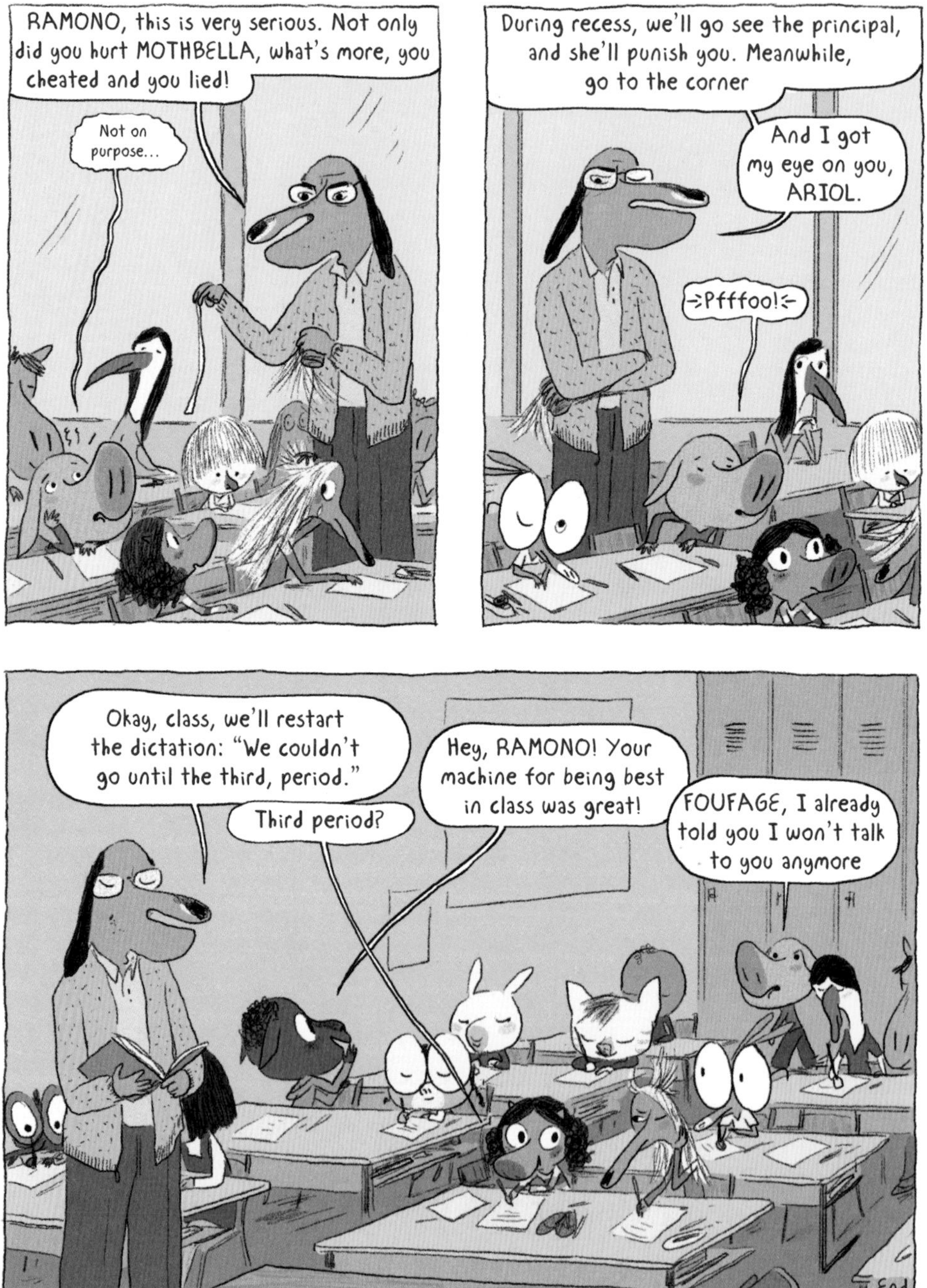
RAMONO, this is very serious. Not only did you hurt MOTHBELLA, what's more, you cheated and you lied!
Not on purpose...
During recess, we'll go see the principal, and she'll punish you. Meanwhile, go to the corner
And I got my eye on you, ARIOL.
Pfffoo!
Okay, class, we'll restart the dictation: "We couldn't go until the third, period."
Third period?
Hey, RAMONO! Your machine for being best in class was great!
FOUFAGE, I already told you I won't talk to you anymore
End

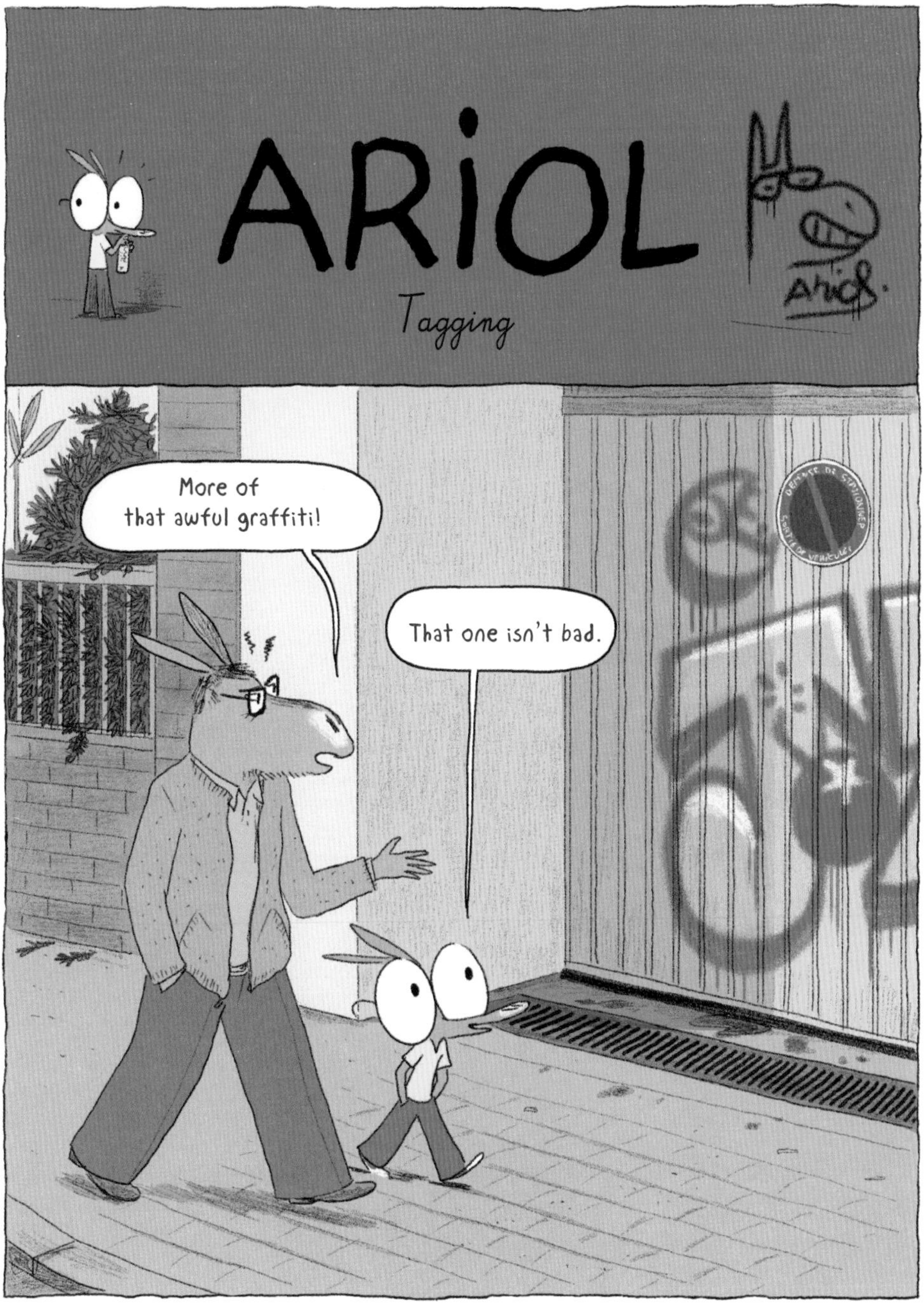
ARIOL
Tagging
More of that awful graffiti!
That one isn't bad.

66

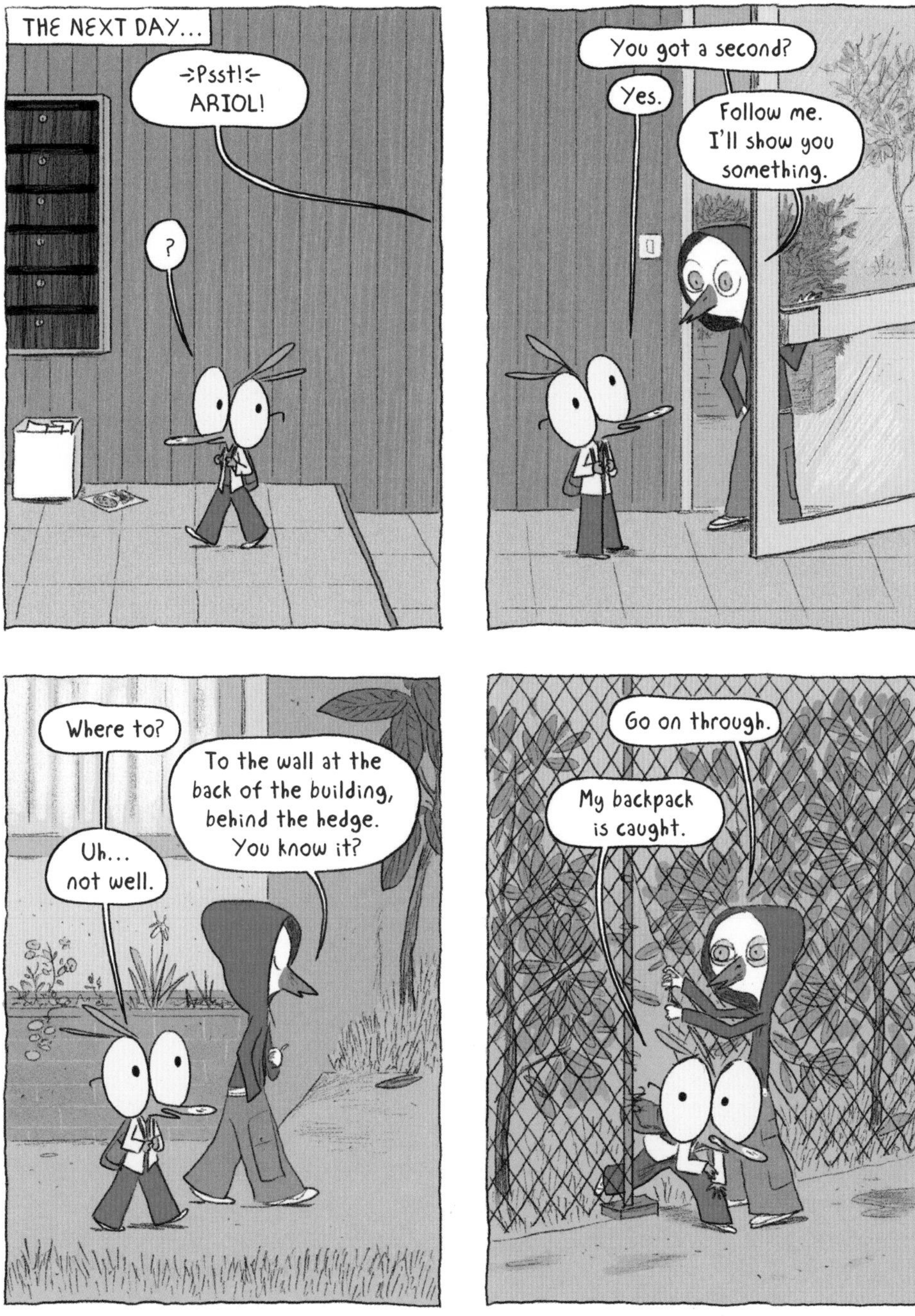
THE NEXT DAY...
⇒Psst!⇐ ARIOL!
?
You got a second?
Yes.
Follow me. I'll show you something.
Where to?
To the wall at the back of the building, behind the hedge. You know it?
Uh... not well.
Go on through.
My backpack is caught.

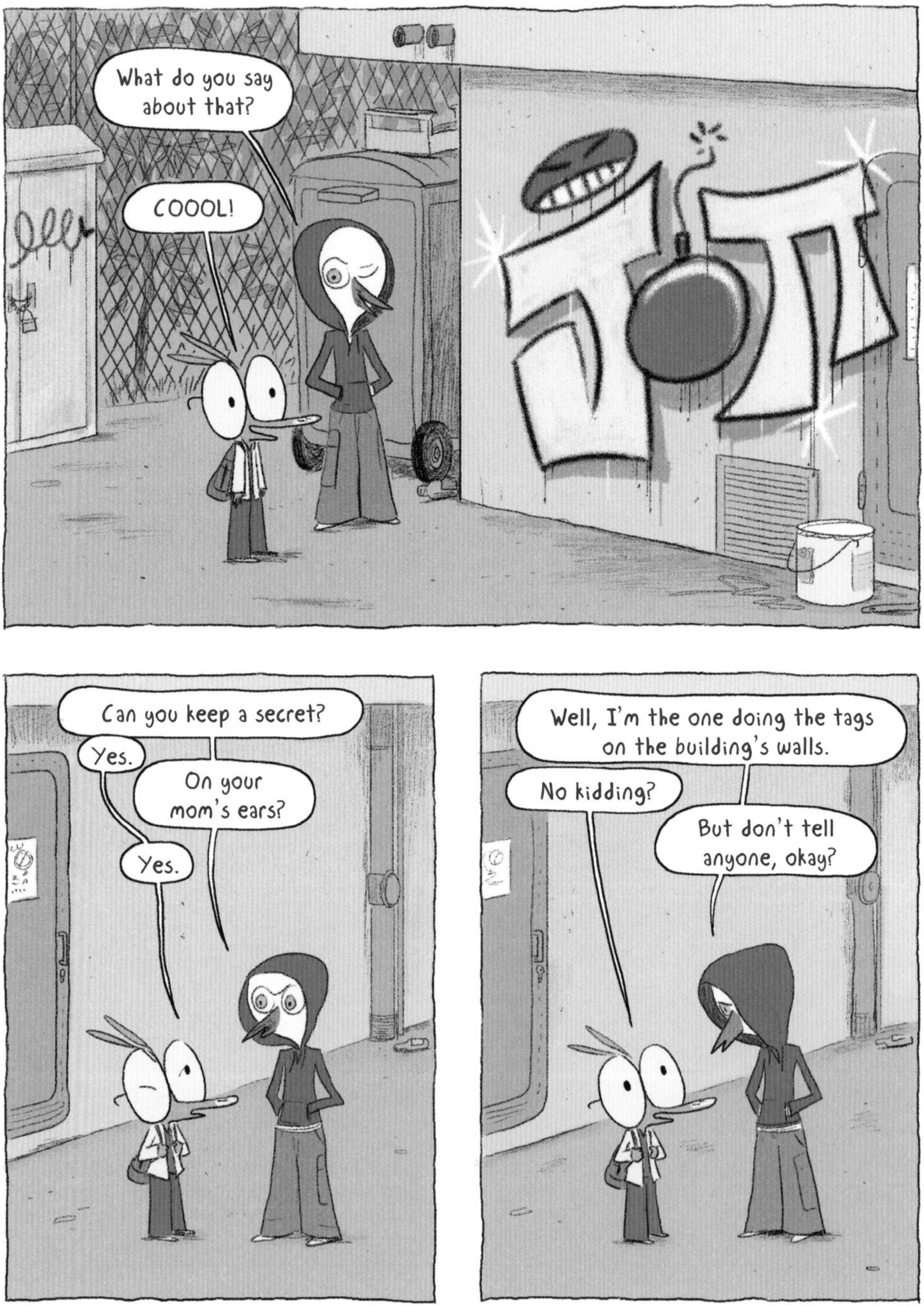
What do you say about that?
COOOL!
Can you keep a secret?
Yes.
On your mom's ears?
Yes.
Well, I'm the one doing the tags on the building's walls.
No kidding?
But don't tell anyone, okay?

69

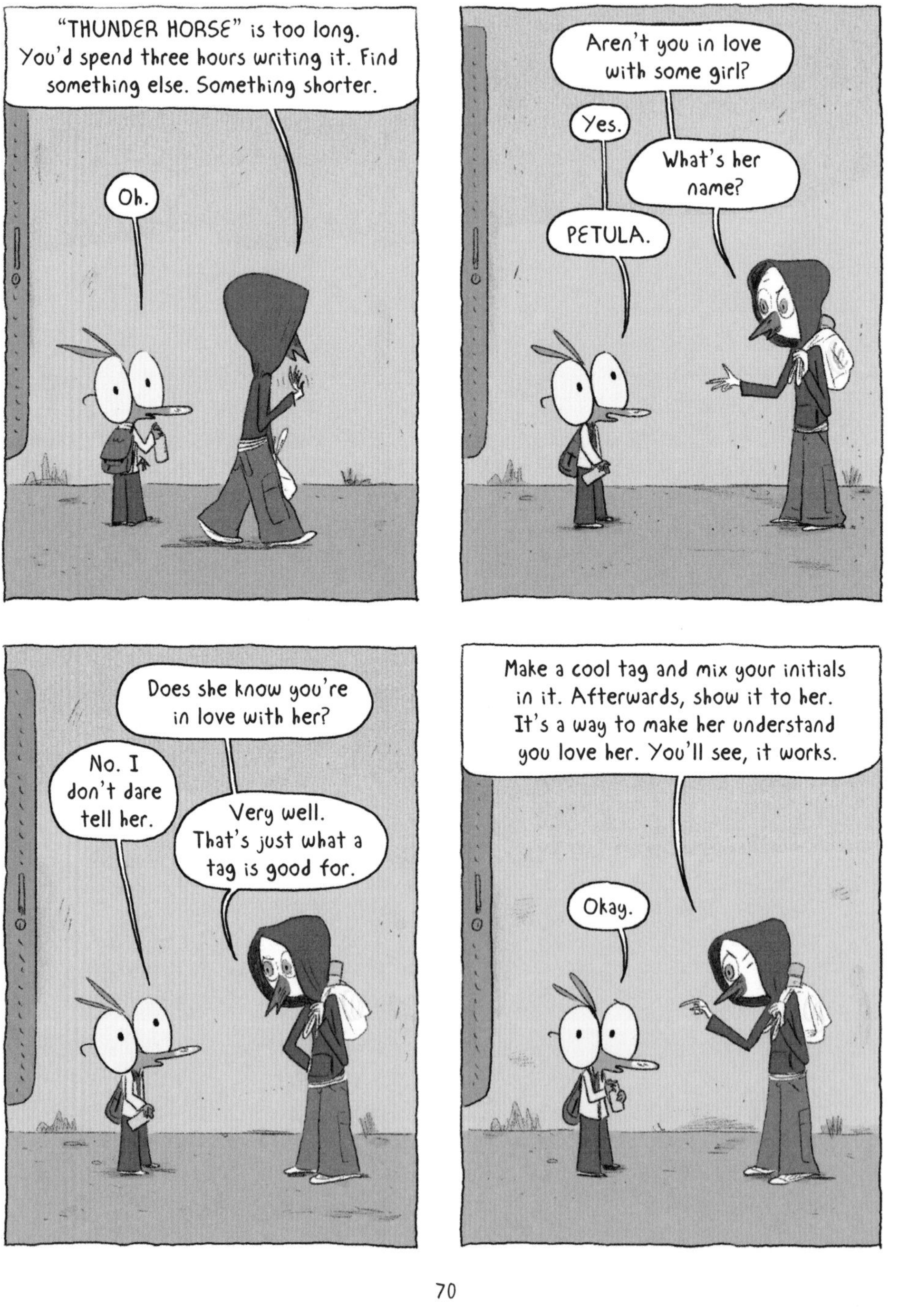
"THUNDER HORSE" is too long. You'd spend three hours writing it. Find something else. Something shorter.
Oh.
Aren't you in love with some girl?
Yes.
What's her name?
PETULA.
Does she know you're in love with her?
No. I don't dare tell her.
Very well. That's just what a tag is good for.
Make a cool tag and mix your initials in it. Afterwards, show it to her. It's a way to make her understand you love her. You'll see, it works.
Okay.

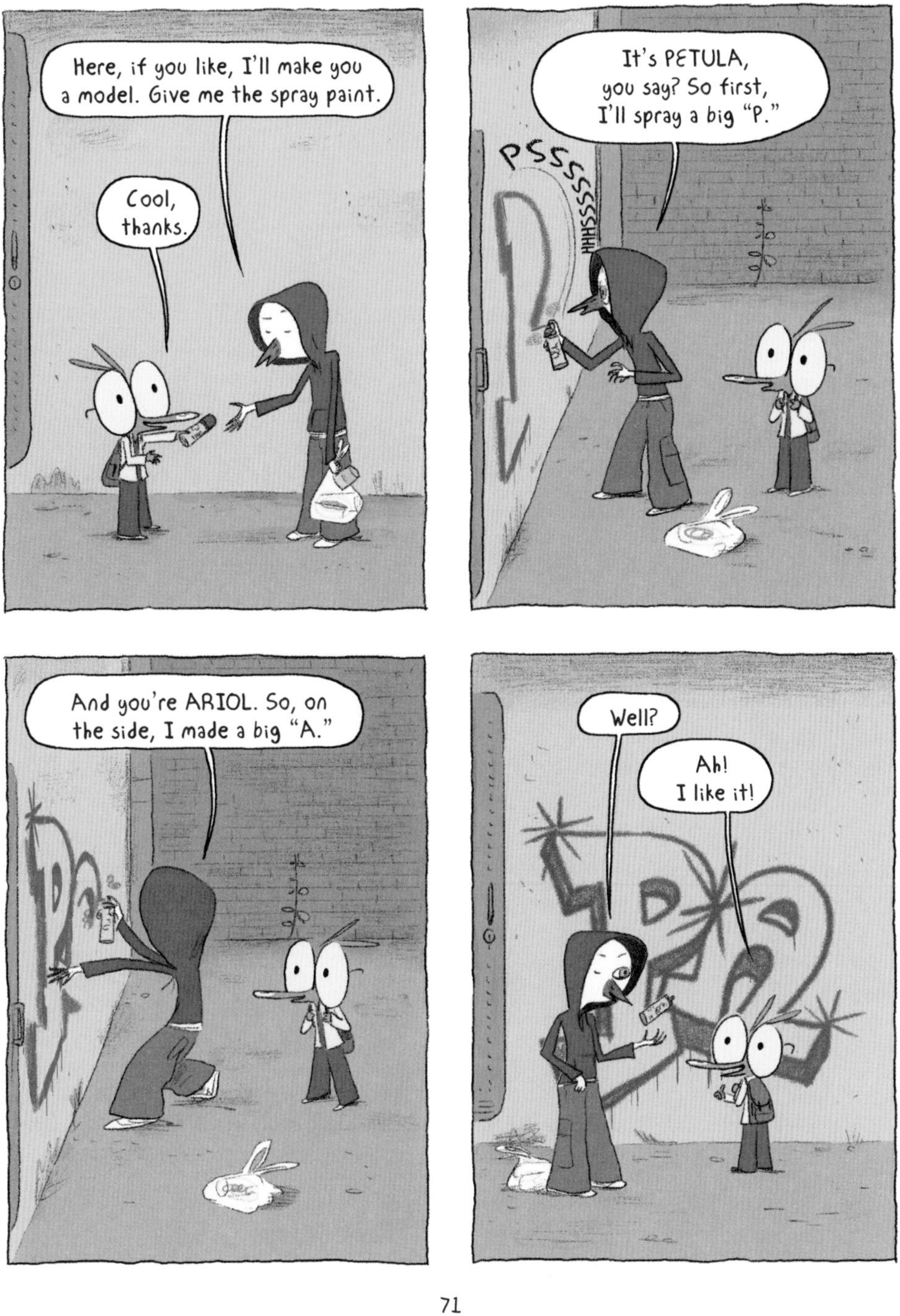
Here, if you like, I'll make you a model. Give me the spray paint.
Cool, thanks.
It's PETULA, you say? So first, I'll spray a big "P."
PSSSSSSSHHH
And you're ARIOL. So, on the side, I made a big "A."
Well?
Ah! I like it!

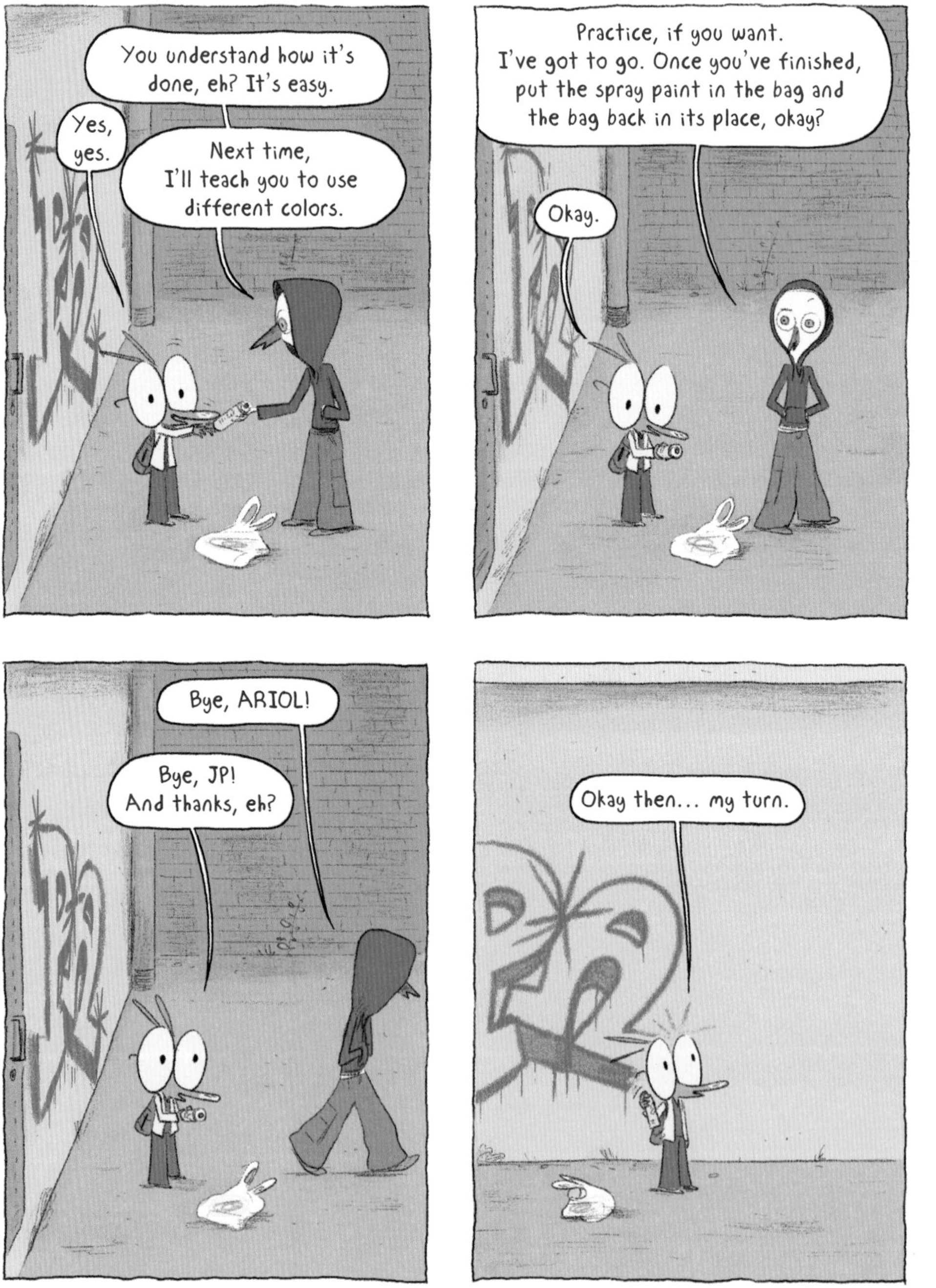

You understand how it's done, eh? It's easy.
Yes, yes.
Next time, I'll teach you to use different colors.
Practice, if you want. I've got to go. Once you've finished, put the spray paint in the bag and the bag back in its place, okay?
Okay.
Bye, ARIOL!
Bye, JP! And thanks, eh?
Okay then... my turn.

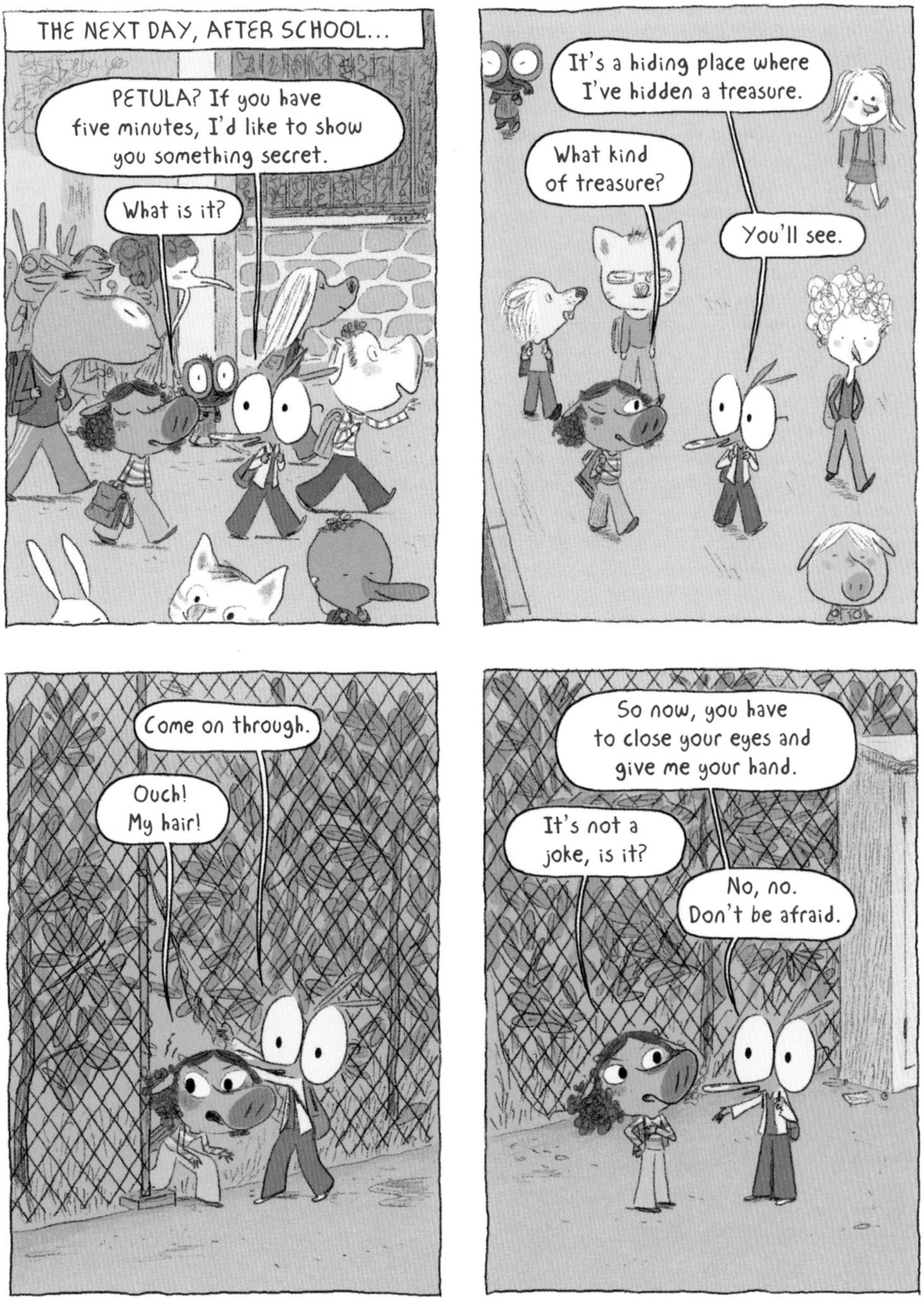
THE NEXT DAY, AFTER SCHOOL...
PETULA? If you have five minutes, I'd like to show you something secret.
What is it?
It's a hiding place where I've hidden a treasure.
What kind of treasure?
You'll see.
Come on through.
Ouch! My hair!
So now, you have to close your eyes and give me your hand.
It's not a joke, is it?
No, no. Don't be afraid.

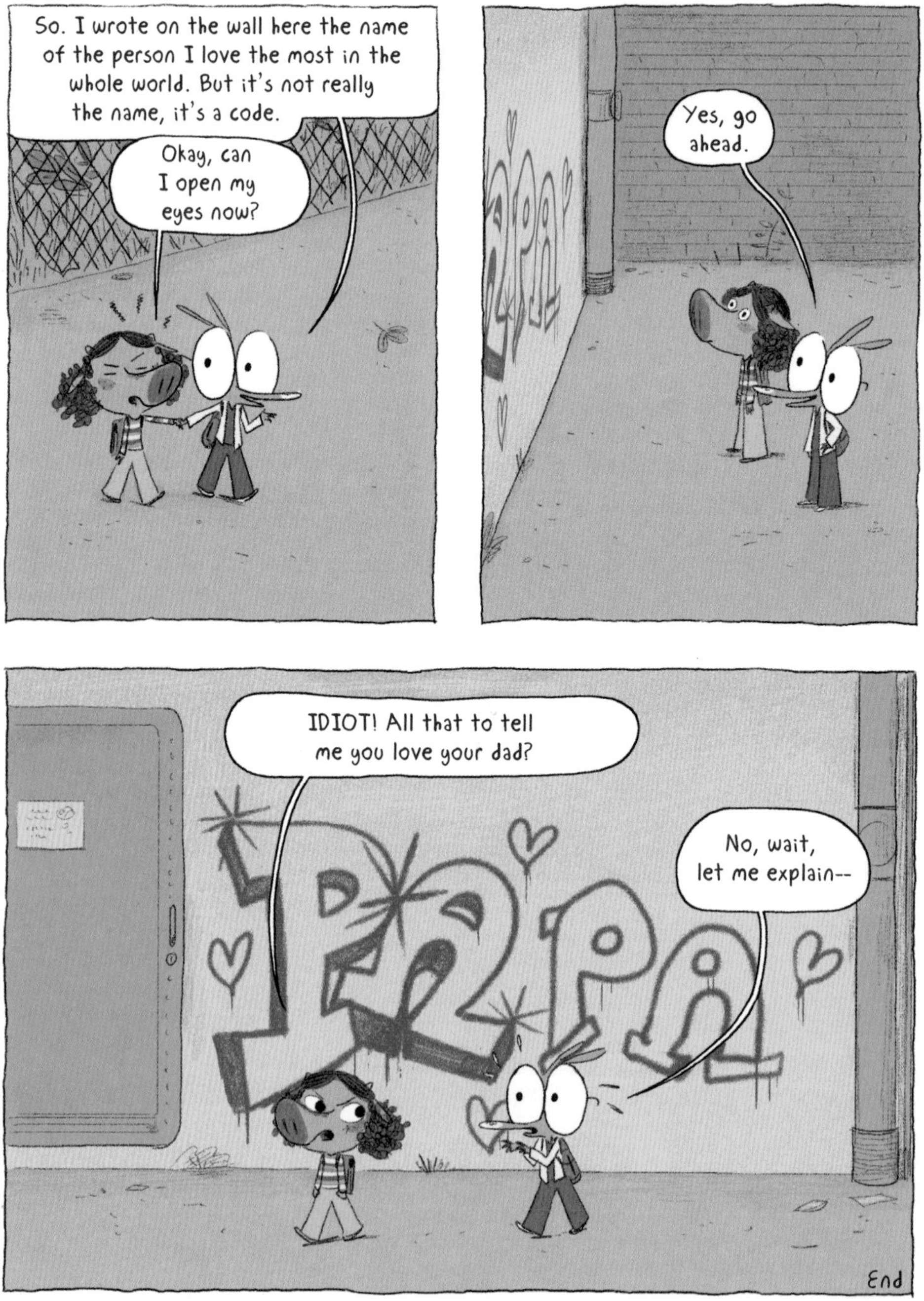
So. I wrote on the wall here the name of the person I love the most in the whole world. But it's not really the name, it's a code.
Okay, can I open my eyes now?
Yes, go ahead.
IDIOT! All that to tell me you love your dad?
No, wait, let me explain--
PaPa
End

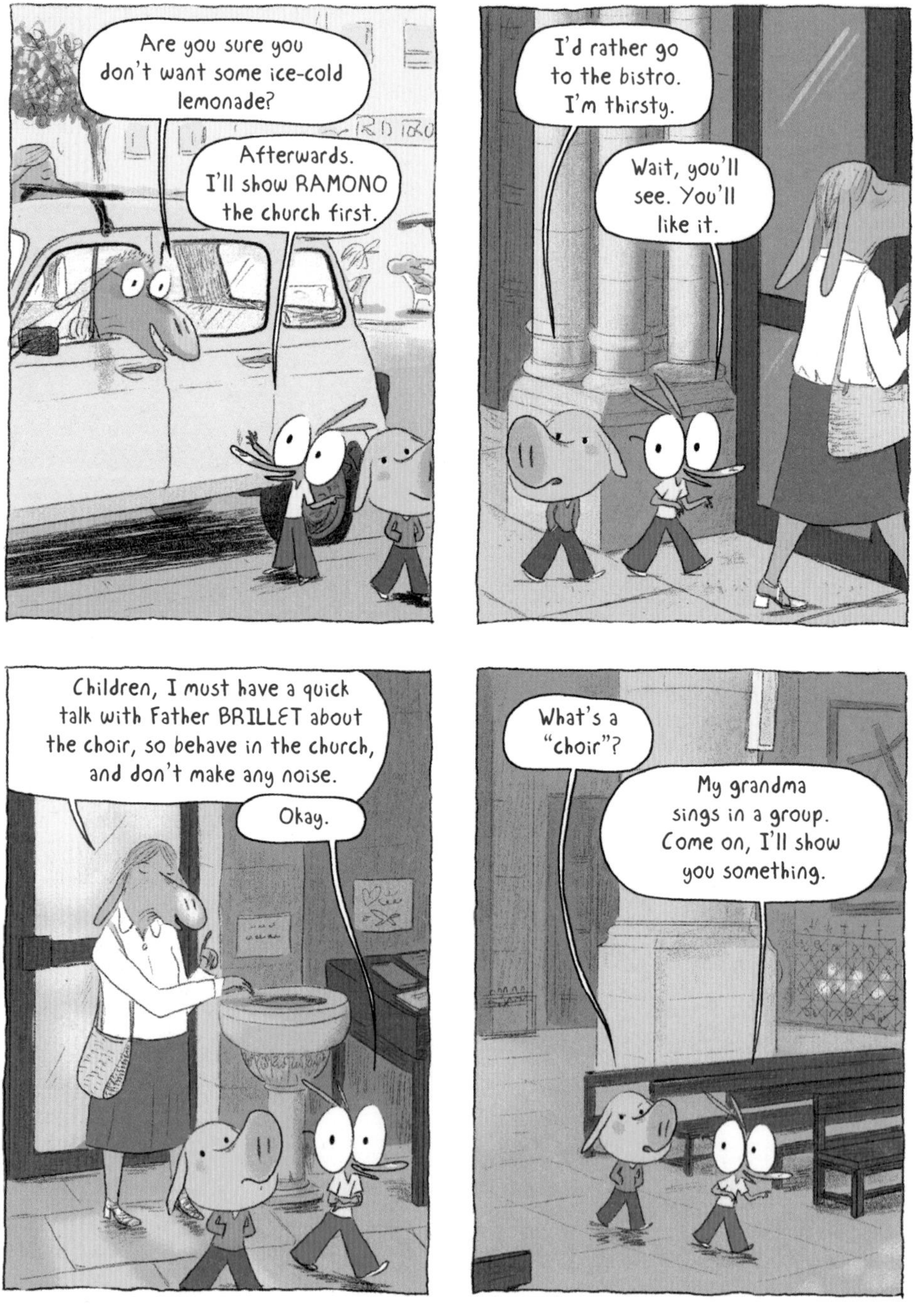
Are you sure you don't want some ice-cold lemonade?
Afterwards. I'll show RAMONO the church first.
I'd rather go to the bistro. I'm thirsty.
Wait, you'll see. You'll like it.
Children, I must have a quick talk with Father BRILLET about the choir, so behave in the church, and don't make any noise.
Okay.
What's a "choir"?
My grandma sings in a group. Come on, I'll show you something.

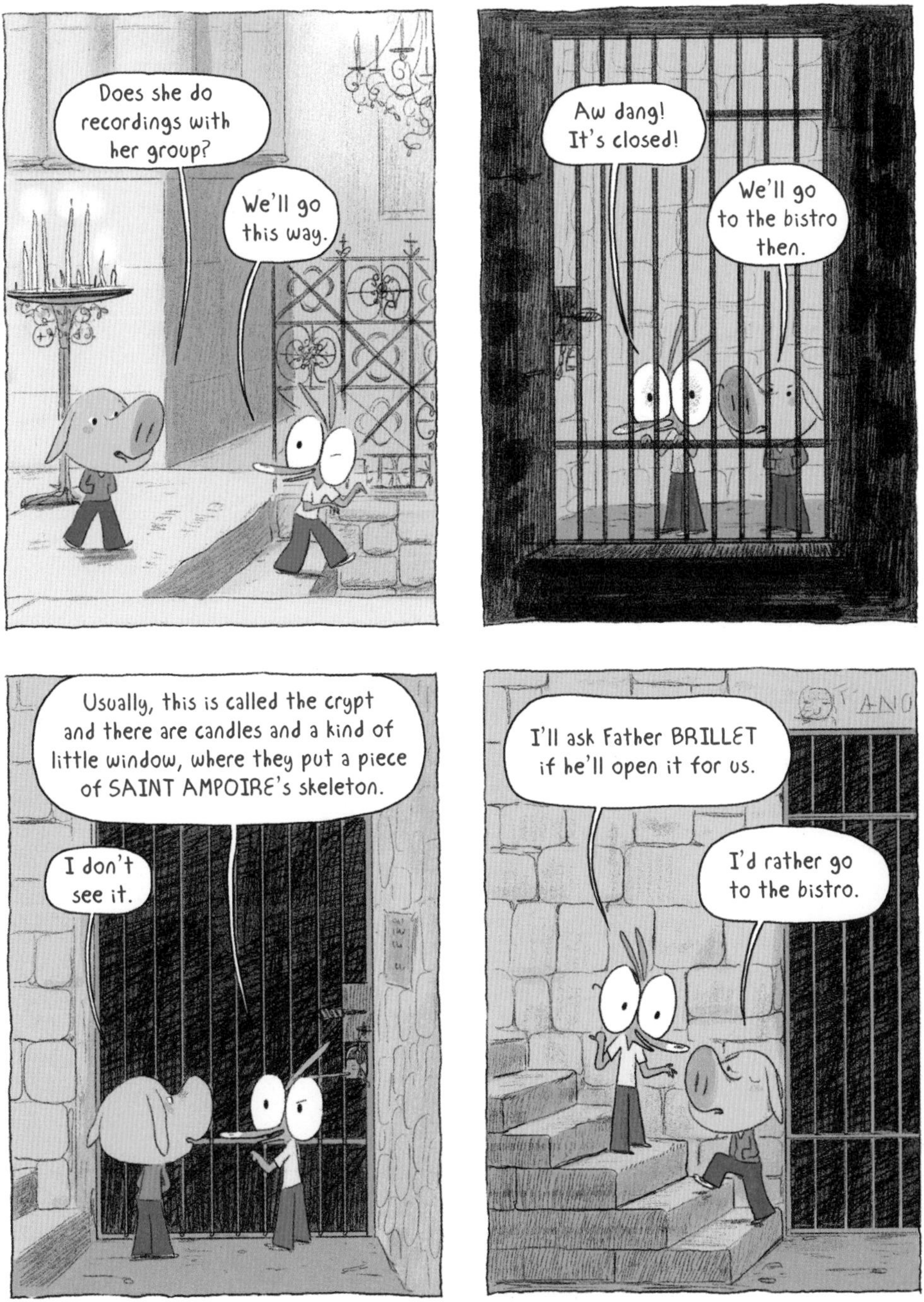
Does she do recordings with her group?
We'll go this way.
Aw dang! It's closed!
We'll go to the bistro then.
Usually, this is called the crypt and there are candles and a kind of little window, where they put a piece of SAINT AMPOIRE's skeleton.
I don't see it.
I'll ask Father BRILLET if he'll open it for us.
I'd rather go to the bistro.

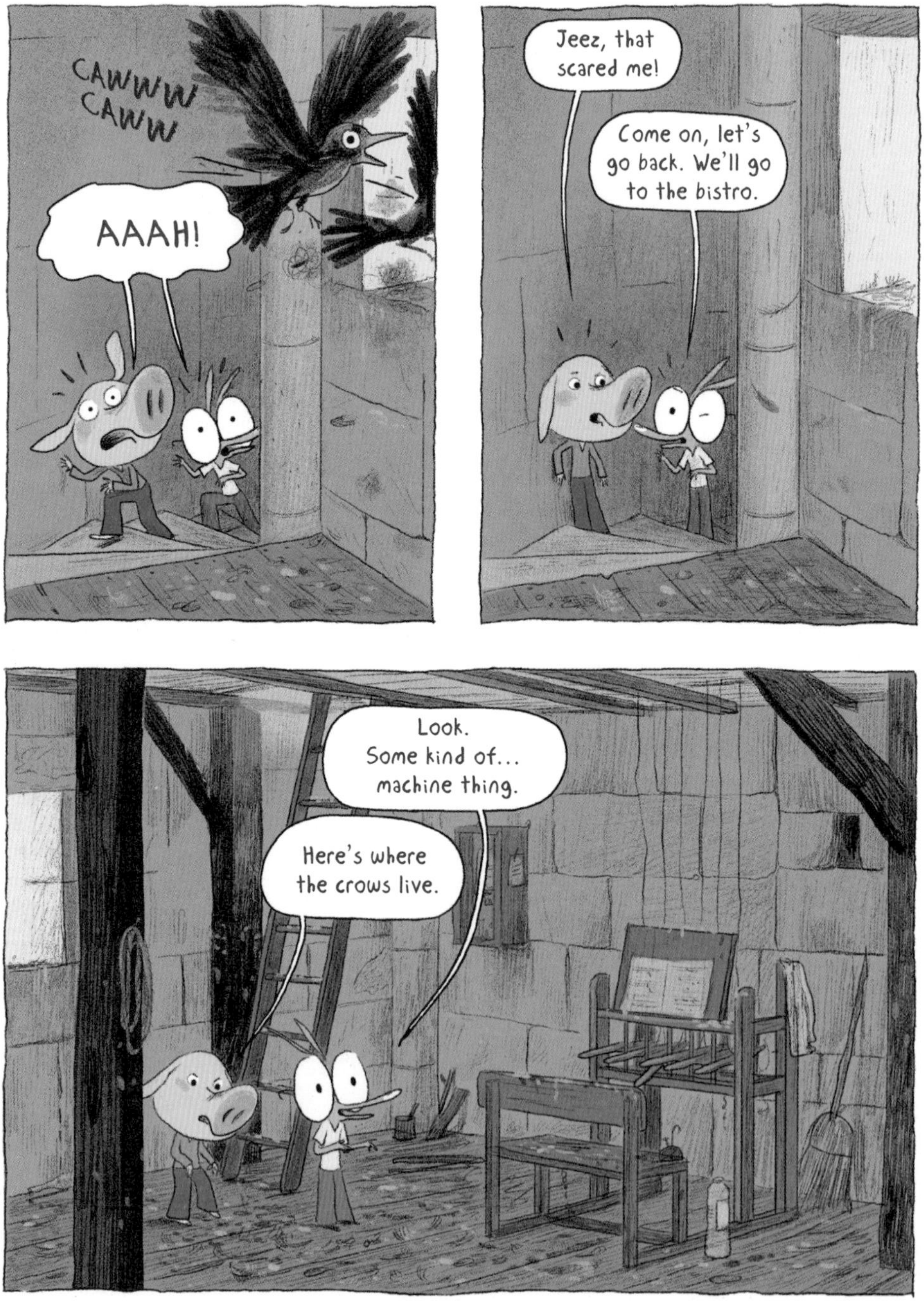
CAWWW
CAWW
AAAH!
Jeez, that scared me!
Come on, let's go back. We'll go to the bistro.
Look. Some kind of... machine thing.
Here's where the crows live.

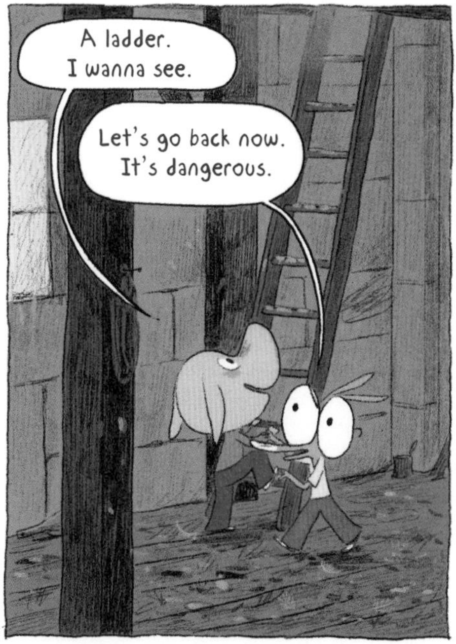
A ladder.
I wanna see.
Let's go back now.
It's dangerous.

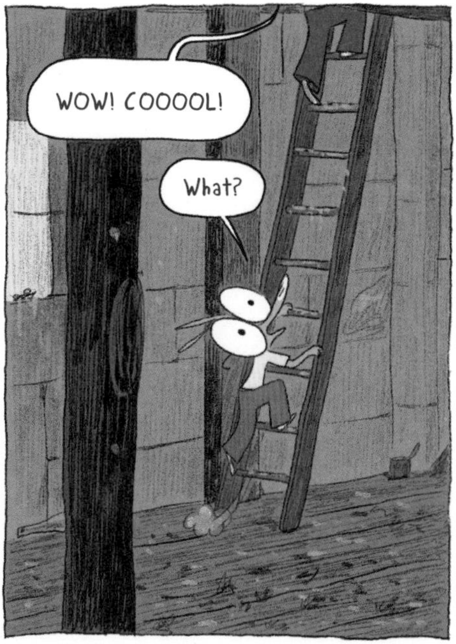
WOW! COOOOL!
What?

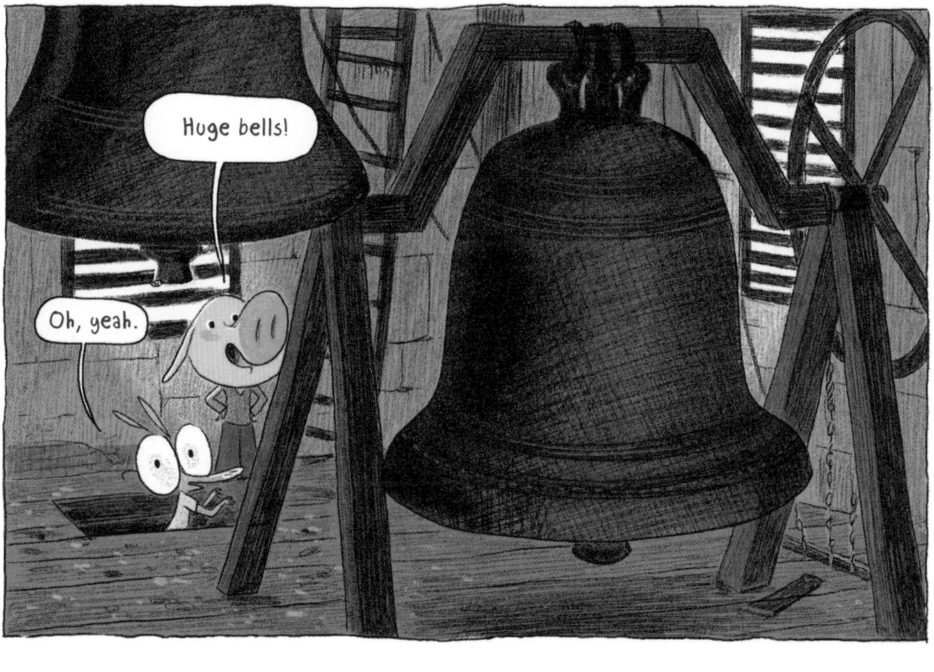
Huge bells!
Oh, yeah.

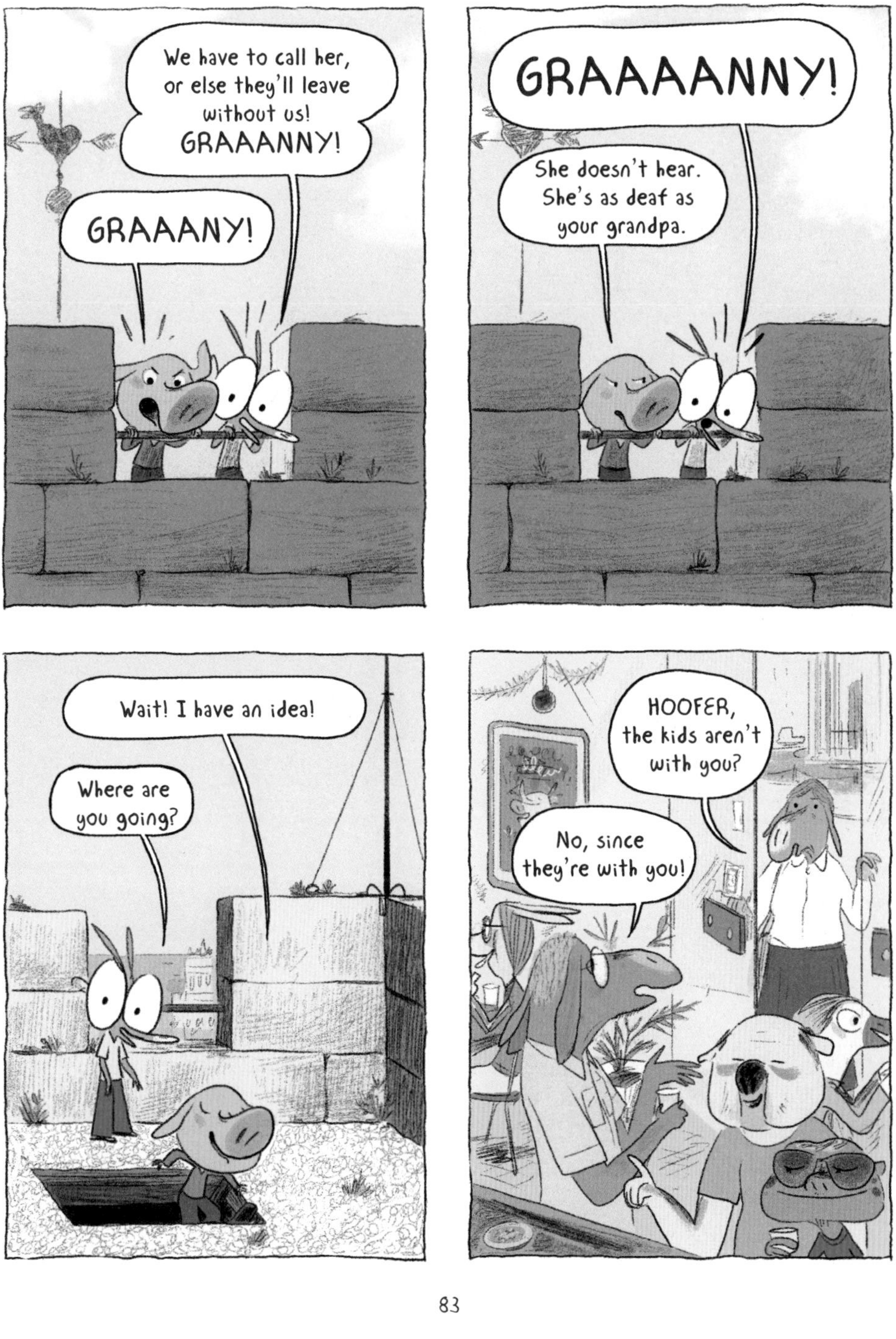

We have to call her, or else they'll leave without us! GRAAANNY!
GRAAANY!
GRAAAAANNY!
She doesn't hear. She's as deaf as your grandpa.
Wait! I have an idea!
Where are you going?
HOOFER, the kids aren't with you?
No, since they're with you!

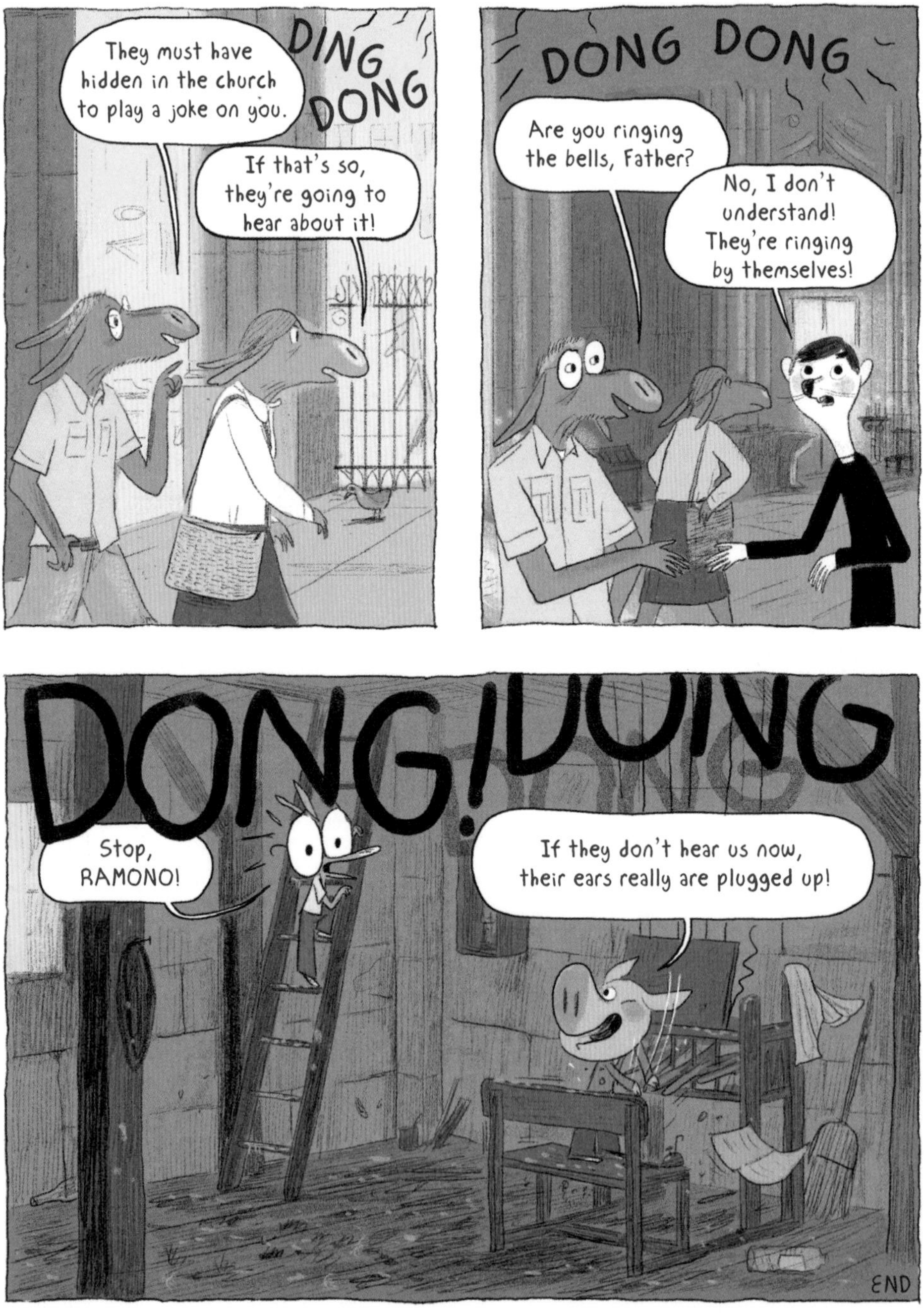

DING DONG
They must have hidden in the church to play a joke on you.
If that's so, they're going to hear about it!
DONG DONG
Are you ringing the bells, Father?
No, I don't understand! They're ringing by themselves!
DONG! DONG
Stop, RAMONO!
If they don't hear us now, their ears really are plugged up!
END

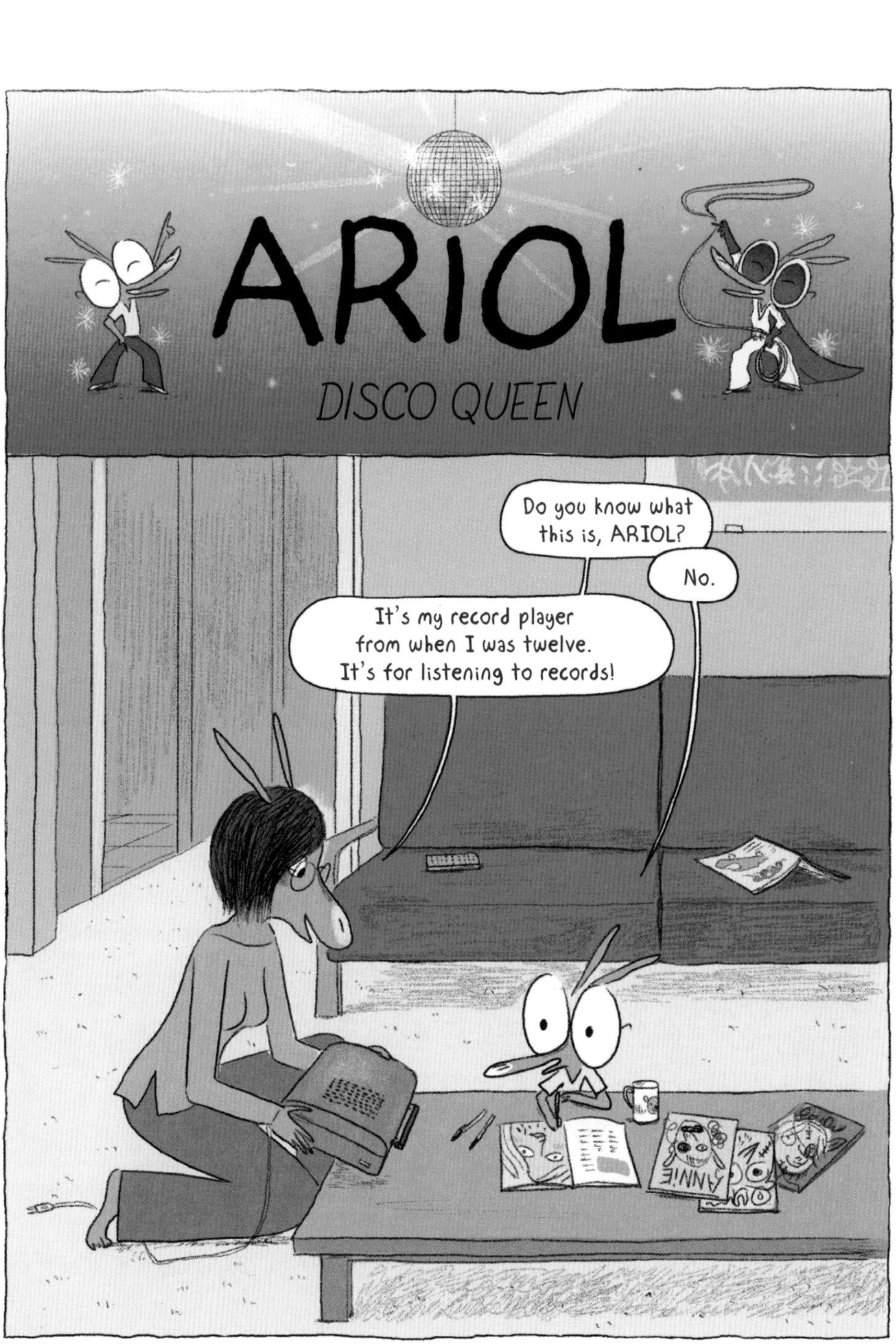
ARIOL
DISCO QUEEN
Do you know what this is, ARIOL?
No.
It's my record player from when I was twelve. It's for listening to records!
ANNIE

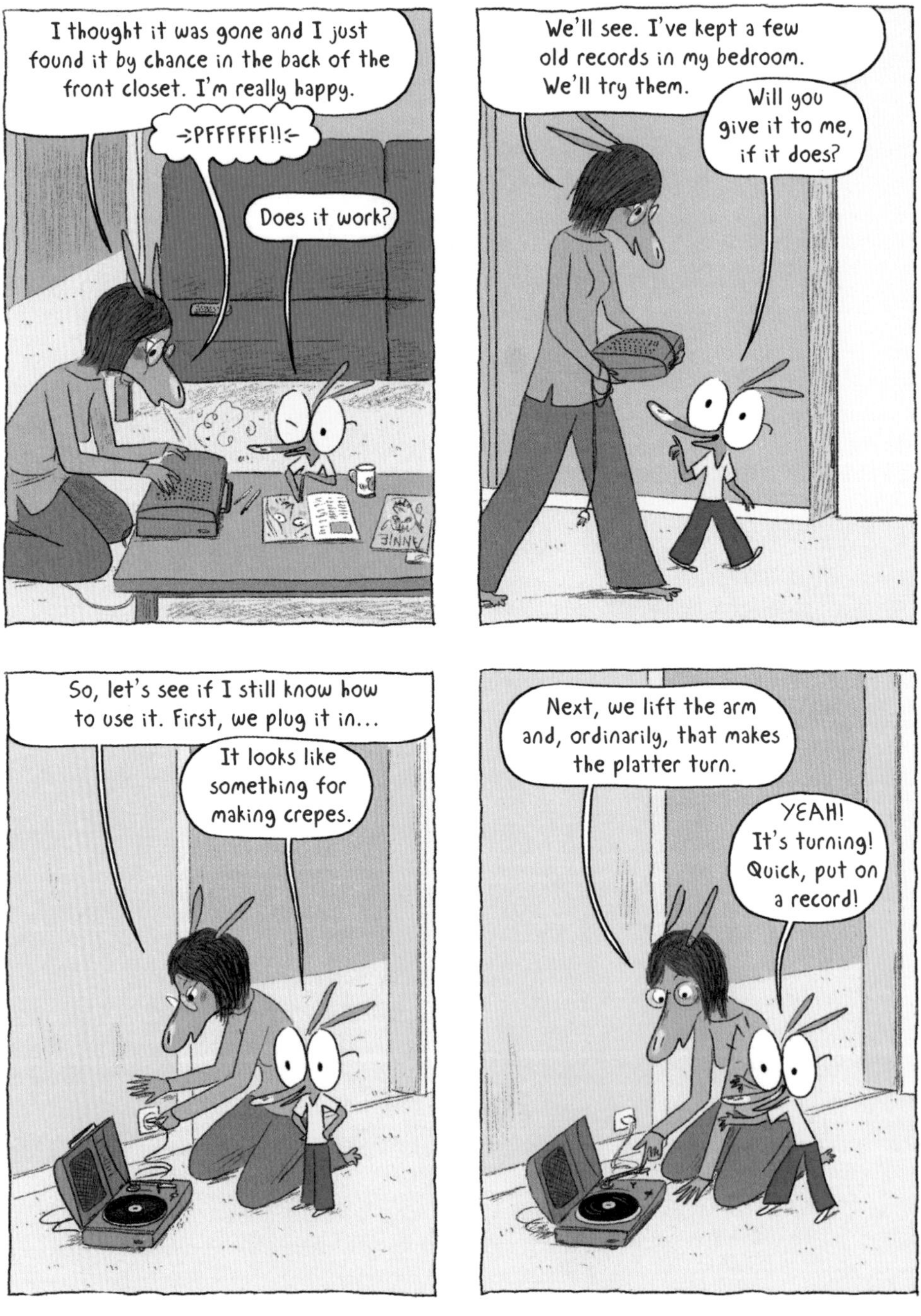
I thought it was gone and I just found it by chance in the back of the front closet. I'm really happy.
⇒PFFFFFF!!⇐
Does it work?
We'll see. I've kept a few old records in my bedroom. We'll try them.
Will you give it to me, if it does?
So, let's see if I still know how to use it. First, we plug it in...
It looks like something for making crepes.
Next, we lift the arm and, ordinarily, that makes the platter turn.
YEAH! It's turning! Quick, put on a record!

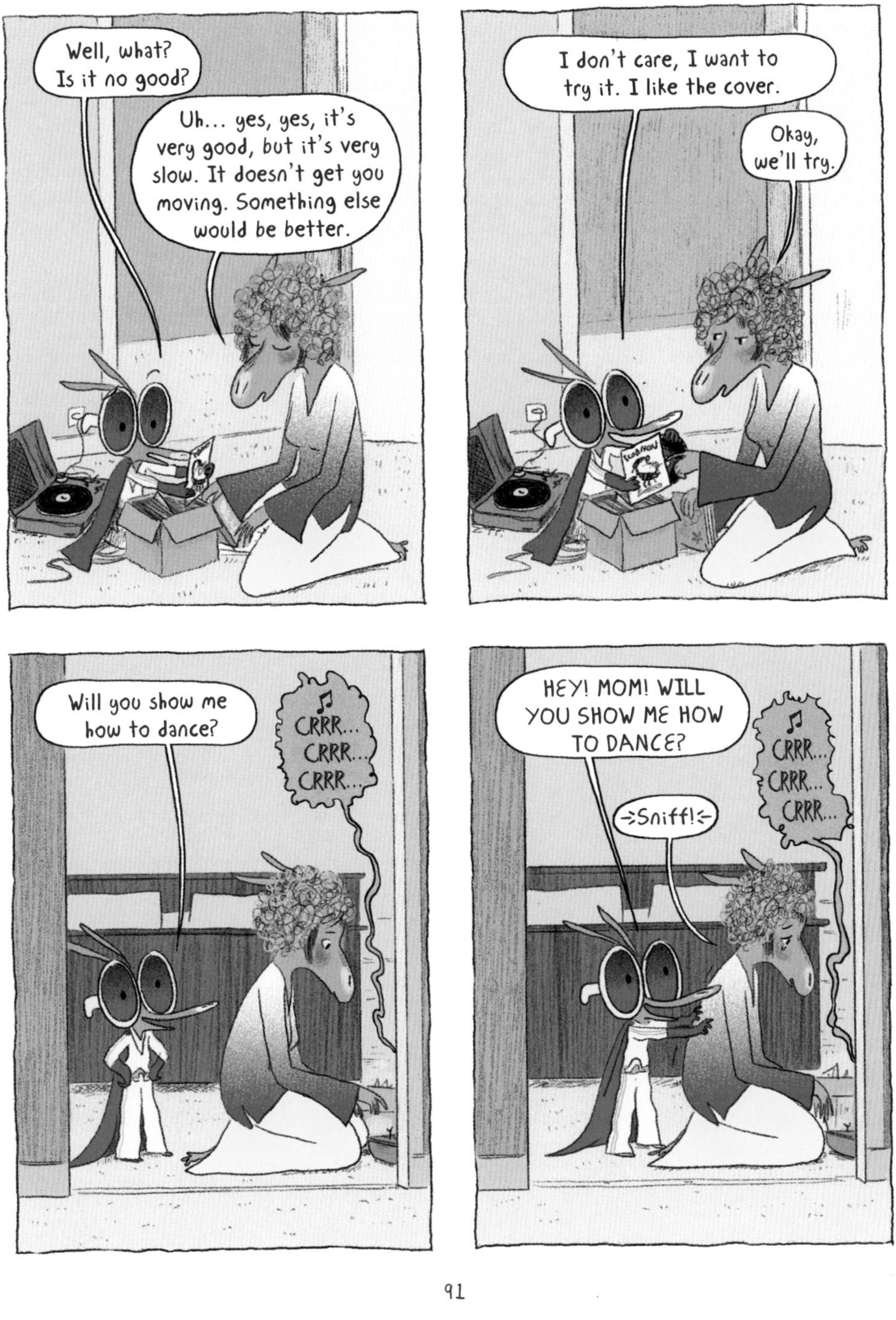
Well, what? Is it no good?
Uh... yes, yes, it's very good, but it's very slow. It doesn't get you moving. Something else would be better.
I don't care, I want to try it. I like the cover.
Okay, we'll try.
Will you show me how to dance?
CRRR... CRRR... CRRR...
HEY! MOM! WILL YOU SHOW ME HOW TO DANCE?
Sniff!
CRRR... CRRR... CRRR...

93

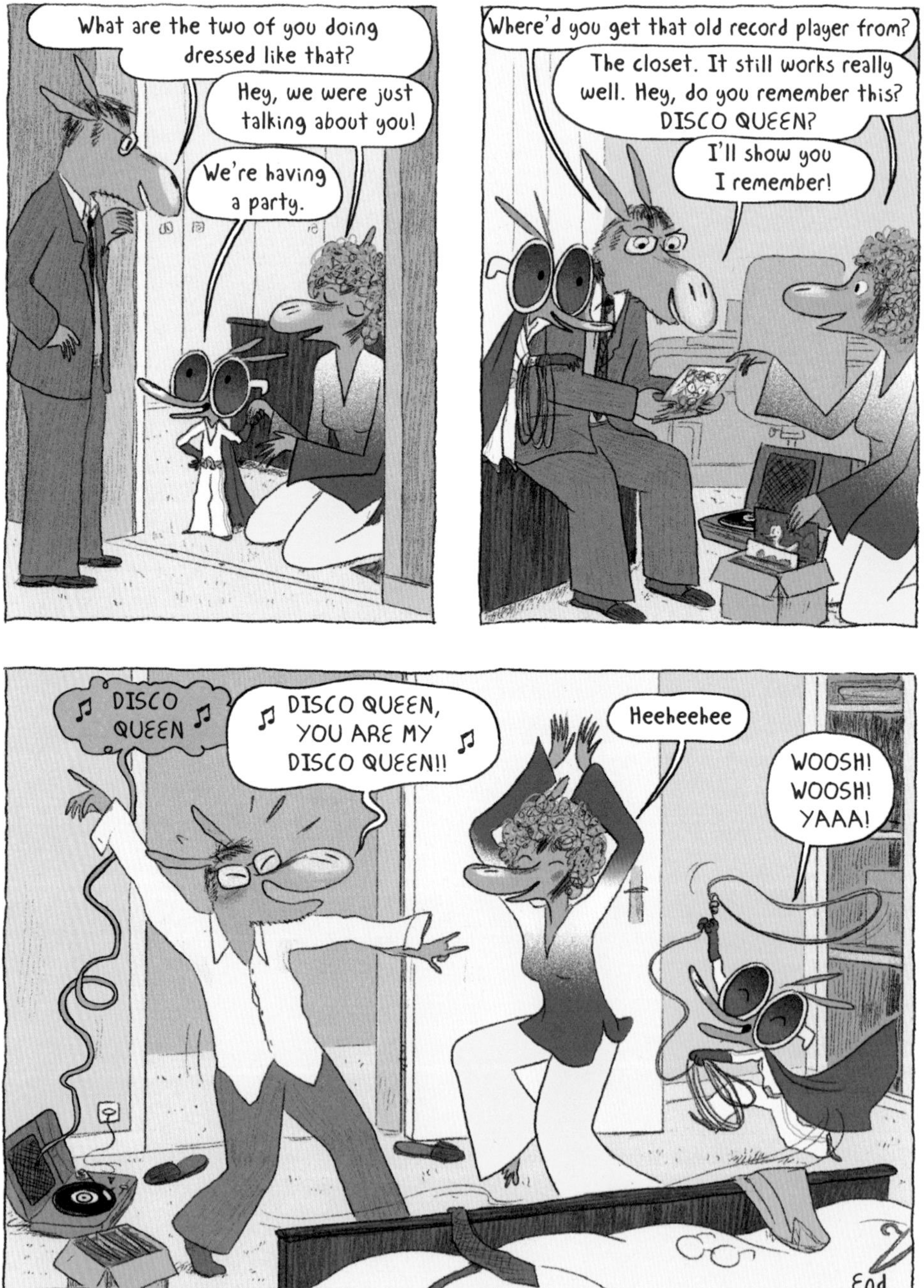
What are the two of you doing dressed like that?
Hey, we were just talking about you!
We're having a party.
Where'd you get that old record player from?
The closet. It still works really well. Hey, do you remember this? DISCO QUEEN?
I'll show you I remember!
DISCO QUEEN
DISCO QUEEN, YOU ARE MY DISCO QUEEN!!
Heeheehee
WOOSH! WOOSH! YAAA!
End

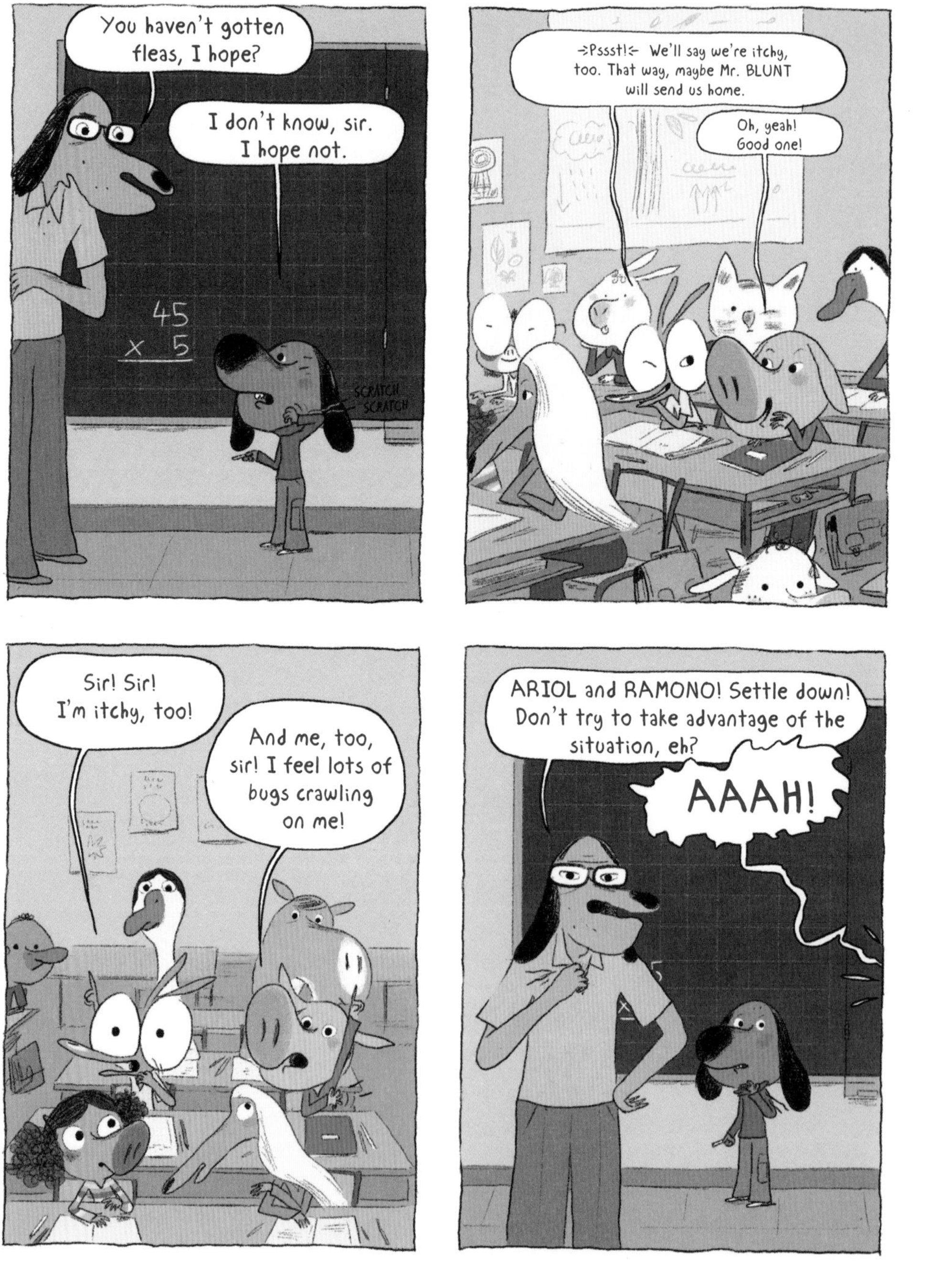
You haven't gotten fleas, I hope?
I don't know, sir. I hope not.
SCRATCH SCRATCH
⇒Pssst!⇐ We'll say we're itchy, too. That way, maybe Mr. BLUNT will send us home.
Oh, yeah! Good one!
Sir! Sir! I'm itchy, too!
And me, too, sir! I feel lots of bugs crawling on me!
ARIOL and RAMONO! Settle down! Don't try to take advantage of the situation, eh?
AAAH!

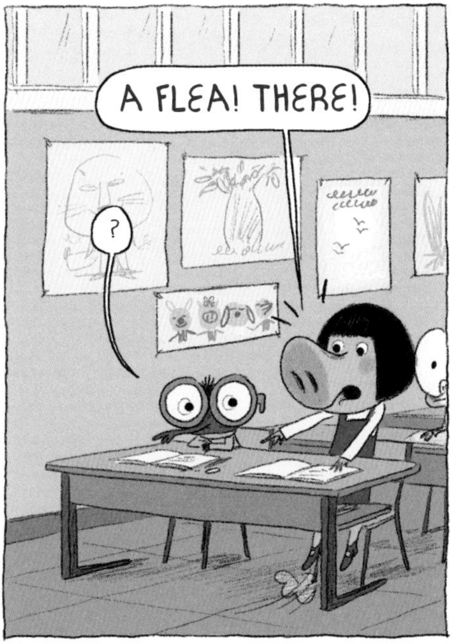
?
A FLEA! THERE!

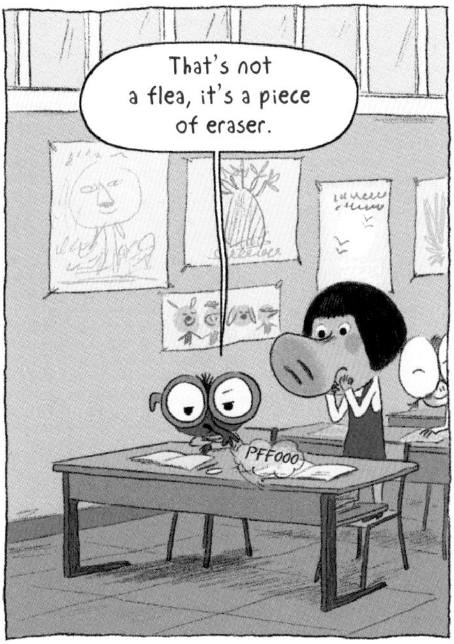
That's not a flea, it's a piece of eraser.
PFFOOO

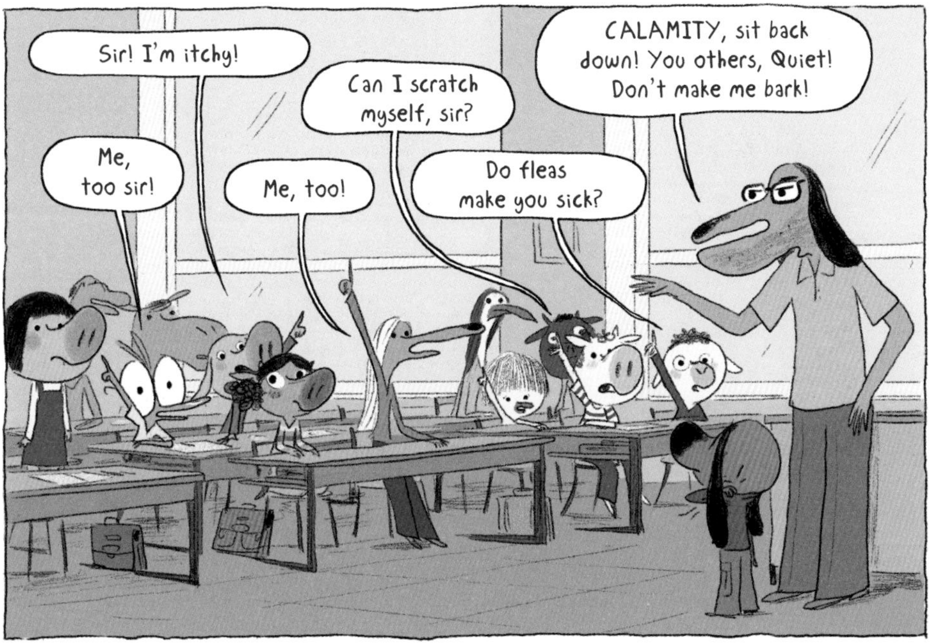
Sir! I'm itchy!
Me, too sir!
Me, too!
Can I scratch myself, sir?
Do fleas make you sick?
CALAMITY, sit back down! You others, Quiet! Don't make me bark!

98

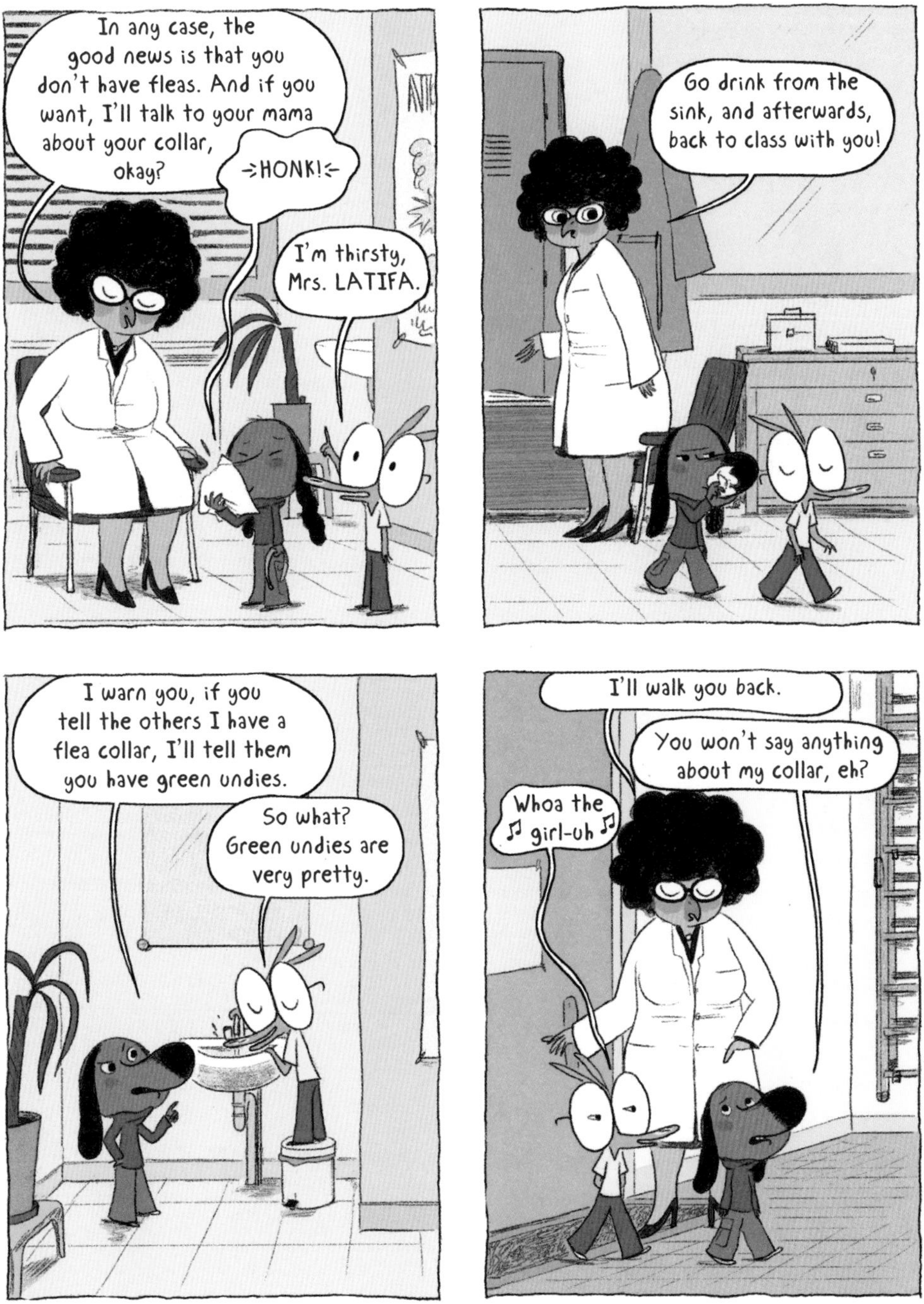
In any case, the good news is that you don't have fleas. And if you want, I'll talk to your mama about your collar, okay?
HONK!
I'm thirsty, Mrs. LATIFA.
Go drink from the sink, and afterwards, back to class with you!
I warn you, if you tell the others I have a flea collar, I'll tell them you have green undies.
So what? Green undies are very pretty.
I'll walk you back.
You won't say anything about my collar, eh?
Whoa the ♫ girl-uh ♫

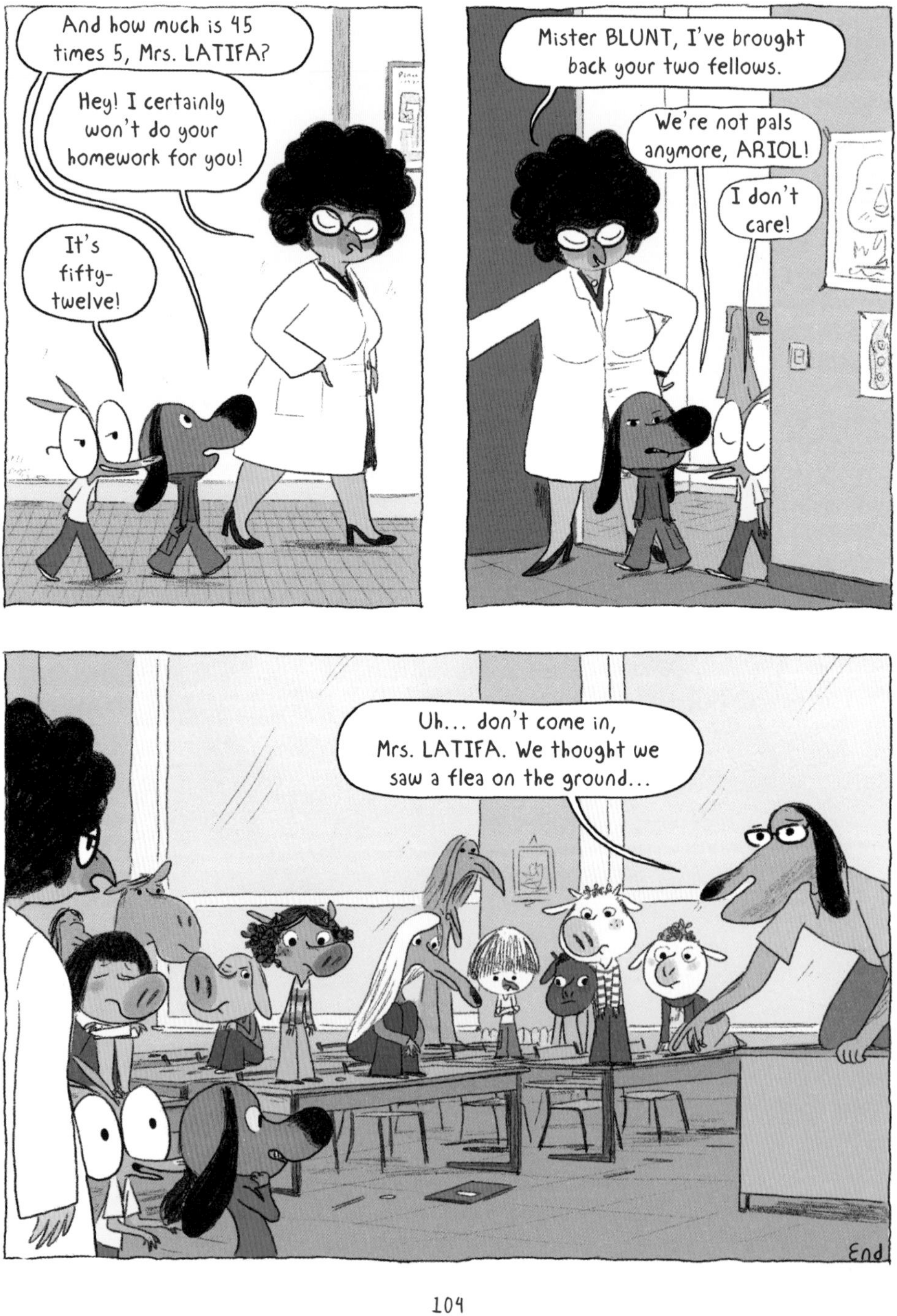
And how much is 45 times 5, Mrs. LATIFA?
Hey! I certainly won't do your homework for you!
It's fifty-twelve!
Mister BLUNT, I've brought back your two fellows.
We're not pals anymore, ARIOL!
I don't care!
Uh... don't come in, Mrs. LATIFA. We thought we saw a flea on the ground...
End

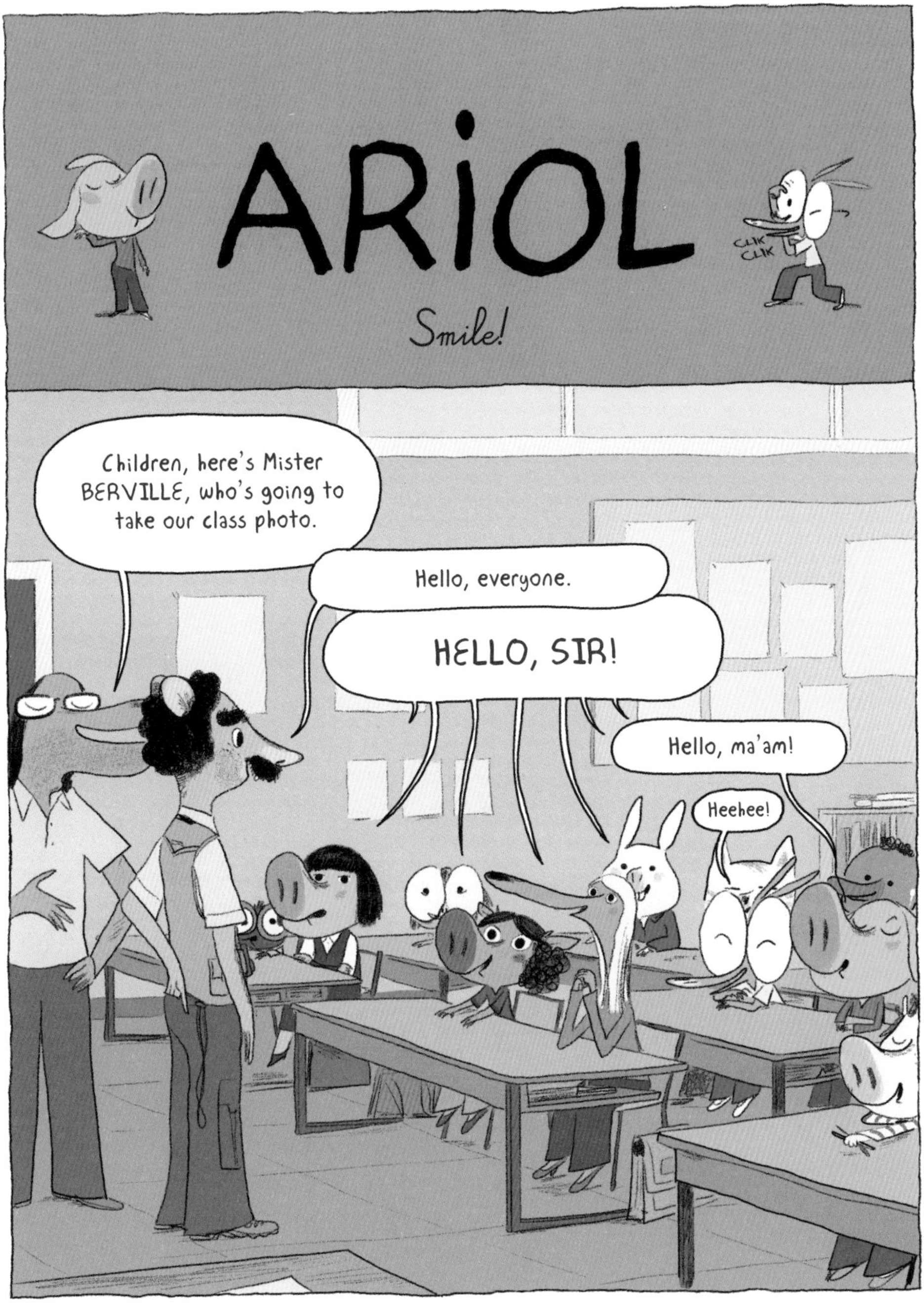
ARIOL
CLIK
CLIK
Smile!
Children, here's Mister BERVILLE, who's going to take our class photo.
Hello, everyone.
HELLO, SIR!
Hello, ma'am!
Heehee!

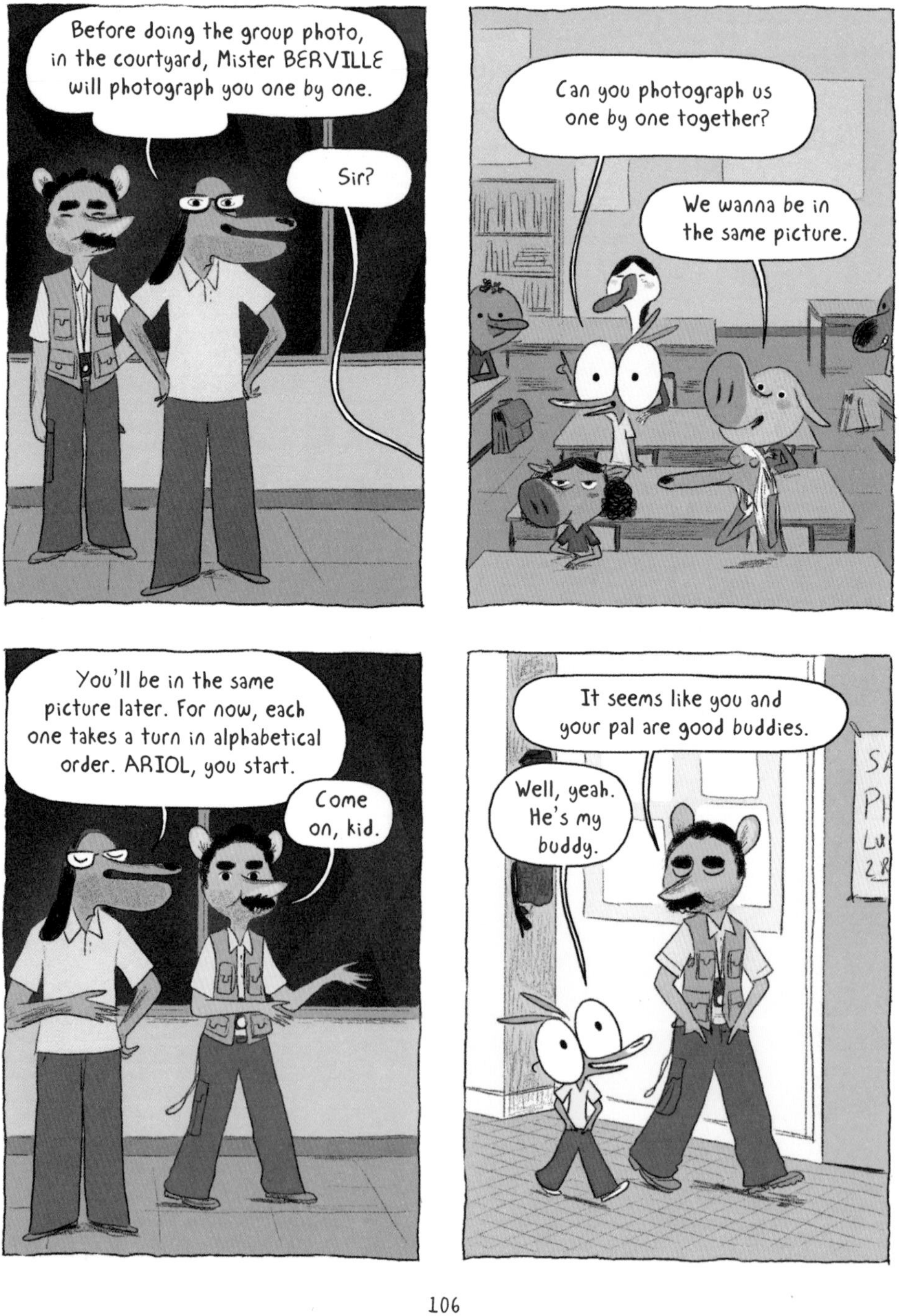
Before doing the group photo, in the courtyard, Mister BERVILLE will photograph you one by one.
Sir?
Can you photograph us one by one together?
We wanna be in the same picture.
You'll be in the same picture later. For now, each one takes a turn in alphabetical order. ARIOL, you start.
Come on, kid.
It seems like you and your pal are good buddies.
Well, yeah. He's my buddy.

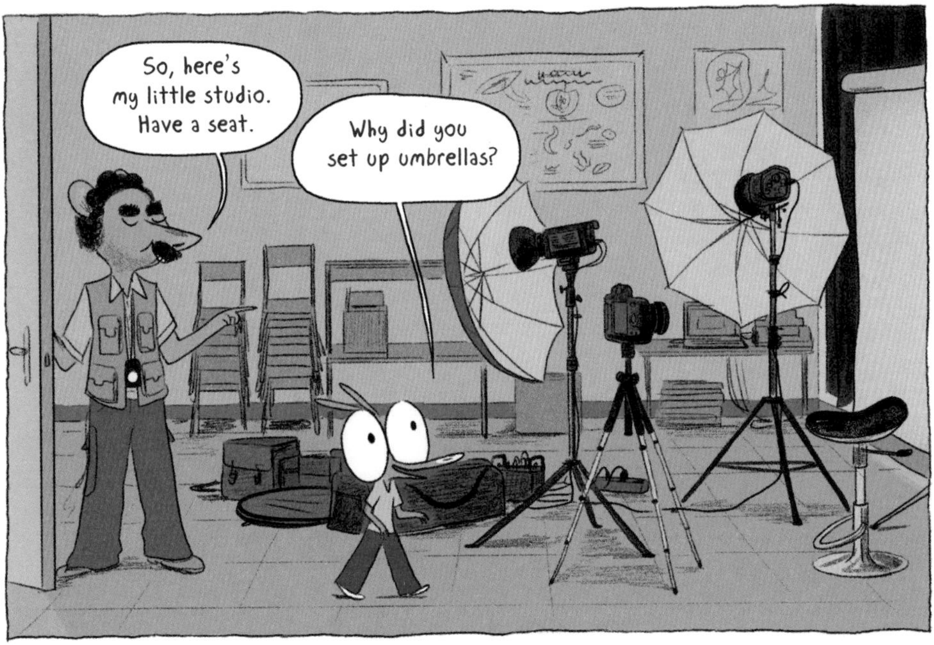
So, here's my little studio. Have a seat.
Why did you set up umbrellas?

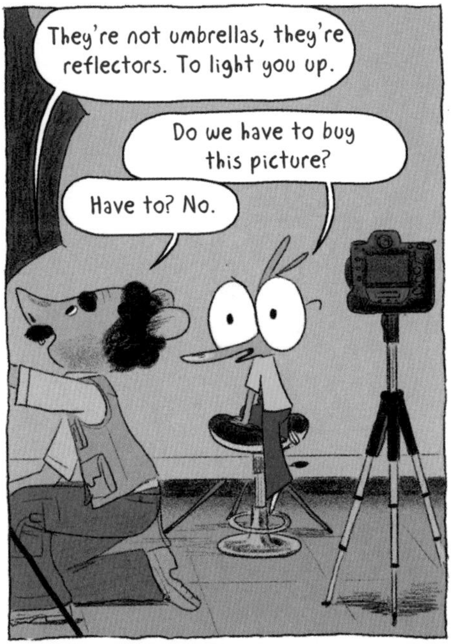
They're not umbrellas, they're reflectors. To light you up.
Do we have to buy this picture?
Have to? No.

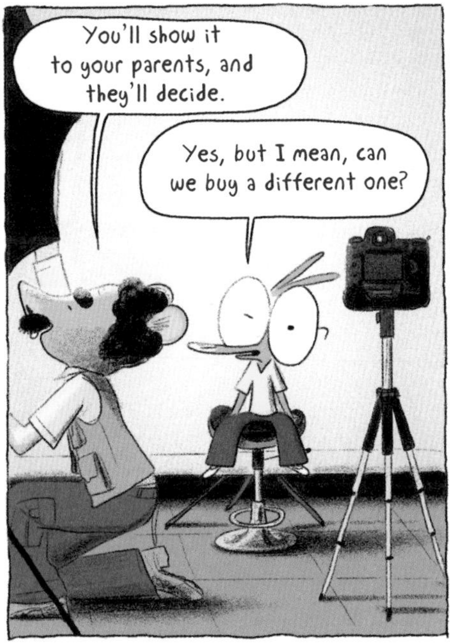
You'll show it to your parents, and they'll decide.
Yes, but I mean, can we buy a different one?

HUP! A flick of the wrist and it rises by itself.

Can I see the photo of ARIOL?

Who's photo?

ARIOL... He's the little donkey who went before me.

AAAH! But for goodness' sake, why are you all asking me for someone else's photo?

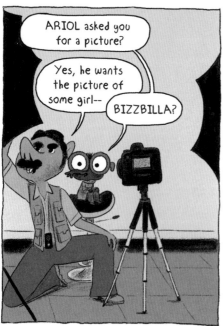

ARIOL asked you for a picture?

Yes, he wants the picture of some girl-- BIZZBILLA?

No, not BIZZBILLA. I forget. A little goat with pigtails, I think.

POF

PETULA?

Yes, that's it, PETULA.

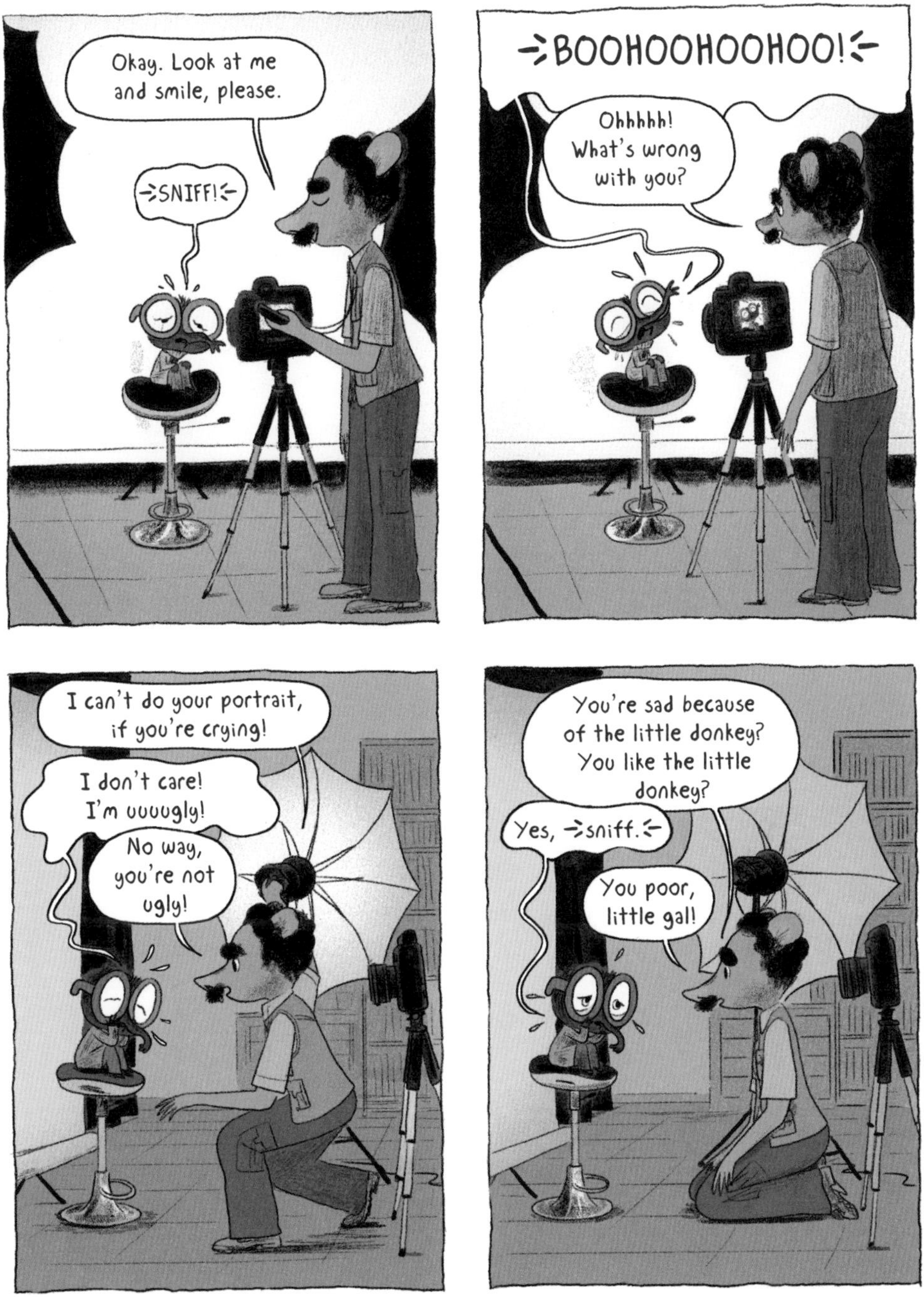
Okay. Look at me and smile, please.
SNIFF!
BOOHOOHOOHOO!
Ohhhhh! What's wrong with you?
I can't do your portrait, if you're crying!
I don't care! I'm uuuugly!
No way, you're not ugly!
You're sad because of the little donkey? You like the little donkey?
Yes, sniff.
You poor, little gal!

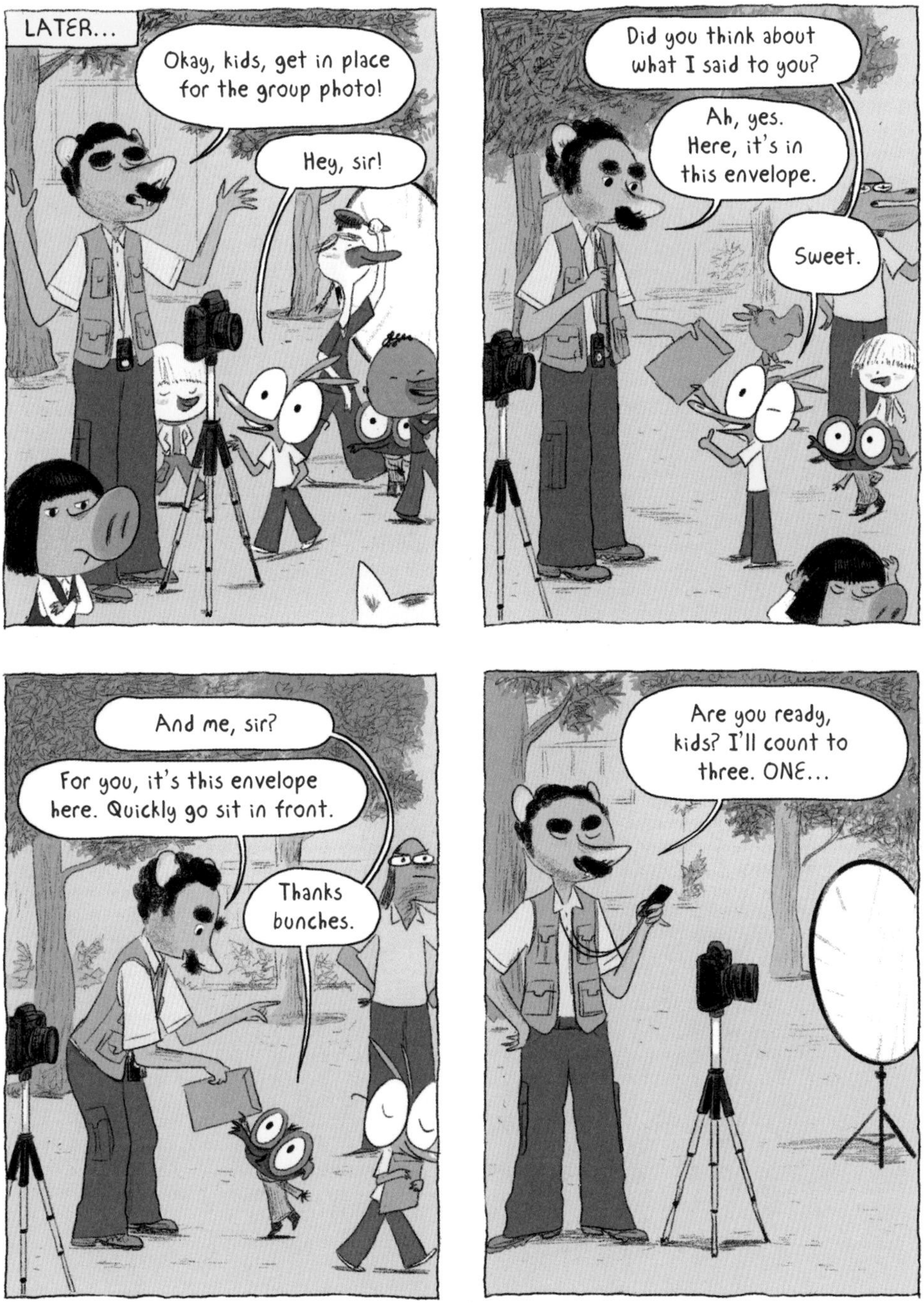
LATER...
Okay, kids, get in place for the group photo!
Hey, sir!
Did you think about what I said to you?
Ah, yes. Here, it's in this envelope.
Sweet.
And me, sir?
For you, it's this envelope here. Quickly go sit in front.
Thanks bunches.
Are you ready, kids? I'll count to three. ONE...

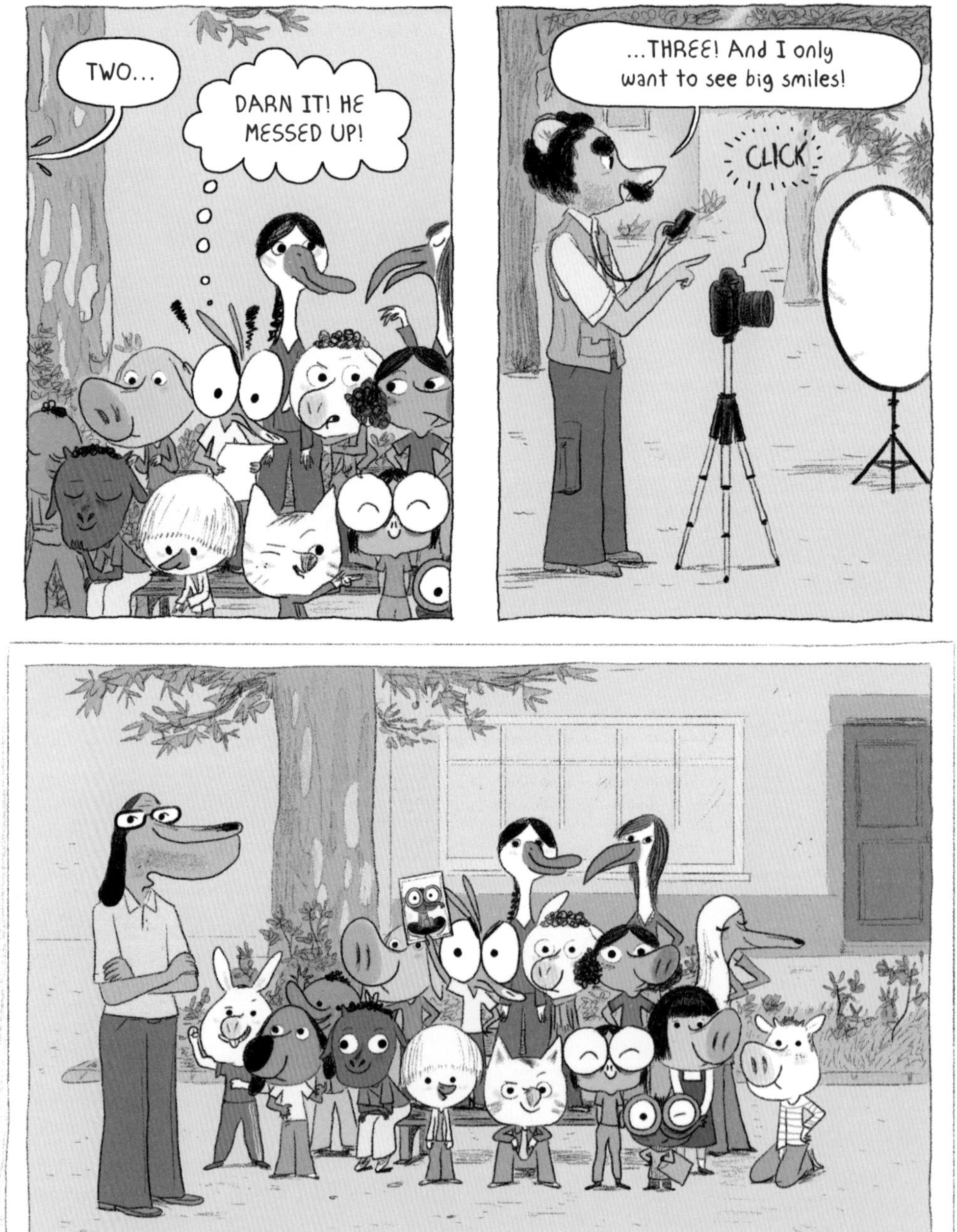
TWO...
DARN IT! HE MESSED UP!
...THREE! And I only want to see big smiles!
CLICK
END

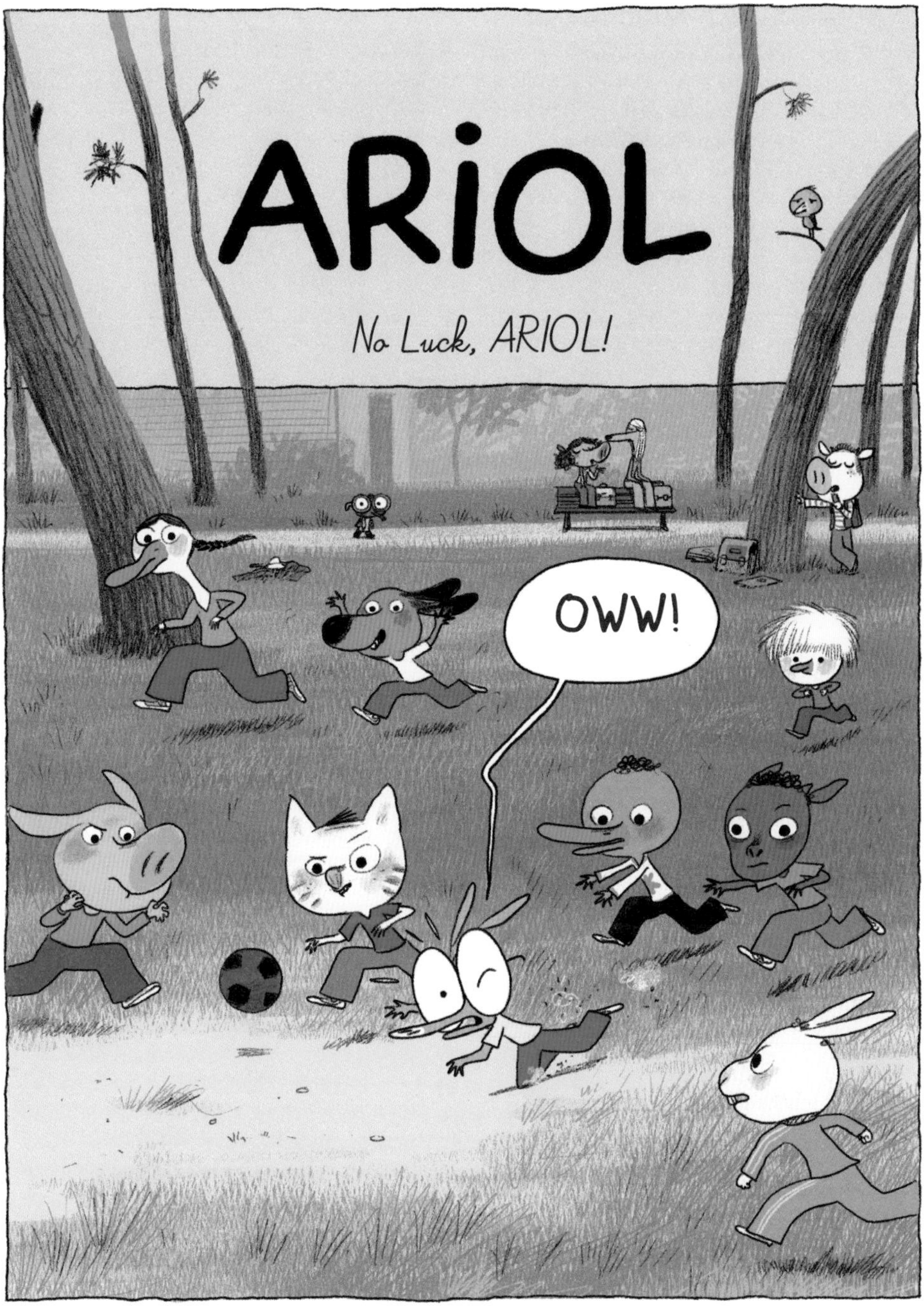
ARiOL
No Luck, ARIOL!
OWW!

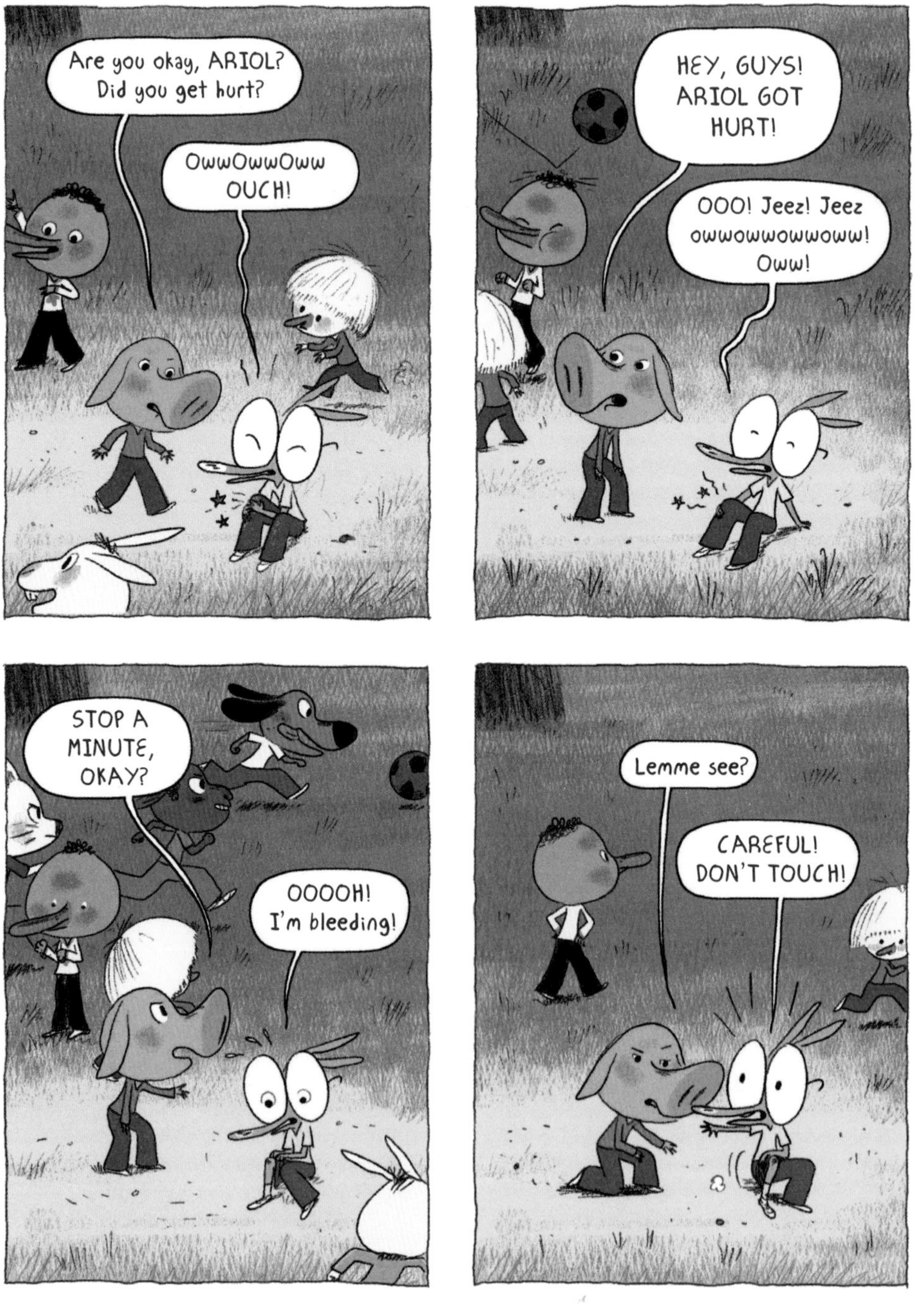
Are you okay, ARIOL? Did you get hurt?
OwwOwwOww OUCH!
HEY, GUYS! ARIOL GOT HURT!
OOO! Jeez! Jeez owwowwowwoww! Oww!
STOP A MINUTE, OKAY?
OOOOH! I'm bleeding!
Lemme see?
CAREFUL! DON'T TOUCH!

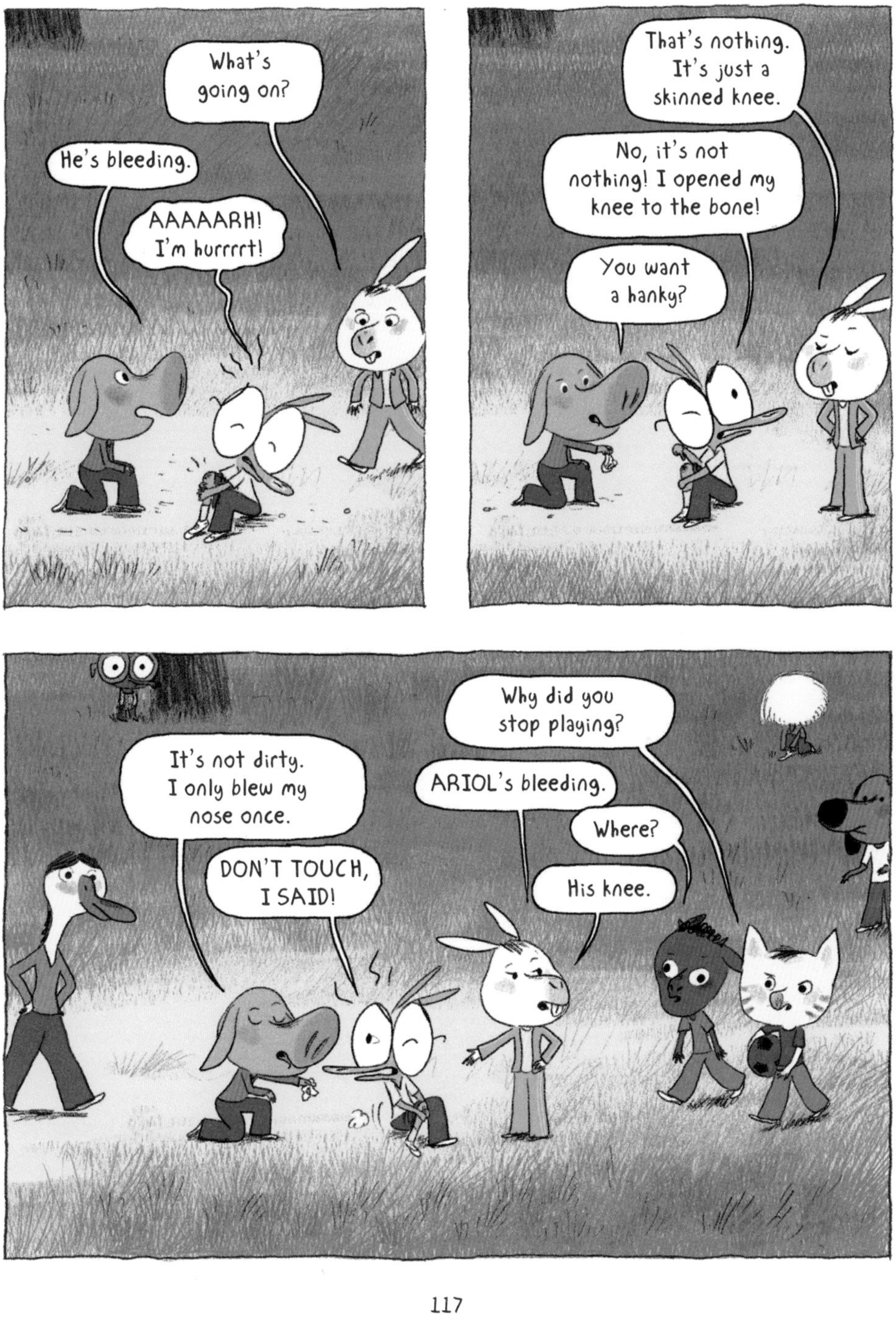
What's going on?
He's bleeding.
AAAAARH! I'm hurrrrt!
That's nothing. It's just a skinned knee.
No, it's not nothing! I opened my knee to the bone!
You want a hanky?
Why did you stop playing?
It's not dirty. I only blew my nose once.
ARIOL's bleeding.
Where?
DON'T TOUCH, I SAID!
His knee.

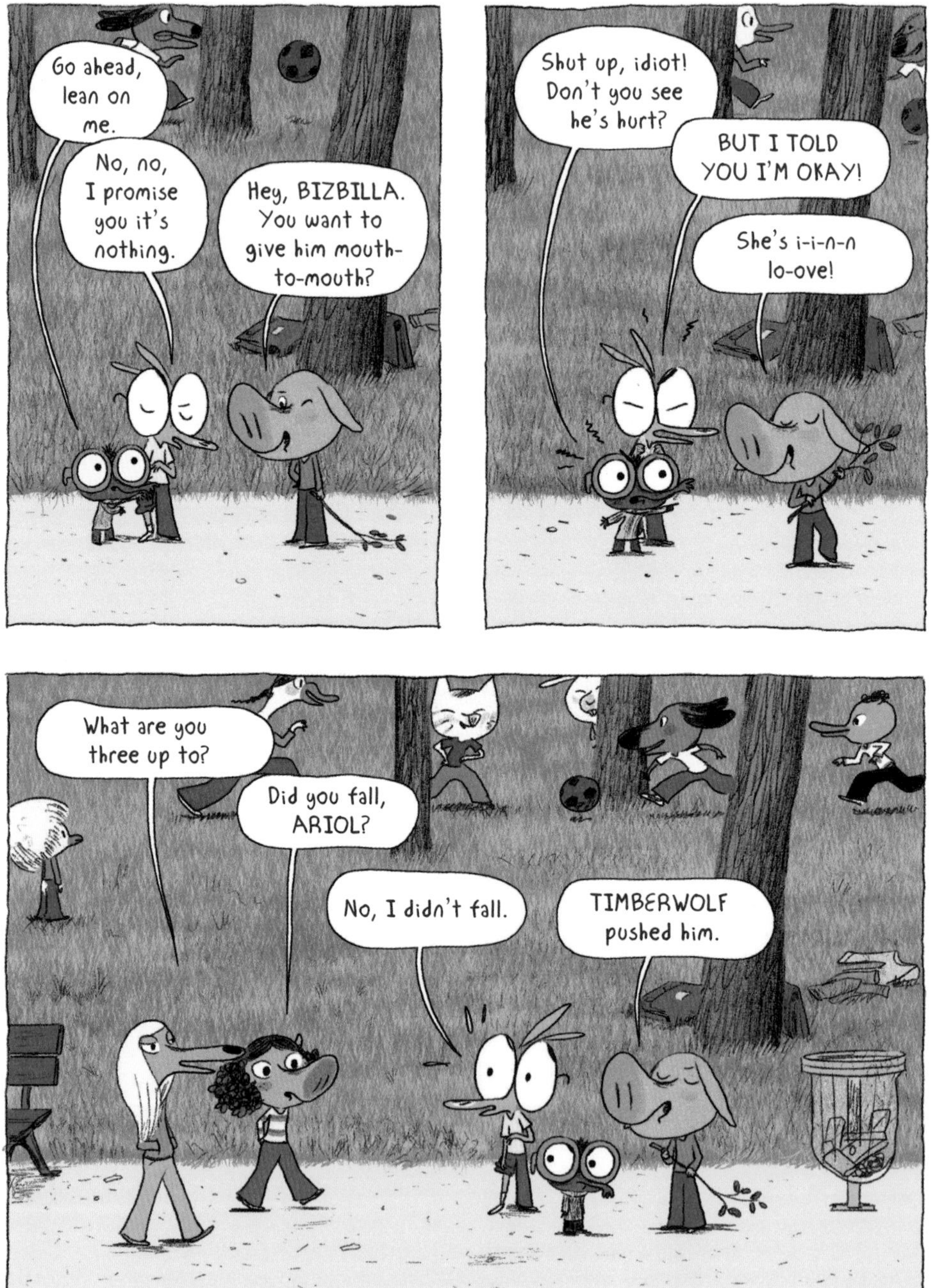
Go ahead, lean on me.
No, no, I promise you it's nothing.
Hey, BIZBILLA. You want to give him mouth-to-mouth?
Shut up, idiot! Don't you see he's hurt?
BUT I TOLD YOU I'M OKAY!
She's i-i-n-n lo-ove!
What are you three up to?
Did you fall, ARIOL?
No, I didn't fall.
TIMBERWOLF pushed him.

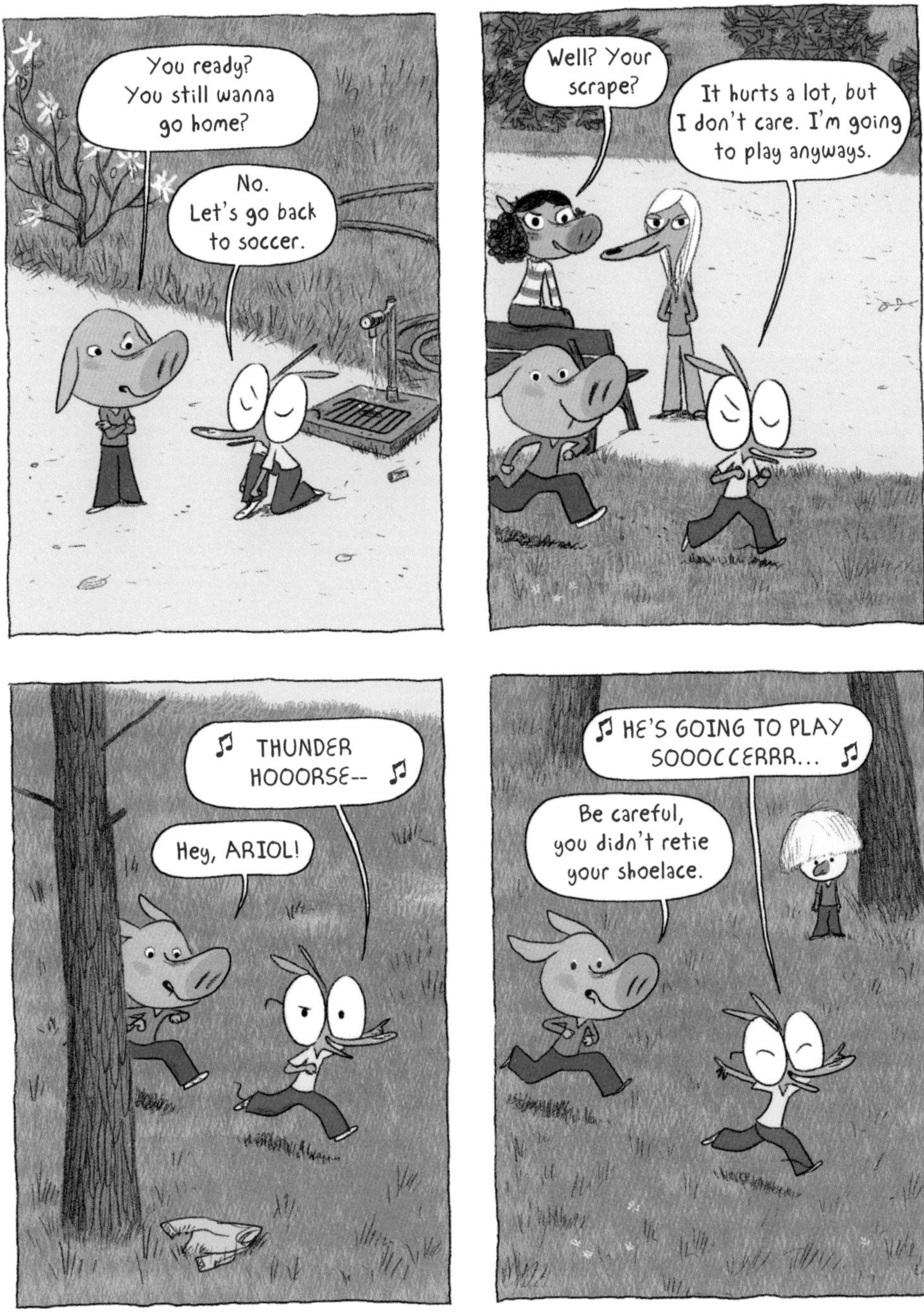
You ready? You still wanna go home?
No. Let's go back to soccer.
Well? Your scrape?
It hurts a lot, but I don't care. I'm going to play anyways.
♫ THUNDER HOOORSE-- ♫
Hey, ARIOL!
♫ HE'S GOING TO PLAY SOOOCCERRR... ♫
Be careful, you didn't retie your shoelace.

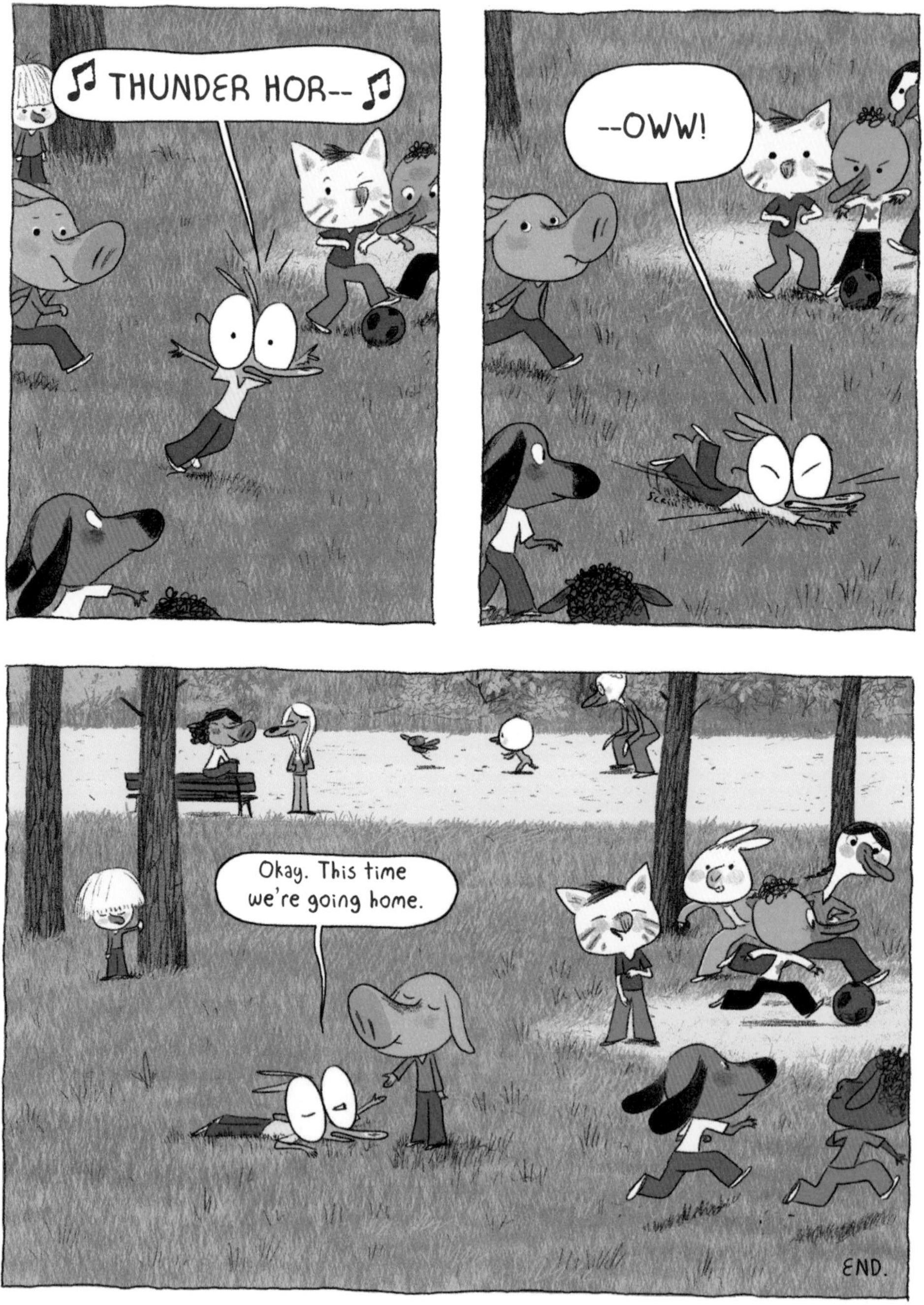
♫ THUNDER HOR-- ♫
--OWW!
Okay. This time we're going home.
END.

WATCH OUT FOR PAPERCUT*Z*

Welcome to the fourth, fuzzy, fantabulous ARIOL graphic novel, by the super-talented team of Emmanuel Guibert and Marc Boutavant, from Papercutz, those homo-sapiens dedicated to publishing great graphic novels for all ages. I'm Jim Salicrup, Editor-in-Chief and Thunder Horse's third biggest fan, and I'm here to recount a recent encounter of the ARIOL-kind.

Last year, none other than ARIOL artist, Marc Boutavant, paid a visit to the United States of America, appearing at such places as the New York Public Library, the Museum Of Modern Art Design Store, and The Miami Book Fair. Everywhere he went he spoke about ARIOL signed, ARIOL graphic novels, and even drew sketches in ARIOL graphic novels. But one of the most exciting stops of Marc's New York adventure was a special signing at Brooklyn's Bergen Street Comics, for it was there that I kind of finally met the entire ARIOL creative team. While Marc was there in-person, Emmanuel Guibert appeared live from France via Skype. Here's a pic of all three of us:

Both Emmanuel and Marc are as delightful as you'd probably imagine the creators of ARIOL to be, if not even more so. Together they answered questions, shared behind-the-scenes stories, and explained how they work together writing and drawing each ARIOL graphic novel. Everyone in attendance had a fun time, and I can't wait to see the two of them again! It was almost like meeting Ariol and Ramono in person!

I also can't wait for ARIOL #5 "Bizzbilla Hits the Bullseye," coming soon! Don't miss it!

Thanks,

Jim

STAY IN TOUCH!

EMAIL: salicrup@papercutz.com
WEB: www.papercutz.com
TWITTER: @papercutzgn
FACEBOOK: PAPERCUTZGRAPHICNOVELS
REGULAR MAIL: Papercutz, 160 Broadway, Suite 700, East Wing, New York, NY 10038

Other Great Titles From PAPERCUTZ™

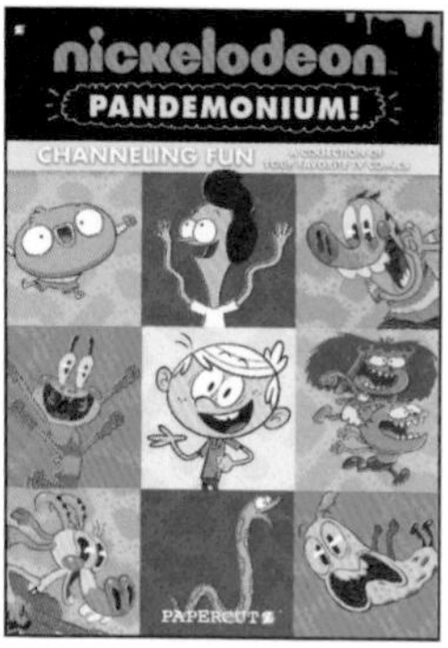
nickelodeon
PANDEMONIUM!
CHANNELING FUN
PAPERCUTZ

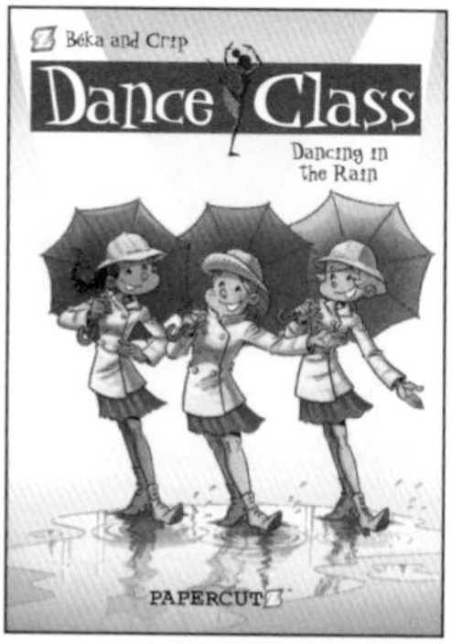
Béka and Crip
Dance Class
Dancing in the Rain
PAPERCUTZ

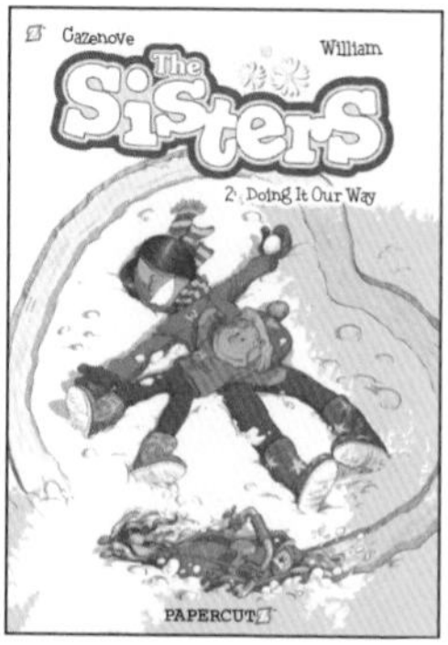
Cazenove
William
The Sisters
2 Doing It Our Way
PAPERCUTZ

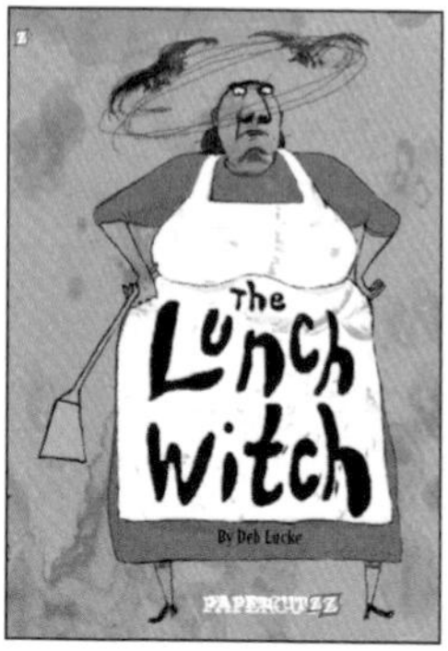
The Lunch Witch
By Deb Lucke
PAPERCUTZ

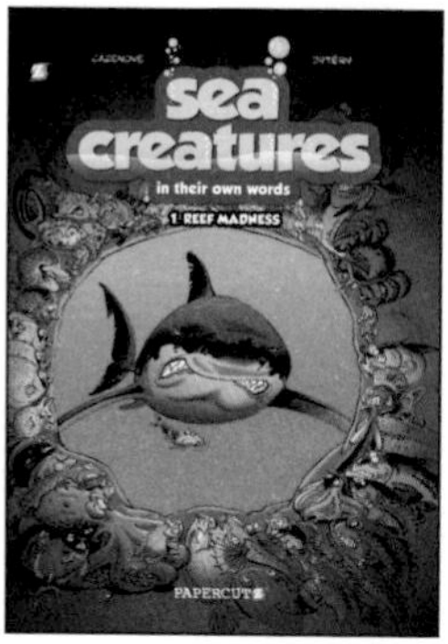
sea creatures
in their own words
1 REEF MADNESS
PAPERCUTZ

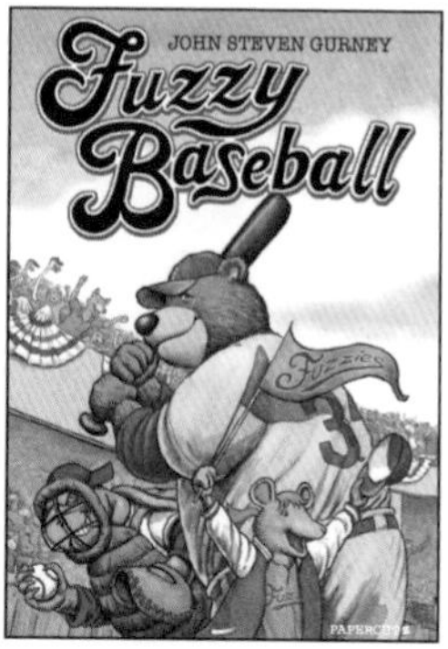
JOHN STEVEN GURNEY
Fuzzy Baseball
PAPERCUTZ

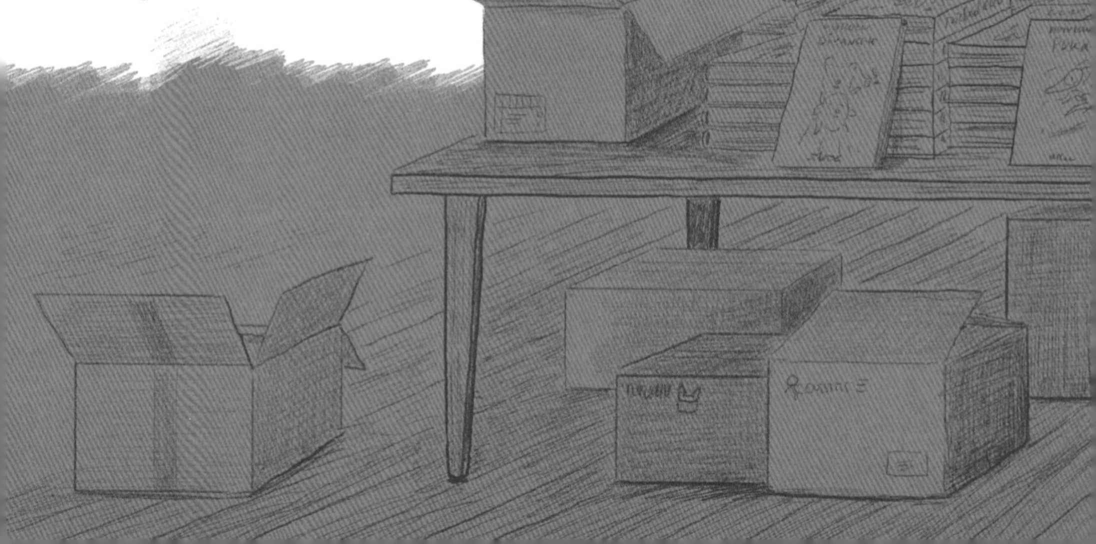

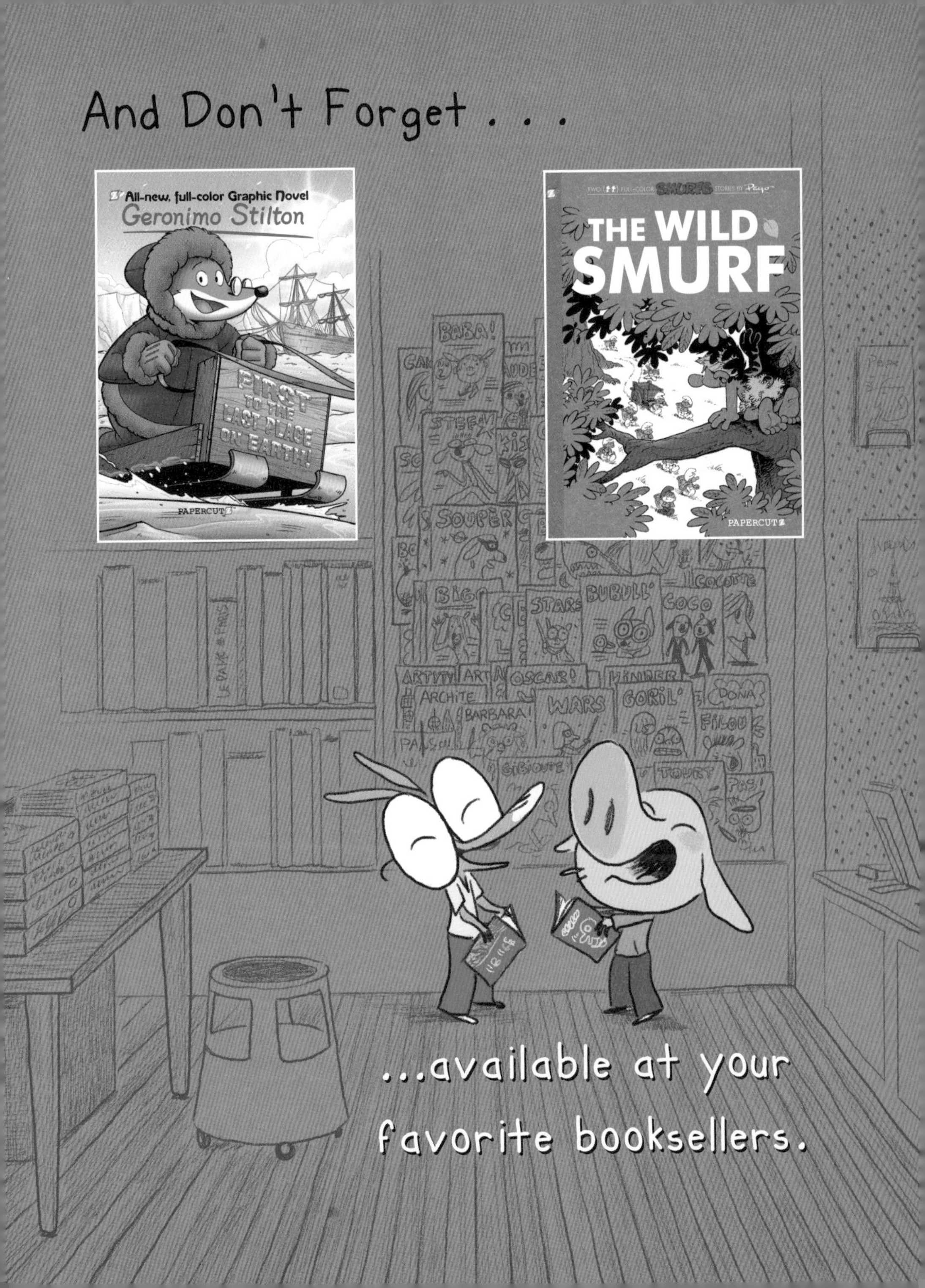
And Don't Forget . . .
All-new, full-color Graphic Novel
Geronimo Stilton
FIRST TO THE LAST PLACE ON EARTH!
PAPERCUTZ
THE WILD SMURF
PAPERCUTZ
...available at your favorite booksellers.